Girls From da Hood 6

Girls From da Hood 6

Ashley & JaQuavis,
and Amaleka McCall

www.urbanbooks.net

Urban Books, LLC
97 N18th Street
Wyandanch, NY 11798

Red Bottom Bandits © Copyright 2011 Ashley Antoinette
The Takedown © Copyright 2011 Amaleka McCall
Beauty and the Streets © Copyright 2011 JaQuavis Coleman

All rights reserved. No part of this book may be reproduced in
any form or by any means without prior consent of the Publisher,
excepting brief quotes used in reviews.

ISBN 13: 978-1-60162-569-4
ISBN 10: 1-60162-569-3

First Mass Market Paperback Printing November 2013
First Trade Paperback Printing April 2011
Printed in the United States of America

10 9 8 7 6 5 4 3 2 1

*This is a work of fiction. Any references or similarities to actual
events, real people, living or dead, or to real locales are intended
to give the novel a sense of reality. Any similarity in other names,
characters, places, and incidents is entirely coincidental.*

Distributed by Kensington Publishing Corp.
Submit Wholesale Orders to:
Kensington Publishing Corp.
C/O Penguin Group (USA) Inc.
Attention: Order Processing
405 Murray Hill Parkway
East Rutherford, NJ 07073-2316
Phone: 1-800-526-0275
Fax: 1-800-227-9604

"RED BOTTOM BANDITS"

Another Ashley Antoinette Classic

Prologue

"God please see us through this . . . please."
The quivering plea that Raegan sent up to her
maker was one of desperation. She was about
to go up against the impossible and the lonely
prayer was all she had left in her bag of tricks.
Her voice broke from anxiety as she continued.
"Watch over us and let us meet back up one day.
Keep my friends safe and help us make it through
this. We are all we got," Raegan said as she stood
with her head pressed against the foreheads of
her best friends Chanel and Gucci. The three
girls stood in a circle, arms wrapped around each
other's shoulders, heads bowed. It was now or
never . . . all or nothing. Their freedom depended
on this one moment. They had done a lot of dirt
together and now it seemed as though karma had
come full circle. Now they stood grasping one

another, hearts racing, tears falling down their tired eyes as they thought about what they were about to do. The odds were stacked against them, but they had no choice but to fight despite how dismal the outcome appeared to be.

"If we don't make it out of this . . . forgive us father for we have sinned . . . in your name we pray, amen," Raegan finished. A hard lump filled her throat as she walked over to the living room blinds and pulled them down discreetly. Red, white, and blue lights lit up the night sky as the police barricaded the city block in an attempt to thwart their escape route. Raegan could hear the pounding inside of her head as the rhythm of her racing heart blocked out all other sound. In all her years on this earth she had never been afraid of anything, but secretly she feared the altercation to come. She didn't want to step one foot outside of the trap house, but she knew that she and her girls had no choice. If they didn't come out eventually the police would come in and she would rather go out under her own terms. She was going to determine how this thing played out and she knew as long as they made the first move they would have the advantage. "We're like sitting ducks in this bitch." Chanel whispered anxiously as she came up over Raegan's shoulder and peeked at the scene outside.

"Then let's stop sitting," Raegan said in a low determined tone. She cocked the pump of the sawed-off double-barrel shotgun she carried with one hand and said, "Fuck it, I'll see you bitches in the Islands."

Chanel racked the automatic AK she carried while Gucci chambered the first round in her semi-automatic 9mm as they burst out of the front door. The three of them rushed out onto the lawn, adrenaline pumping, fear pulsing through their bodies as they shot it out with the Flint Police Department. Desperation caused them to fire their weapons endlessly and their marksman aim was enough to give the officers outside the shootout of the century.

Boom! Boom! Boom!

Raegan was so swift with the shotgun that you would have never thought she had to reload her weapon. There was nothing hesitant about her trigger finger. As she came out blazing, bullets flew past her head as she inched as quickly as possible to her car.

The melody of the police sirens harmonized with the gunshots as the girls popped off, serenading the streets.

The three girls exchanged fire with the entire police force and held their own as they each tried to escape to their prospective cars. They had been together their entire lives but the time had come for them to separate. It was time to fly solo. Although their chances of escape were slim to none they knew that by splitting up they increased their chances of eluding capture and avoiding the sticky situation. The cops couldn't focus on all three of them at once, so they each took their own risk as they cleared a path for themselves, popping off recklessly. They were too hot and they needed to split up before making their way to the Virgin Islands.

"Aghhh," Raegan shouted mercilessly as she fired over and over again. Hitting an officer was not her objective . . . she only meant to incite fear. She was skilled enough with her aim to come dangerously close to homicide without actually committing it. Killing a cop was the last thing she needed to add to her hood resume so she was cognizant of exactly where her bullets struck. Her hair whipped wildly around her face as she turned quickly to check on the status of her girls. Her mouth fell open in horror as she noticed an officer sneaking up behind Gucci. It was as if the entire scene was playing out in slow motion before her.

"Nooo! Guch!" she shouted. Gucci turned her head toward Raegan's voice and her eyes opened in horror when she saw Raegan pull a handgun from her back waistline. With precision, Raegan let off a shot that laid the officer out—dropping him where he stood before he could ever pull his trigger. In the blink of an eye things had gone from bad to worse. As a matter of fact things were already at worse . . . now they were just out of fucking control. The consequences of her actions were now irreparable and tears of regret immediately surfaced in her horrified eyes.

"Oh shit!" Gucci yelled as she realized how close she had come to death. Raegan's hand shook as she looked at the smoking gun in her hand. In a split second the situation had escalated, but before she could even process what had happened a blinding pain shot through her as her body jerked forward. Her mouth fell open in agony, but no sound came out. Her eyes watered as she looked Gucci in the eyes desperately begging for help without uttering a word. Her hand fell over her right shoulder as she realized she had been shot. It seemed as if the entire police force had her in their crosshairs. By killing one of their own, Raegan had become public enemy number one. She crouched down to shield herself from the bullets that were flying her way. Enraged Gucci blazed off, aiming at the officers behind Raegan. Regan was frantic and in shock as she pulled a bloody hand away from her body. She grimaced in excruciating pain. With one of their own laid out in the dirt, the officers became even more relentless in their pursuit.

"Raegan go!" Gucci yelled as she continued to fire cover shots. The automatic machine gun that Gucci spewed was enough to give Raegan time to run. Raegan snapped out of her daze and scrambled to fire her gun with her left hand. Her entire right side was on fire which hindered her shot. With her left arm, Raegan shot wildly and ran for dear life until she finally reached her car. Gunshots shattered her rear window and bullets riddled the body of her car as she pulled off, her tires burning rubber as her foot pushed the gas pedal to the floor. Her car tipped to the side until she finally gained control of the vehicle's speed as she sped away. As her eyes darted wildly in her rearview she saw that Chanel was long gone and that Gucci was still going gun to gun with the cops. Everything in her wanted to turn around and help her friend, but knew that she couldn't. *Gucci will make it out . . . she has to,* Raegan thought. She was bleeding profusely onto the leather seats and she knew that she needed help, but there was nothing she could do but keep driving. The sirens behind her indicated that the cops were following her. The logical thing to do would be to give up . . . to pull over the car and surrender, but there was no way she was going to prison. Nothing in her would allow her to surrender. She would make those crackers chase her from one coast to the other before she gave up. *I've got to shake these squad cars,* she thought as she pressed the Acura to the max while bobbing and weaving through traffic. The traffic light in front of her turned yellow signaling for her to slow down, but instead she sped up, flying through the intersection and causing the cars that had the right of way to hit their breaks fiercely. When the officers following her tried to follow suit they were hit with a sudden surprise as a semi-truck smashed into the side of their vehicle.

Screech!

The sound of tires wailing as cars tried to avoid the pile up accident was all that Raegan heard as she kept it moving. "I have to get out of this car," she whispered frantically as she bent a sharp right. She drove the Acura for ten more miles before she finally ditched the car on a suburban street. Grabbing a jacket out of the backseat she tried to hide her injured shoulder as best she could, but the blood quickly seeped through the fabric. There was nothing inconspicuous about her appearance. She was hot and she needed to get the hell out of dodge. She grabbed her empty gun and hid it inside the jacket as she weakly walked. She was trying to put as much distance behind her as she possibly could, but she wouldn't get far on her feet. She was losing too much blood. She needed a car. Her blood speckled the pavement as she trudged along begrudgingly. As her head began to spin she stumbled slightly, beginning to feel faint. Grateful for the night's shadow, she sat down on the street curb to reserve her strength as she tried to piece together a plan in her head. *I have to stop this wound from bleeding,* she thought as she held onto her arm, applying pressure and grimacing at the same time. As she came to a corner house she noticed a man leaving his home. Black baggy jeans, a black jacket, and matching fitted he secured his front door never noticing Raegan as she approached. She pulled her chrome .45 from her waistline, knowing that it contained no bullets. *He doesn't know that,* she thought, deciding to use the empty pistol as leverage. She walked directly up on him and put her gun to the back of his head.

"If you move I will pull this trigger you understand?" she asked, her voice unwavering.

Surprised that the voice behind him came from a woman he nodded in shock.

"Open the door and go back inside," she instructed as she looked around anxiously.

The man did as he was told, not wanting to buck because he had too much to lose. He had no idea how he had been caught slipping—by a bitch no less. She could feel his shoulders tense as she pushed him forward into the house. She was straight pump faking, holding up the guy with an empty gun. As long as she kept control this would play out in her favor.

"Put your hands up," she said.

The guy gripped the duffel bag that he held in his hand and spoke calmly. "You don't have to do it like this," he said.

"Shut up and open the door," Raegan ordered.

The guy turned his key in the lock and opened up his front door as Raegan guided him inside.

"Sit down," she stated harshly as she kept her gun trained on him.

The guy knew that he didn't have much to lose. He didn't know Raegan but he knew her type. If she had enough balls to run up on him then she had enough balls to kill him. Deciding to go for broke he spun around unexpectedly and grabbed her arm forcefully as he slammed her into the wall.

"Aghh," she yelled as she fought ferociously with him for control of the gun. With her injured arm it didn't take much effort for him to overpower her. Snatching the gun from her hand he pushed her away from him. Without hesitation he aimed at her head and pulled the trigger.

Click!

Heaving from the altercation, he looked at the girl in exasperation. "Fuck is you doing? You robbing niggas with empty guns?" he asked in disbelief as he tossed the .45 onto the ground. Enraged he cleared the space between them and hemmed her up. He wrapped his hands tightly around her neck, choking her out as he lifted her off of the ground. "Who sent you?!" he yelled through clenched teeth, his temple throbbing in rage.

"Who sent you?!" he shouted. He demanded answers, but the tight hold he had on her neck prevented her from answering. She clawed at his hands as her eyes burned in desperation. She scratched and clawed violently, reaching for his face as her nails dug into his skin. She was fighting him with all of her might, but her blows and protests were in vain. He was literally squeezing the life out of her.

"Please . . . " she gasped as her face turned red and the room began to close in around her.

Her eyes pleaded with him as he scanned her, reading her, observing her. He saw that she was soaked in blood and shaking in fear. She could feel the life leaving her body as he choked her ruthlessly. Reluctantly, he loosened his grip on her.

Cough! Cough!

Raegan choked as she gulped in air, bending over as she welcomed the oxygen into her burning lungs. Her legs gave out under her as she slouched onto the floor.

The guy looked down at Raegan silently wondering what events had brought her to his home that night. As Raegan struggled on the floor the guy looked at her curiously. Anger turned to sympathy when he noticed that she was in tremendous pain.

"Why are you here?" he asked, his voice skeptical and stern.

Raegan looked up at him grimacing as her shoulder continued to bleed profusely. She didn't have a choice but to answer him. She had invaded his home . . . if he shot her dead it would be justified.

"I need help," she whispered.

"You've got a funny way of seeking help ma," the guy replied sarcastically. A part of him wanted to slap the taste from her mouth for running upon him toting a gun, but the desperate look in her eyes told him that she was between a rock and a hard place. He didn't know the circumstances that had placed her in his presence, but for some reason he didn't feel right just putting her out and leaving her on stuck.

"I'm sorry," she replied with tear filled eyes. "I wasn't going to shoot you." I just needed to clean up and I needed a car. Nobody sent me. I'm hurt and I couldn't make it much further on foot."

Her voice was shaking and the fear he noticed in her was enough for the guy to let down his guard. He reached his hand out to help her up from the floor.

Wide eyed, she stared at his hand unsurely.

"You gon' stay down there all night or what?" he asked. "You bleeding all over my Brazilian hardwoods ma. Get up."

Raegan grabbed his hand with reluctance as her fear was replaced by her embarrassment.

"Look, I'm sorry. I just need to get out of here," she said in a panic as she turned for the door.

"I don't know why you're running, but you won't get very far with that arm," he commented. "It looks like you need a doctor."

"No!" Raegan shouted in protest. "No doctors! No hospitals and no fucking doctors." She held her injury tenderly as the thought of being apprehended overwhelmed her. There was no way she could walk into a hospital without being arrested. The police knew that she had been hit and would surely have units posted at all the local hospitals, anticipating her arrival.

"Okay, okay," the guy replied. "At least clean yourself up. There's gauze and peroxide underneath the bathroom sink."

Raegan nodded her head and answered. "Where is it?"

"It's upstairs . . . first door on your left," he replied.

Raegan hesitantly walked toward the bathroom. She was sure that he would call the police on her as soon as she disappeared from sight, but she planned on being long gone before they ever got there. *I just need to get myself together first,* she thought as she entered the bathroom, frantic. She grabbed a towel from the countertop and turned on the faucet. Her bloodstained hands painted the sink as the water flowed onto her palms. She removed her shirt and the sight of the gaping hole in her shoulder made her gasp in shock. A knock at the door caused her to jump in fear. Holding her breath, she stared into the mirror's reflection, eyeing the door behind her. She just knew that the police were standing on the other side of it. Her nerves were quickly eased when the guy peeped his head inside. He immediately noticed the terror in her eyes and said, "It's just me." He stepped inside and reached beneath the sink and removed a first aid kit. "Let me see your shoulder."

Raegan turned toward the guy and winced as he began to clean her wound.

"What's your name?" he asked.

"Raegan . . . Sonny Raegan," she replied.

"Who shot you?" he asked as he did his best to clean the crusted blood from the gaping hole in her shoulder.

"The police," she answered.

He hesitated and looked her in the eyes, his gaze revealing his disbelief. "You're running from the police?" he asked.

"My girls and I . . . we got into some trouble," she replied, not giving him too much information. "We never had anything, no one ever gave us anything. It was always a struggle . . . from day to day. We got tired of struggling . . . tired of being the have-nots."

The guy taped her shoulder and handed her a bottle of aspirin.

"What's your name?" he asked as he applied pressure to her arm.

"Oww . . . Jesus! Can you press any harder!" she shouted in annoyance as extreme pain took over her entire body. Her skin was pale and sweat shone on her brow as she cringed.

"Look, pressure is the only thing that's going to stop this bleeding. You've got a bullet in your arm. You can let me do this or you can take your pretty ass to the hospital or you can run out of here and leave a trail of blood behind you. Choose one." he said authoritatively, speaking to her as if she were an unruly child.

She sighed knowing that she didn't have many options. "Fine, but be easy . . . it feels like I'm being shot all over again," she complained. She turned her head and closed her eyes in impatience as she anticipated the agony to come. "Who are you anyway?" she asked rudely as if he had invaded her home.

"Brelin Nolen," he answered shortly.

"Raegan," she replied. "Sonny Raegan."

"I would say it's nice to meet you, but considering—"

"Ha ha," she said as she looked him in the eye sarcastically. For the first time she inventoried the man in front of her. His dark as night skin and beautifully white teeth were so attractive to her. His clean-shaven face was sculpted perfectly with the exception of a tiny scar that rested above his left eyebrow. Handsome was an understatement. He had a grown man appeal that gave her butterflies; and the stern, disapproving look that he gave her made her feel as if he was one of the few men in the world who could put her in her place.

"I'm no doctor but I did the best I could," he said. "There's a clean shirt in the master closet." He nodded toward the door and began to exit the room.

"Why are you helping me?" Raegan asked.

"I haven't figured that out yet," he replied as he walked out.

Raegan quickly dressed and returned to the living room where Brelin waited patiently. "What's next?" he asked.

"I have to get out of this city," she stated surely.

"Can I give you a ride somewhere?" he asked.

She thought about saying yes, but quickly dismissed the notion. She couldn't afford any slip-ups. Brelin was just one more person who could get her caught. *I've already been in his presence for too long,* she thought as she shook her head. "No thank you. I'll be fine."

Brelin stood to his feet and walked close to her. She could tell from the look on his face that he didn't believe her. "Well look, I'ma hit you with some paper. It'll be enough to call you a cab and get yourself a room for the night." He peeled off ten hundred dollars bills from the stack he retrieved from his pocket and placed them in her palm.

"I can't . . . you don't even know me," she said.

"You can stick a nigga up, but can't take a genuine offer," he asked with a chuckle.

She smiled back and closed her hand around the money. "Thank you. I swear one day I'll pay you back."

He nodded his head to make her feel better but they both knew that they wouldn't cross paths anytime in the near future. Brelin could tell that Raegan prided herself on her independence so he didn't rob her of her dignity by refusing her. As he stared at her almond colored face he wondered what had brought her to this point. Her beauty hid her cruel intentions, which made her a deadly threat. He knew that she had broken many hearts in her day.

"Can I use your phone?" she asked.

He grabbed his cell phone and tossed it to her, then listened as she called a cab company. As she hung up the phone she gave him a weak smile.

"I'll wait outside for my ride. You don't want to be mixed up in the mess I've gotten myself into," Raegan stated sincerely with regret in her voice as she tossed his phone back to him.

As Brelin watched her walk out of the door he couldn't help but wonder where she had come from. The old saying that looks could be deceiving was absolute—Raegan was the epitome of that. He felt guilty as if he owed her more than what he had given her and his conscience weighed heavily upon him. Everything in him told him that he was playing with fire, but he ignored his instincts and ran out of the door after her. He stopped dead in his tracks and his heart sank when he looked at his empty driveway. *Fuck,* he thought as he looked at the vacant space that his Benz used to occupy. He pulled out his phone and started to dial 911, but stopped when he saw the message that Raegan had left in an open text.

I don't ride in cabs. Thanks for letting me
borrow your car. I'll return it, I promise.

                                                        -R

Taken aback by Raegan, Brelin had to smile.
He shook his head because there wasn't a nigga
walking on two legs that could pull one over on
him, but within a matter of minutes a beautiful
woman had walked into his life and suckered
him out of his whip. He had never encountered
a woman so slick. He was definitely intrigued.
As he walked back into his home, he dialed his
insurance company as he shook his head in
disbelief. *That bitch is crazy as hell,* he thought
as he chuckled to himself while shaking his head.
I hope she gets away.

Raegan tried to drive the speed limit as she
made her way out of town, but her nerves caused
her foot to be heavy on the gas. As she passed a
highway sign she noticed that she was 150 miles
from the Ohio Turnpike. Once she was a couple
states over she would be able to relax. With her
fake passport gripped tightly in her hand, she
breathed deeply. All she had to do was make
it to Florida. There was a boat waiting there to

take her and her girls to paradise . . . if they ever made it. A honking horn behind her caused her to check her rearview mirror and her heart sank into her stomach when she recognized the car. A Lincoln Town Car followed behind her, blowing to get her attention. She frowned in confusion. "What the fuck are you blowing for?" she complained to herself as she rolled her eyes. "Damn it . . . today is not the fucking day. It's a red light you idiot!" she shouted. The car pulled up beside her and the back window slowly rolled down. As Raegan realized who was in her presence, she felt all of the blood drain from her face. His face was her worst nightmare—the last person she wanted to see. Without thinking she pressed the gas pedal down to the floor.

"Fuck! How did he find me?" she asked as she instantly took off. No matter how fast she drove she couldn't shake the tinted car.

Boom!

The driver crashed into the rear of her car causing Raegan to swerve into oncoming highway traffic. She cut the wheel to the right and barely missed a collision only to be rammed from behind again.

"Agh!" she screamed in a desperate attempt to maintain control of the car. The driver pulled up to Raegan and rolled down his window.

"Pull over!" he shouted as he lifted a pistol up to show her he was strapped.

Raegan grabbed the pistol from her passenger seat and held it up as she raised an eyebrow in rebuttal. *Nigga, you're not the only one who can pop something,* she thought angrily as she kept driving like a bat out of hell. There was no way she was stopping that car. She knew who sat in the backseat of the town car and she most definitely wasn't trying to see him. She could only imagine the type of revenge he sought and tears came to her eyes. She held on tightly to the steering wheel and then slammed the car into the driver's side door.

"Get away from me," she shouted as she rammed the car again, this time making the town car rub against the metal divider on the side of the road. Sparks flew as the metal clashed but Raegan never let up on her gas. Her eyes bugged in horror when she saw the town car recover and she knew that her escape was impossible when the driver resumed his speed. He stuck his gun out of his window and fired two shots, deflating both of her passenger side tires.

The Benz fishtailed out of control as she desperately fought to maintain control of the car. The world around her was like one carousel of confusion as she spun wildly, gripping the steering wheel. The collision that stopped it all wrecked her brain on impact as her head jerked back. The foggy haze that enveloped her made it hard for her to process her thoughts. Her mind said, *run!* But her body didn't listen. She saw a figure looming over her as her car door was opened.

"No," she protested as she slapped at the hands that snatched her from the car. She scratched and swung, but her efforts were futile. The large driver picked her up, bear hugging her, as he carried her to the tinted town car. Kicking, screaming, and spitting, Raegan did all she could to free herself but she knew that there was no getting away—not from this. The back window rolled down.

"Get in the car."

As soon as she heard his voice the fight within her left her body. The emotional dams she had built up broke as tears flowed down her cheeks.

"Don't do this," she whispered as she looked him in the eyes. She could see the resentment, the rage—the need for vengeance in his deadly stare.

Her plea fell upon deaf ears as she watched the tinted window roll up and she was forced into the car. As she sat, trapped in the backseat, fear filled her. She closed her eyes and cried silently as she thought about all the things she had done to bring her to this point.

Chapter One

One year ago

"Get him out of me now!" Raegan shouted as she pushed with all of her might. "Now . . . get him out!" At twenty-two, Sonny Raegan was about to give birth to a baby . . . a boy . . . a son that she planned to name Micah II. Her heart pounded with the intensity of stampeding horses as she gripped the hand of the nurse that stood near her bedside. She had been in labor for ten hours and it was nothing like the fairy-tale day she had made up in her head. It was her first child and she had been distracted by the ideal of having a baby. She had imagined children's birthday gatherings, adorable blue outfits, and nursery rhymes. She was inexperienced in motherhood and knew nothing about the labor pains, stretch marks, and the unending turmoil that came along with giving birth. After ten months, forty weeks; and countless hours of bloated feet, morning sickness, and a huge belly; the day had finally come for her to meet her baby.

"Okay Raegan, breathe sweetheart . . . you have a few seconds before the next contraction comes," Dr. McEwen stated as she looked up at Raegan through her blood stained thighs.

Raegan collapsed her head against the pillow and gasped for air as she looked around the room. It was full of people—nurses and doctors and orderlies—all there to help bring life into the world, but their presence wasn't enough. She was surrounded by a room full of people but none of them mattered. The one person who was missing, the one person who had promised he would be there, was nowhere to be found. Micah had left her to bring their son into the world on her own.

"I need my phone . . . I need to call his father. He can't come yet. Micah has to be here," she pleaded as her emotions took over and tears emerged in her young eyes.

"You don't have time to make a call, Raegan. This baby is crowning and it's time to push," the doctor said.

"Please . . . just one call," Raegan begged.

The doctor nodded and a nurse handed her the hospital phone. She felt intense pressure between her legs and fought the urge to push as she dialed Micah's number. Whatever bit of strength she had left abandoned her when she heard the voice of a woman answer the phone.

"Hello?"

The air deflated from Raegan's lungs. "Who is this?" she questioned weakly.

A vice grip of anger made her heart feel as if it would explode as she replied, "Who am I? Who are you? And why you answering his phone?"

Raegan was asking questions she already knew the answers to. *He's fucking around on me,* she thought as she gasped for air. *I'm lying here giving him a baby and he's with another woman.*

"Raegan, it's time. Put down the phone. Your baby needs you to be strong," Dr. McEwen said.

Reluctantly Raegan hung up the phone and gripped behind her knees as she pulled them to her chest. With a broken heart she pushed out her son. The moment she saw him he became the love of her life. His subtle cry broke through the air like the scent of soul cooking on a Sunday morning. He was the spitting image of his father and she couldn't wait to show Micah what a beautiful combination the two of them had created. She was young and naïve. Raegan was sure that her new found love for her child would be shared by his father. So positive that this baby would keep him faithful, she couldn't wait to get home to start her new life as a mother. She had given Micah a family, a seed to call his own. She was sure that this cemented her spot in his life. As she looked down at her baby she smiled and pulled him to her as she kissed his forehead. "I love you Micah," she whispered. As she sat alone in the cold, sterile room, she had never felt so alone. There were no cards, no family members around to give their unwanted advice, and no father doting over his newborn child. It was just the two of them and as she fell asleep with him in her arms her joy quickly transformed to sadness.

As Raegan watched the city streets pass her by she felt a calm that she never knew existed. Her baby lay sleeping on her lap as she made her way home. She couldn't believe that the man who had fathered her child had missed the birth, but she told herself that it didn't matter because once he laid eyes on their son he would be smitten. Other chicks wouldn't be able to compete now that she had given him an heir. He would choose her, he would wife her—he had to. After all of the things he had promised her and all of the people she had defied to be with him; it was time for him to return her loyalty. As the cab crept up to Micah's home, butterflies filled her stomach. "We're home baby boy," she cooed as she grabbed the bag of baby products she had accumulated from the hospital. She looked at the meter and said, "I have to go get some money out of the house. I'll be right back."

The driver nodded and Raegan exited the vehicle. She shielded her son from the cold winter wind as it bit at her, almost knocking her off her feet.

She stepped inside and the heat instantly melted away the stiffness that clung to her bones. Afraid that she would wake her baby, she didn't announce her presence. Instead she crept inside as she made her way to their bedroom. Everything in her wanted to cuss Micah out for not being there for her but she contained her anger. No matter how much she showed her displeasure she couldn't change the fact that he had missed the most important day in her life. *Just be cool Raegan. It doesn't matter. As long as he is here for us now, just let it go,* she told herself.

When she entered the bedroom she lost all composure and her knees became so weak that she had to reach out, gripping the wall just to steady her balance. Her breaths became so shallow that it felt as if she would suffocate. The empty feeling she felt in her chest hurt worse than anything she had ever felt. Before her eyes, lying in the very bed in which they had conceived their son, lay Micah sleeping beside another bitch. She had only been gone for two days and already he had replaced her. She never thought he would have the audacity to bring another girl into their home, but the proof was in the pudding. He couldn't lie his way out of this one. Her eyes scanned the room and the evidence of his night of passion gave away his indiscretions. The condom wrapper on the bedspread, the black panties on the floor, the ruffled bed sheets beneath them, the way the girl's legs were intertwined with his—they painted a perfect picture of what had gone on the night before. Her heartbreak turned to rage as she walked out of the room, careful not to wake the sleeping couple. *This nigga want to play games with me,* she thought. *He got this bitch in my house . . . in our bed.* She went to the spare closet and grabbed a suitcase as she began to fill it with some of her possessions. She took some of his as well, grabbing his Rolex and diamond chain. Micah wasn't a huge player in the game. He was getting little money—bill money and usually had some spare change to floss with so when she hit his stash she only pulled out ten stacks. It wasn't much but it was enough to give her the confidence to leave a no good nigga with no good intentions. Raegan put on a pot of boiling water as she walked outside to return to the cab. She put her baby's blanket on the seat, then placed him gently on top of it and then put her bag inside.

"Give me five minutes. I need to handle something real fast," she said as she handed the cab driver a hundred dollar bill. She walked back inside with the determination of a woman scorned. Her insides rattled with every step she took, but she shook off the pain and made her way back to the pot she had prepared on the stove. As she grabbed the potholders and lifted it from the blue fire that danced beneath the steel, she halted as she looked out of the window at her awaiting cab. Her heart beat with intensity and adrenaline pumped through her. She headed up the steps and into the bedroom. She pulled back the covers and poured the scolding water right onto Micah's crotch.

"Aghh! Shit!" Micah screamed as he awoke in tremendous pain and the girl beside him scrambled to get out of the bed. He jumped up grabbing his manhood as he looked at Raegan in surprise. "Fuck is you doing?"

"Fuck am I doing?" she shot back. "What the fuck are you doing Micah? I just had your son yesterday and you were laid up in this bitch with her?"

"Bitch I should kill you," he shot as he lunged toward her and pinned her to the wall. Raegan's head hit the drywall hard, cracking it as Micah choked her.

"Fuck you," she said with teary eyes.

"Micah stop," the random girl said as she tried to pull him off of Raegan. "Let her go."

"Bitch nobody's talking to you," he seethed as he slapped her hand off of him.

"I give you a son and you give me an ass whooping. Is that how this works?" Raegan asked. Micah grabbed Raegan's vagina roughly, threatening to rip the stitches that kept her insides from falling out and causing her to cry out in pain.

"Say you're sorry bitch," he demanded.

Before the words could leave her mouth, the girl behind him lifted the steel pot and hit Micah upside the head with all of her might.

Micah turned to react, but Raegan grabbed the lamp off of the dresser and swung it at the back of his head. It shattered over him as glass stuck in the back of his neck and blood dripped from his open skull. She had split him open down to the white meat and felt no remorse as her emotions cheered her on.

Raegan and the girl attacked him simultaneously as he tried to shield himself from the blows. Raegan was swinging with all of her might while the girl was using her stiletto heels to pound out his face.

"You dirty dick-ass nigga. Fuck you!" Raegan shouted as she backed up from him. "Stay away from me and my son!" She backed out of the room as the other girl slipped into her dress. Micah lay bleeding crumpled on the floor as Raegan walked out disgusted at herself for ever loving his bum ass.

When she finally made it outside she almost cried when she saw her suitcase sitting on the curb and her baby lying on top of it. The cab was long gone and her son was crying at the top of his lungs. "Oh my God. I'm so sorry . . . mommy's so sorry," she whispered as she rushed to pick him up. She noticed that her bag was open slightly and her stomach sank as she knelt to examine the contents of her bag. The money was gone. She was broke and she had just bitten the hand that fed her. Hopeless, she knew that she couldn't go back inside. It was official. She and Micah were over. She had no choice but to start walking. She cradled her baby, trying to warm him in one arm as she carried her suitcase in the other. As she walked her tears froze on her face and her baby's cries broke her heart. "We don't need him boo. We've got each other."

Beep! Beep!

The sound of a car horn caught her attention and the girl who she had caught with Micah rolled up beside her.

"Hey get in," she said.

Raegan kept walking and didn't look the girl's way.

"Look I can give you a ride. It's cold out here and you're walking with a baby. He's going to get sick," the girl reasoned. "I can take you wherever you need to go."

Raegan hesitated, knowing that she had no real destination. As much as she wanted to turn down the ride, the thought of warm heat lured her to the car.

"I didn't know he had a girl," the girl said as she drove off. The heat instantly settled the baby down. "I didn't even like that nigga. I was gonna rob him. I just wanted to find out where he kept the safe."

"What safe? That small balling ass mu'fucka didn't have no safe. He had shoe box money," Raegan scoffed as she shook her head from side to side.

"Look. I apologize. I hope you don't have any ill will toward me," the girl said. "I'm Chanel."

Raegan wanted to beef out with the girl, but inside she knew that she had set herself up. She had invested her all into a man who had invested nothing. His disloyalty was inevitable. If it had not been this girl it would have been the next.

"Raegan," she replied.

"Where can I drop you off at?" Chanel asked.

Exhausted Raegan sighed and responded, "There's a shelter on—"

"You're gonna stay at a shelter with your baby?" Chanel asked. "You don't have any family?"

"No," Raegan said shortly. "The shelter will be fine."

Chanel shook her head and headed toward her own house. "A shelter isn't fine. You can stay with me for a few nights until you make arrangements."

Raegan wanted to protest but knew that she didn't have many other options. "You don't even know me."

"I know but I feel bad just dropping you at a shelter with a newborn. I have a roommate, but we live in a four bedroom so we have plenty of room," she answered. "I know you have to be exhausted. Once you rest up you can decide what your next move is. Besides I feel bad. I feel like if it wasn't for me you would be at home with your man."

"Highly unlikely," Raegan said.

"Well I hope you burned his dick off . . . broke nigga don't deserve to ever get any pussy," Chanel stated.

The girls broke out in laughter as Chanel headed home. As soon as Raegan stepped foot inside Chanel's home she could tell that the girl was getting a bit of money. "My girl Lisa stays here, but you'll hardly ever see her. She's a good girl . . . a college student. Her head is always in the books so she won't even know you're here," Chanel said as she showed Raegan to one of the spare rooms.

"Thanks for this," Raegan said gratefully as she held onto her sleeping baby.

"Thanks for what?" Chanel replied as if it was nothing and to her it was no big deal. Real bitches did real shit and there was no way that she could see herself leaving Raegan and her son out in the cold. She invited Raegan to her home partly out of guilt, but mostly out of sympathy. She knew what it was like putting your trust into a no good ass nigga. Chanel had been burnt one too many times, so she felt Raegan's pain.

"Get you some rest girl. I'll watch your baby so you can catch a few hours of sleep. You look like you're about to pass out," Chanel offered.

Raegan reluctantly handed Chanel her son. She didn't want to give him to her, but she was so damn tired. Chanel could see the lioness in Raegan coming out over her baby cub.

"I'm not on no petty shit," Chanel said to ease Raegan's concerns. "I'm just trying to help. I don't think with my heart . . . I think with my pocket book. After I pulled off I didn't think a second thought about your man and I don't judge you for fucking him up. I'm just glad you didn't fuck me up."

Raegan chuckled as she handed Chanel her son. "Thanks."

"You're welcome. What's his name?"

"Micah . . . Micah II," Raegan replied.

Chanel brought the swaddled baby up to her face and kissed his nose. "Come on Micah . . . let's go talk shit about your bullshit ass daddy," she cooed. She gave Raegan a knowing look and Raegan chuckled as she shook her head and retreated to her room. She didn't know that she had just made a lasting friend. In fact, she didn't know Chanel from the next girl, but she appreciated her in that time and in that moment nonetheless.

Knock! Knock! Knock!

"I swear to fucking God if that knocking wake this baby up I'ma slap the black off of somebody," Chanel whispered as she looked at the sleeping infant that slept beside her.

Lisa appeared at Chanel's door, her headscarf covered her short tapered haircut, and she folded her arms in annoyance.

"You expecting somebody? It's three o'clock in the morning," she complained. She didn't notice the baby in the room until she walked into the room. Her eyebrows arose in confusion. "Whose baby?"

"A friend of mine. She's in the spare room. Can you answer the door before he wakes up?" Chanel asked. "You know I don't let niggas know where I live so that has to be for you."

Lisa walked out of the room, her slender long legs leading the way. Snatching the door open, she was ready to go off, but the sight of DCs finest caused her spark to fizzle out.

"Can I help you officers?" she asked, her displeasure apparent.

"We are looking for a Sonny Raegan," one of the officers stated.

"Who?" Lisa asked.

"Ma'am does a Chanel Rodgers live here? We need to speak with her. She was with the young woman we are looking for," the officer stated impatiently.

"Hold on. I'll be right back," Lisa said defensively as she began to close the front door. One of the officers placed his foot over the threshold to stop it from closing completely.

"Can we come in ma'am?" he asked.

"Do you have a warrant?" she shot back. She didn't know what kind of trouble Chanel was in but she wasn't about to just feed her to the wolves.

"No . . ."

"Then no you can not come in. I'll be right back," she stated as she closed the door. She sprinted upstairs and into Chanel's room.

"Fuck is wrong with you? Why are you running?" Chanel asked.

"The police are at the door asking about you and a girl named Sonny Raegan," Lisa informed as she shrugged her shoulders.

"The police?"

The voice came from the hallway and both girls looked up as Raegan walked into the room.

"I take it you're Raegan," Lisa stated.

"Yeah," she replied.

"Well the police are here for you," Lisa said.

"Lisa, you have to tell them she's not here," Chanel stated.

"No, it's okay. I'll see what they want," Raegan said. Chanel gently grabbed the baby and followed Raegan down the stairs and to the front door.

She opened the door with a pounding heart and stared the officers directly in the face, while both Chanel and Lisa stood behind her.

"Are you Sonny Raegan?"

"Yeah that's me," she answered unsurely.

"You are under arrest for kidnapping and assault, turn around please ma'am."

"What?" Chanel exclaimed as Raegan was put in handcuffs.

"Wait . . . I didn't kidnap anybody. He's my son!" she shouted as they pulled her out of the house against her will. "Wait!" she protested.

"I was there . . . hold up! You guys are making a mistake," Chanel shouted. The sound of commotion awoke baby Micah and his screams mixed in with the confusion to create chaos. Chanel handed the baby off to Lisa as she followed behind the officers as they carted Raegan away. Her bare feet froze from the snow-covered ground but she marched behind them, throwing insults and objections at their backs.

"Please . . . don't do this. I can't go to jail. I just had a baby. He needs me. This is wrong. It's a misunderstanding," Raegan pleaded.

Chanel stood pissed off and shaking her head in disgust as she marched back into the house.

"What was that all about?" Lisa asked.

"Some bullshit. Her whack ass baby daddy playing games and telling lies. Can you watch him while I go downtown to see about getting her out?" Chanel asked.

Lisa nodded her head. "Yeah of course. Go ahead."

Lisa stood rocking baby Micah in her arms as Chanel stormed out of the house and disappeared into the night.

"I'm not giving Micah full custody. Fuck that! He wasn't even there when my baby was born. Now all of a sudden he want to be there fulltime!" Raegan shouted as she ice grilled her attorney. Livid, her foot tapped against the floor and her sharp breaths could be heard across the room.

"You don't have a choice. The judge has already ordered that your son be turned over to his father. He made you look extremely violent to the judge. You can always appeal to the family court later, once this has died down. You're lucky that the kidnapping charges were dropped and that you only received community service for the assault. This could have gone an entirely different way," the state assigned attorney stated with little patience. "You're unemployed and you attacked your child's father. When your situation has improved we can revisit the idea of you regaining custody."

Raegan dropped her head and allowed her tears to surface as her heart broke in half. "Everything's going to be okay Raegan. You have us," Chanel said as she reached over and hugged Raegan. Lisa gripped Raegan's hand in support and gave her a weak smile as she held onto baby Micah. The threesome had become extremely close. Two months had passed since the day that life had introduced them to one another. What had started out as an awkward situation had blossomed into a valued friendship. Chanel and Lisa had accepted Raegan and her son into their lives without hesitation. Micah had pressed full charges against Raegan out of spite and had tied her up in the legal system. The girls had taken good care of baby Micah while his parents battled it out, but the fight was over and they all had to say their good-byes to baby Micah. Raegan had lost and it felt as if she were handing her child over to a stranger.

Lisa handed Micah over to Raegan. She cradled him in her arms and kissed his forehead before she got up and reluctantly walked out of the room.

Micah stood with a smirk on his face as he reached out for the baby. "Give me my son," he spat.

"Why are you doing this Micah? Because I caught *you* cheating? You didn't even want him. Why are you taking him from me?" she asked.

"Bitch you took from me so now I'm taking from you. You should've left my paper where you found it," he seethed as he stared at her in contempt. "You give me my money I might give you your brat back."

Raegan shook her head in disgust. "You doing all of this over $10,000?" she asked. "You bitter, broke bastard!"

Micah put the baby in a car seat and then turned away from Raegan.

"I want my baby!"

"I wanted my money! We can't always have the things we want," he mocked as he left the lawyer's office feeling as though he had gotten the last laugh.

Chapter Two

Nahvid sat behind his cherry oak desk as he leaned back in his executive chair and he focused on the man speaking before him. He only half listened as exhaustion plagued him. He was a man who wore many hats. His many businesses kept him busy, but it was his dealings in the street that caused the bags to form beneath his eyes and made his heart heavy. He had planned to give the streets up a long time ago, but they always pulled him back in. The streets had chosen him back when he was a young kid coming up in Baltimore and they had a hold on him. He couldn't let go. He had a strange fear of going broke despite the millions of dollars he had in the bank. He feared poverty—it was his only fear. He had been down skid row and he refused to go back. He was addicted to it all.

The Money.

The Power.

The Prestige.

"I swear Nah, the cops took that shit out of the trunk of my car and kept it moving. They robbed me."

Nahvid folded his hands on top of his desk and stared the man in his eyes. *This stupid mu'fucka,* he thought in frustration. Nahvid didn't care to hear the tune the guy was singing. He wasn't interested in hearing sob stories. Nahvid was about his paper and if the nigga didn't have it, a conversation was not going to be the consequence. Nahvid wasn't about talk and his silence put fear in the young hustler's heart. Nahvid had been in the game long enough to know guilty men couldn't handle silence—they needed the noise to distract from the lies they told. Silence intimidated liars and they dominated the conversation so that the others didn't have time to dispute their stories. So as the hustler went on and on he dug his grave deeper and deeper.

"Yo my man . . . all that you're talking is good is irrelevant. Do you have my money?" Nahvid asked sternly.

"That's what I'm trying to tell you. I got pulled over and the cops took the weight out of my car," the guy rambled.

"And yet you sit in front of me," Nahvid responded sarcastically.

"Man, I swear on my moms . . . those pigs were dirty. They just took the weight and let me go. If you hit me with something I can flip it and work off my debt to you fam," the guy stated. He tried to put on a brave front but the quivering in his voice gave him away. "Come on Nahvid man. I've known you since the sandbox fam. I know how you get down. I didn't steal from you. I'm good for it Nah. Just let me pay you back a little at a time."

Nahvid's brow bent low as if he were highly offended. "Did I hit you with the work a little at a time?" he asked.

At a loss for words, the man didn't respond.

"Then I don't want my money a little at a time. Now I'ma ask you again. Do you have my money?"

The hustler shook his head and lowered his eyes to the floor as if he were a little boy being scolded by his father.

"Then you know who you need to go see. Right now this is about you. You go see my man Reason and I'll keep it about you. If you run then I'ma make it about that wife and those two kids you got out there in Southeast," Nahvid stated.

He didn't need to make eye contact or even raise his voice for his threat to hit home. He simply picked up his phone and proceeded to handle the day's business as the hustler stood to his feet. The color left the man's face as he stared at Nahvid in desperation.

"You can see yourself out fam," Nahvid stated shortly as he nodded toward the door.

Nahvid put the call in to his right hand man Reese "Reason" Grimes and with the snap of a finger a man's life was on a countdown. "Make it clean . . . no headshots. I've known the nigga awhile. Let his wife have an open casket," Nahvid instructed before hanging up the phone.

The sound of glass breaking caused him to stand to his feet as he pulled his .45 out of his desk drawer and made his way toward the noise. When he entered his kitchen he lowered his pistol and leaned against the wall as a shallow pit filled him stomach. He knew it was her without even seeing her face. Her slender frame and long jet-black hair were embedded in his memory. Even through the stench that covered her body, he recognized her scent. His eyes watered as he watched his mother rummage through his refrigerator, desperately shoving anything into her mouth that she could find.

He wanted to be disappointed in her, but this had become a routine long ago. Crack binges, clean binges, crack binges, clean binges. She never stuck to one thing for too long. Her crack addiction was too much for her to handle. She had a monkey on her back like none he had ever seen. She was part of the reason he entered the dope game in the first place. Being born to a drug addicted mother he knew that the taste of crack had already been introduced to him. He was born hooked and he knew that crack was destined to be a part of his life. Instead of smoking it, he chose the lesser evil and sold it. It was either one or the other. He walked up behind her and wrapped his arms around her waist, holding tightly as he hugged her from behind.

"Hey Nita," he said, calling her by her first name as he always had.

Nita stopped scrambling and calmed down. Her son always soothed her soul. She rested her head on his strong chest and replied. "Hey baby."

"When did you get out?" he asked. "I thought you were going to try this time."

"I did try those mu'fuckas kicked me out the program," Nita shouted.

"Kicked you out for what?" he questioned. He took her hand and turned her toward him.

"Don't lie to me Nita. What did they kick you out for?"

Nita lowered her eyes and shuffled her feet nervously. "I brought a little something into the center with me . . ."

"Ma . . ." Nahvid sighed in disappointment.

"Just a little bit. To hold me over you know . . ." she explained.

"No Nita. I don't know," he countered. "You got to get off of this shit. You're killing yourself."

"We all got to go sometime," she said as she pulled a cigarette from her bra and put it in her mouth. She lit it and only took one pull before Nahvid snatched it from her lips and broke it in half.

"You're pushing it old lady," he said with a smile.

"Old lady? Who you calling old? Huh? I remember back in the day when I was the finest thing walking these streets. I was on the scene, let me tell you . . ."

"Yeah yeah yeah. I've heard it all before," he teased as he put his arm around his mother's shoulder and pulled her close.

"Let's go take a hot bath and then I'll take you out to eat," he said.

He escorted his mother upstairs, his heart delighted by her presence. He sat on the toilet as she bathed herself. He wanted to give her privacy, but he was afraid that she would hop out of the window and be disappear like a thief in the night. They reminisced about the good ol' days. When she spoke of her past . . . before the drugs . . . before the shame . . . her eyes sparkled clear and vibrant. He had no memory of her before crack. All of his stories were filled with dark times so he didn't share them. He simply listened to her and let her talk until her heart was content. He enjoyed her presence. It wasn't often that he got to indulge in her and he cherished every fleeting moment that they shared. He told himself that he was going to get his mother clean. The day she got clean would be the day he gave up the game. *She's going right back to rehab in the morning,* he thought. As he held out a towel for her she stepped out of the tub and he wrapped her up, ensuring that she was warm. Despite her flaws, his mother was his world. He adored her and it tortured him to see her in pain.

"I love you Nita. You're my favorite girl in the world. You show up and then you leave me. You hurt my heart Nita. Every time you leave you kill me. Stop running. You've got to get clean," he whispered.

"I know Nahvid. Mama will baby. I promise. I will."

Nahvid pulled his grey Range Rover up to the rehab center as his mother cowered in her seat beside him.

"You can do this Nita. I'm going to be behind you every step of the way. This time I'll be here everyday to visit. Twice a day if they let me," he said.

He noticed that his mother was silent. He could see through her; she was intimidated by the inevitable hard journey to come. He got out and helped his mother from the car before accompanying her inside.

"They're not going to let me back in here Nahvid," Nita said shamefully.

"Don't worry about it. They will let you in. You wait right here," he replied as he motioned for one of the seats in the reception area. He knew that the rules to the rehab were strict, but the $25,000 knot in his pocket ensured Nita's re-admission. Nahvid walked in and made the arrangements with the director. Hopeful that this time would be different he went to retrieve Nita, but when he saw the empty chair she had been sitting in, he knew that she was long gone. His heart sank into his stomach as disappointment filled him. He should have known that she wouldn't go through with it. She wasn't ready to let her pipe go and there was nothing he could do to change that fact.

Raegan walked into the rehab center; her attitude at an all time high. She couldn't believe Micah had taken their son from her. *Now I have to go in here and deal with these people,* she thought as she snatched the door open. She was so pissed off that she didn't realize that someone was coming out at the exact same time and she collided into him with full force. She lost her footing on the ice beneath her and went flying to the ground. Her head smashed against the pavement sending a blinding pain shooting through her.

She sat up as she winced in pain, instinctively reaching for the back of her head.

"Are you okay?" Nahvid asked as he knelt down beside her.

"Umm yeah . . . I'm sorry I didn't see . . . oww," she moaned as she stopped midsentence to touch her tender head.

"Let me help you up," he offered as he scooped her legs and lifted her from the ground before setting her on her feet.

Raegan cleared her hair from her face and he was taken by surprise at how beautiful she was.

Damn, what is she doing sucking on a pipe? He asked himself, instantly assuming that she was an addict. He shook his head in disgrace. "You a'ight?" he checked once more.

She nodded as she brushed herself off. "Yeah I'm fine. Thanks."

She walked inside of the building and he made his way to his car, each dismissing the other without a second thought.

Raegan sighed as she shifted her weight from foot to foot. Chanel was late and Raegan was more than ready to go. Her first day of community service had left a bad taste in her mouth and she wanted nothing more than to get home and scrub the smell of crack off of her. The door opened and a chocolate girl exited the building. Her gray eyes mesmerized Raegan; she was taken aback by how pretty the girl was. She caught herself staring and turned her head.

"I wish this bitch would hurry up, it's cold as hell out here," she uttered to herself.

"You ain't lying," the girl whispered back. "You're the new girl right?"

"Oh no I'm not a patient here. I'm just volunteering," she said.

"Do I look like a crackhead to you?" the girl asked with a laugh. "Damn that's fucked up. I need to put myself together a little better if I'm coming off like that."

Raegan laughed and replied, "My fault girl. I'm bugging. You just kinda assume that everybody in this place have problems bigger than your own, you know?"

"Problems I've got—an addiction, not hardly," the girl replied. "I'm Gucci."

"Raegan."

A car horn honked and Raegan looked up hoping it was Chanel.

"That's me . . . I'll see you tomorrow though Raegan," Gucci said.

Raegan nodded as she watched the girl step into the black Mercedes. It was sitting right with all black everything and she shook her head as she thought, *damn wish it were me.*

Honk, honk!

Chanel pulled up just as Gucci rolled off.

"Hurry up bitch, we're going out tonight. It's time to cheer you up!"

"How the hell you get tickets at this concert. K. West has been sold out for weeks!" Lisa yelled as she made her way to the center of the front row.

"One of my niggas got 'em for me," Chanel replied.

"You don't need to rob this nigga then, he's a keeper," Raegan said. The girls were laced thanks to Chanel's latest sponsor. He was so friendly with the paper that she didn't have to rob him. He kept her pockets full of money. He had plenty of it and didn't mind sharing. Raegan's black Prada dress looked as if it were painted on and red bottom Louboutins made her shine like a star in a crowd full of duds. Her hair was pulled high off of her face in a genie ponytail. Everything from her eyebrows to her manicure was on point and the attention she was getting let her know she had put herself together right.

The entire front row was full of DCs finest and the crowd went crazy when the soulful rapper hit the stage. The concert was nice but it was the intermission that was the real show. Everybody was dressed in their best as they walked around the Verizon Center trying to be seen.

"It's so much potential in here," Chanel said, eyeing potential victims for her latest scam.

"Damn girl take a night off. Ain't your pussy tired," Lisa stated seriously.

"Ain't your third of the rent late bitch?" Chanel shot back. "You need to let me put you up on game so you can get your paper up."

Lisa stuck up her middle finger as Raegan shook her head. A crowd of girls crowded around a group of guys standing against the wall and as Raegan walked by she noticed the guy who had knocked her off her feet earlier that day. Their eyes locked and she slyly looked away and turned up her sexy as she walked subtly, precisely knowing that he was looking at her ass. She glanced back and to her dismay the guy wasn't looking. She peered at him curiously and smiled as she kept walking. Raegan had never been one to play her cards too closely. She wasn't obvious or desperate and there were plenty niggas in the building showing her mad love. *His loss*, she thought as she kept it moving with her girls.

***

Nahvid smirked as he sipped his Rémy and stood amongst his circle, shutting down the event as usual. It never mattered who came to town. In DC Nahvid was the celebrity. That was his city.

"Shorty bad as hell. That's you?" Reason asked as he leaned into his man curiously.

"Nah," Nahvid replied. "I saw her earlier at the rehab center when I was fucking with my moms."

"Bitch a piper?" Reason asked in disbelief. "They making em' like that now?"

"I don't know. I ain't never seen none like her," Nahvid stated. "She probably work there or something."

"You don't mind if I get on that?" Reason asked.

Nahvid wanted to tell him to fall back because Raegan definitely had him curious but he didn't want to rain on his man's parade. There were enough women at the event to go around so he nodded toward her. "Go ahead fam—do you."

Nahvid watched as his man approached Raegan. He silently hoped that she turned Reason down. Nahvid didn't want a chick that was easy to get so this was the perfect test to see what type of lady she actually was. Reason had women standing in line to deal with him so he was a catch around the city. If she turned him down it wouldn't be for his looks and Nahvid was eager to see how she handled herself, amongst a hood legend. He played the cut as his man went fishing.

"Yo' can I talk to you ladies for a minute?" Reason asked as he approached them, while looking Raegan up and down.

"What's your name ma?" he asked.

"Raegan we're going to keep walking, we'll be at the little girl's room," Chanel shouted.

"Okay, I'm coming right behind you," Raegan responded. She looked at the guy in front of her. "My name's Raegan," she responded.

"Raegan and Reason goes well together," he said with a charming smile.

"It's corny," she shot back with a smirk.

He laughed at her blunt nature, his ego slightly bruised as he rubbed his goatee. "You hard on a nigga huh? I'm just trying to get to know you beautiful," he said as he put a hand to his heart as if she were breaking it.

Raegan rolled her eyes and shook her head. She could tell that Reason's lines were well rehearsed. "How many chicks have you come at like that tonight?" she asked.

Her question caught him off guard because he suddenly became dumbfounded. The look on his face gave him away.

"That many?" she asked. "Listen brother let me give you some game. Women don't like being a part of a herd. It's not good to hear when its not meant exclusively for you."

She walked away leaving him staring at her backside as she entered the bathroom.

Nahvid chuckled as he watched his man throw up the white flag in surrender. "Was it that bad?" he asked, still laughing when Reason approached.

"Bitch was cold," he replied as he shook his head. "She's a crackhead."

"Why she got to be on crack fam?" Nahvid asked playfully.

"Cuz the ho got to be high to turn me down," Reason replied. His feelings seemed genuinely hurt for all of ten seconds until his trained eye sought out another lady from the crowd.

Nahvid's interest in Raegan doubled just from the way she had handled herself. *I'll see her around,* he thought.

The after party was jumping. The parking lot of the Park Hyatt Hotel looked like a foreign dealership as the East Coast's biggest players came out for a night on the town. DC wasn't the only city in the building. New Yitty, Baltimore, and even Norfolk had come out to play. The girls parked their cars a block away from the hotel, along with the other ordinary folks with ordinary cars and made their way to the party. The entire hotel had been reserved for the after partiers with the famous rapper promising to make an appearance.

As Raegan walked through the parking lot she noticed Gucci standing near the black Benz she had gotten picked up in earlier that day. She was stunning from head to toe, dipped in gold. Gold dress, gold jewelry, gold everything, reminding Raegan of a hot girl from the eighties. Raegan had to admit that Gucci's man kept her fly and she waved on her way inside the building.

As soon as they got inside, Chanel found her victim for the night. "I'll probably meet you guys at home. Here are my keys. I see something I like over there," she said before making her way across the room.

"Want to get a drink?" Lisa asked.

Raegan was about to say yes until she saw Micah walk into the hotel. She turned to Lisa. "No I'm not feeling that well," she lied. "I think I'm going to just catch a cab home."

"You sure?" Lisa asked.

"Yeah I'm sure. It stinks in here all of a sudden. Too many grimy niggas," Raegan responded. Her stomach turned and she felt sick as she tried to remain inconspicuous while heading toward the door. It was inevitable for Micah to see her. When he laid eyes on Raegan she could see the idea of revenge in his stare. He blocked her path.

"Fuck you going?" he asked harshly as he gripped the top of her arm. "What you rushing off for?" His tone was taunting as if he dared her to pop off.

"Let me go Micah!" she said between clenched teeth as she pulled her arm away from him. "Where is my son?"

"I should fuck you up for that little stunt you pulled," he threatened as he backed her into a corner. His hostility was evident. He stood so close to her that it appeared as though they were an intimate couple, but behind the visage his hand was wrapped tightly around her small neck. She struggled against him. "Stop," she whispered as he put one hand up her dress. She pulled at his hand, desperately. "Stop Micah!"

Her voice was loud but the music was louder and her protests were swallowed up in the sea of chatter.

No one would have even noticed how he was handling her if Nahvid hadn't been watching. He had spotted her from across the room and as he made his way over, his temperature rose in anger. He could see the look of concern on Raegan's face and although he did not know her, he wanted to.

"Is there a problem, my man?" he asked.

Micah turned and looked at Nahvid, but didn't loosen his grip.

"Nothing that concerns you," he shot.

"Yo, you don't know me and I think you want to keep it that way. I'm not on no rah rah shit fam. I don't do that. So I'm gon' say this one time and how the rest of your night play out is up to you. Walk away," he said with malice in his tone.

"Didn't I tell you mu'fucka . . . " Micah got loud and turned toward Nahvid, which proved to be the biggest mistake of his life. Nahvid never traveled without his goon squad and they were waiting, more than willing to put in work.

Out of nowhere his li'l niggas mauled Micah causing Raegan to turn her head. "No please . . . make them stop," she said, thinking that Micah might harm their son just to get even with her.

Nahvid frowned in confusion. He wasn't beat for the drama. "Just a minute ago the mu'fucka was choking you. Now you saving him?" He was about to dismiss her as a birdbrain, until she explained.

"He has my son. He's petty and is keeping him away from me out of spite. I don't want him to do anything to my baby just to get back at me," she pleaded softly.

Nahvid looked across the room at Reason and nodded toward the mob. He knew that was his cue to stop the commotion.

"Carry him out," Nahvid instructed as he led Raegan out of the building.

"Thank you," she said gratefully.

"You're welcome."

As Nahvid looked down at her, he had a million questions he wanted to ask; but he barely knew her and he didn't want to pry into her personal life too soon. She had just told him she had a kid—that he could deal with, but he wondered what other skeletons she had in her closet.

"I need to find my girls. I'm just trying to get out of here," she whispered as she wrapped her arms around herself, shivering from the winter cold.

He removed his Armani jacket and placed it around her shoulders. "Don't let my man mess up your night, ma."

"My night? Ha! That's funny. Try my life," she exclaimed as she shook her head. "I can't believe I ever fucked with him."

"I saw you. I kind of bumped into you earlier . . ."

"Oh yeah, that was you. I have a knot the size of a baseball on the back of my head thanks to you," she said half joking. She smiled at him and his heart fluttered. He was never a sucker for women, but Raegan was interesting. She was something different . . . new.

"My fault ma. You got to let me make that up to you sometime," he replied.

"Anytime," she answered. "I'm Raegan by the way."

"Like Ronald?"

"Like Sonny," she said with a chuckle. "My last name's Raegan, but I've gone by that since I was a kid," she explained.

"Sonny Rae. I like that. I'm Nahvid," he introduced.

"It's very nice to meet you Nahvid," she said. She discreetly looked him up and down, admiring his almond colored skin, chinky eyes, and full lips. He was the most handsome man she had ever seen. It was more his style than anything that attracted her. He had a grown man vibe to him that made her cream her panties.

"I'm about to shake this shit though. It's not my type of scene," he said. "Here's my business card," he said. "You let me know when I can take you out for dinner. You know? To apologize for knocking you off your feet."

"I will. Have a good night Nahvid," she said. She stood on her tiptoes to kiss his cheek and whispered, "Thank you for handling that mess for me earlier. You didn't have to but I'm glad you did."

Raegan hopped into the first cab she saw and this time when she looked back at Nahvid, he was watching.

Chanel looked around the hotel room as her eyes adjusted to the dark. The sound of snoring beside her let her know that her victim was asleep and it was time for her to make her move. She slid from underneath him, slowly, carefully so that she didn't wake him. She wanted to wash the smell of sex from her body, but she didn't have time. *I'll do that when I get home. Right now I just need to get the money and get out of here,* she thought. Locating her clothes she slid into her dress and heels quickly, then rifled through the LRG jeans that were strewn on the floor. *Bingo,* she thought as she threw it into her clutch bag and headed for the door. She cracked it slightly, not wanting to allow any light into the room. Before she could step one foot outside the door, a forearm came from behind her and slammed it shut.

"Bitch where you going?"

She turned around to face the man she had just slept with hoping that he hadn't seen her rob him. "Empty that bag bitch," he said as he put the chain lock on the top of the hotel door.

Chanel held onto the clutch and ran for the door, but was pulled back by her weave. The guy violently dragged her all the way back to the bed.

"You want to rob me bitch? You can keep it. But you about to earn that paper. Get on your fucking knees," he ordered.

"Look you can have it back. Just let me go," she begged.

The dude grabbed his gun off his nightstand and without warning pistol whipped her until she fell to her knees. Blood seeped from her mouth as she cried. "Grimy-ass bitch . . . you gon' take that paper with you, but you gonna work for every dollar. Open your mouth."

Chanel sobbed and keeled over as she begged him. "Please don't."

"Don't cry now ho. Get up!" he shouted as he kicked her in the ribs.

Chanel crawled to her knees and reluctantly opened her mouth as the guy removed his dick. He peed all over her face and inside her mouth as she spit it out while turning her face. Shoving himself down her throat, he choked her as he fucked her face. He grinded so hard that it felt as though he would take her head off. There was nothing gentle about his stroke. He was punishing her. Chanel had been hustling and scamming men for a long time but never had she been caught. If she had known that this would be the repercussions to her actions she would have never done it. Chanel gagged and scratched at his abdomen, but his grip on the back of her head was so tight that she couldn't move. After releasing in her mouth he slapped her across the face, the gun cutting into her cheek as her head snapped to the right.

"Please . . ." she cried as she spit out a combination of semen, blood, and urine.

"Please what bitch?" he asked. "Say you're sorry."

"I'm sorry!" she cried, still on her knees. She tried to climb to her feet, but he knocked her back down.

"Sit the fuck back down. I didn't tell you to get your ass up!" he shouted as he pointed the gun in her face, daring her to move. The guy retrieved his money out of her bag and peeled it off, flicking at her, making it rain all over her. After degrading and defiling her, he was letting her keep the cash. It was never about that. He had punished her because of her disrespect.

"You can have that little paper bitch," he stated. "Now get the fuck out."

Her greed wouldn't allow her to leave the money on the ground. She hadn't gone through this pain and humiliation for nothing. She came there for the money and she planned on leaving with the money. She picked up every bill and then scrambled from the room, grateful to leave there with her life.

Chanel stumbled into the house. She was barely able to keep her balance as the room spun wildly. Her head pounded to the beat of a faraway drum as she reached for the light switch. She was too embarrassed to wake her room-mates. She didn't want Raegan and Lisa to see her at her lowest point, but when the stairway light illuminated she knew that she would have to face them.

"Chanel is that you?" Lisa called out from the top of the stairs.

"Y . . . y . . . yeah it's me. I need help," she replied back her voice trembling.

Raegan and Lisa rushed down the steps and stopped in shock when they say Chanel bleeding all over their hardwood floors.

"Oh my God. Who did this to you?" Raegan asked as she ran to her side. The strong stench of urine filled her nostrils as she led Chanel to the couch. "Sit down."

"What happened?" Lisa grilled.

"The nigga I was trying to hustle caught me," Chanel admitted.

"I told your ass this would happen," Lisa said. "You should have stopped while you were ahead. You wasn't getting big money from those niggas. You're risking your life for chump change and shopping money."

"Money is money and no matter what you say I needed it. This is all I know. This is my hustle," Chanel defended.

"Then you need a new hustle hun," Raegan said sincerely. "I feel you chasing the American dream. You want your piece of the pie. I understand that, but if you gonna do it why not go all out? Why the nickel and diming?"

"What do you mean?" Chanel asked. "What I'm supposed to strong arm niggas? I'm only one bitch."

"And I'm one bitch and that makes two. Niggas do it all the time. Sticking mu'fuckas for they paper. If we can hit just one good lick than we can all be set for a while," Raegan said. She couldn't even believe the words that were coming from her mouth, but her motivation was her son. She wanted to give Micah his money back so that he would return her son.

"I'm for that and that bitch-ass nigga who fucked me up is first on my list," Chanel stated as she wiped her eyes.

Lisa stood with her hands on her hips, shaking her head. "Are you two fucking serious? Raegan . . . look at her. She in here smelling like piss, her mouth all busted up and you want to get in on that scheming bullshit?"

"All we have to do is do it once and do it right. I see those school loan bills that's piling up on your dresser Lis. One good robbery will catch you up," Raegan said convincingly.

"So what you bitches are bank robbers now. Y'all gonna take a bank?" Lisa asked incredulously.

"Not a bank. A stash house," Raegan concluded.

"Niggas be having at least a hundred thousand in they stash spots. Not to mention the coke that be lying around," Chanel said growing excited. This was the payday she had been looking for . . . the one that she needed to leave the game alone for good.

"You bitches are crazy. I don't want a damn thing to do with this one. Good night," Lisa said as she walked away from the conversation. She didn't even want to know too much about it. She couldn't tell what she didn't know.

"We can do this Raegan," Chanel said.

"I know . . . I need this money too Chanel. You know that's the only way Micah is going to let this beef with me go," Raegan replied. Her eyes bugged out as she thought of who they would target. "I know a nigga too. He picks up this girl from the rehab center all the time."

"How you know he papered up? Just because he's hustling doesn't mean he's doing it right. He could be an ol' hustling backwards ass nigga," Chanel asked.

"Trust me he's not just doing it for the lifestyle. He drives a Benz, keeps his girl laced . . . I saw them tonight at the after party. He's getting it. I know it," Raegan said surely.

"Then let's do it," Chanel said as she lifted her hand to give her girl some play.

Raegan cringed and said, "I'll give you a high five *after* you take a shower. You kinda stink."

Despite her pain, Chanel burst into laughter as Raegan chuckled too. In the back of her mind Chanel vowed that she would get revenge on the guy who had fucked her up. She would make sure that their paths crossed again one day, but in the meantime they were about to get money.

Chapter Three

For the next few days, Raegan made friends with Gucci. She made it a point to find out something new about her boyfriend each day. Raegan's suspicions were right. According to Gucci, her boyfriend Jamie was the perfect lick. Raegan felt bad because she genuinely liked the girl, but her boyfriend had to get it.

"Hey is everything okay?" Gucci asked as they sat at the reception desk filing patient forms.

"Yeah, why do you ask?" Raegan responded, hoping she wasn't acting suspicious. It was awkward sitting next to the girl when Raegan knew in the back of her head that she was plotting on her man.

"I saw what happened last night . . . at the after party. Dude was way out of line," Gucci commented.

"He's my child's father," Raegan admitted.

"What? And he fooling on you like that?" she asked.

"We have a lot of issues with one another. I'm not fucking with him. He took my son away from me," Raegan stated. She didn't know what possessed her to tell Gucci her business. She kicked herself for being so loose at the lips.

"That's foul," she replied.

"The messed up part is he wants me to pay $10,000 to get my own baby back," Raegan said.

Gucci was silent. She could hear the yearning in Raegan's voice. She couldn't pretend to empathize with Raegan. She didn't have children. In fact, she didn't want them. She was too afraid of what her mother's genes might do to her own kids.

"For what it's worth I can tell you love your baby. Don't let him beat you girl," Gucci stated as she stood from her seat. Raegan half smiled as she watched her walk away. Her conscience nagged at her to change her plans but it was too late. Chanel was already in place. She had followed him around for days until he led them straight to his stash house. Today was the day that Raegan gave the go ahead and there was no turning back. With their finances in dire circumstance, it was now or never. They had watched his every move and had his routine down to a science. It was time to set their nerves aside and make this money.

At the end of the day Raegan left fifteen minutes early so that she and Chanel could already be in place when Gucci's man came to get her. They watched as Gucci came out of the building and got inside his car and when he pulled off, he never even suspected to check his rearview mirror. He had no idea what was about to take place.

Gucci sat back in the leather seats and sighed.

"What's good, baby girl? You don't got no love for your man?" Jamie asked as he reached over and palmed her thigh tightly. Gucci leaned over and kissed his cheek, but he turned his head and dodged her.

"You know what I'm talking about ma. I just rode all the way across town to pick you up. Come put in some work," Jamie said as he lifted out of his seat slightly and grabbed his crotch suggestively.

Gucci wanted to tell him to kiss her ass. That maybe she would want to please him if he approached her differently, but what could she say. She needed him. He may not treat her the best,

but he kept her stable. The cash and gifts he
threw her way made life bearable. Without him
she was be on stuck. He was her man and she
wanted to show him she appreciated the things
he did for her, no matter how small. She slid
her head between his legs and took him into her
mouth, tears filling her eyes. Gucci would have
gladly done what it took to please her man if he
didn't constantly make her feel as if she had to.
With him, it wasn't her choice to please him. It
was a requirement that he had made clear from
day one. He held her head and she finished the
job as they pulled into her driveway.

"Go grab you an overnight bag. You're coming
over tonight. I'll take you shopping in the morning," he promised. To most girls the offer would
be romantic, exciting, but to Gucci it felt like a
demand. But instead of standing up for herself
she told him to wait a quick minute and ran into
the house to retrieve a few items. She was labeled
weak minded, not because she wanted to be but
because she didn't know how to be any way else.

When she arrived home she avoided his stare
and got out of the car with a short good-bye. She
was halfway up the walkway when he called her
name.

"Guch!"

She turned around and walked back to him, standing outside his window. He put his hand out the window and placed ten hundred dollar bills in her hand. "Pay a bill or something, make sure your moms is straight," he told her.

She nodded her head.

"What do you say?" he asked.

"Thanks daddy," she said as she backpedaled into the house.

She quickly peeked in on her mother and nodded to the nurse that was on duty.

"How you doing today ma?" she asked as she bent and kissed her on the forehead.

Her mother turned her head away and peered at the nurse. "She mean, Gucci."

Gucci arched her eyebrows and glared at the nurse. "What did you do to her? Did you hurt her?" she asked directly.

"No—no. I just helped her get dressed for the day. She was upset and crying about it, but I would never—"

Gucci put her hand up already knowing that her mother was giving the nurse a hard time. She didn't like to be undressed by strangers. Past ghosts made her weary of everyone but Gucci. "It's okay ma. I'm home now. Don't worry.

Nobody's going to hurt you." She was used to taking care of things. Gucci's mother had relied on her ever since she was a young kid. Significantly disabled, her mother didn't function well mentally. Southern born, she was labeled slow, even the most minute tasks seemed impossible for her to learn and Gucci had always been the glue that held everything together. Gucci was a product of her mother's rape. A nurse who had been hired to take care of her mother had molested her for years and it wasn't discovered until she went into labor with Gucci. Now here she was at twenty-three, burdened with the task of caring for a woman who had never wanted her in the first place. The man who raped her would whisper in her ear.

"Ooh this some good coochie," he would say.

So when she gave birth to her baby all she could say was the word coochie, but she was so slow that she mispronounced the word.

"Gucci . . . Gucci," she said repeatedly. She said the word so much that the nurses put it down on the birth certificate. No, Gucci's name had nothing to do with fashion. It was a direct reflection of her mother's rape and it was a ghost that haunted her even to this day.

If Gucci had the money she would put her mother in an adult facility to make things easier. A professional home could take better care of her mother than Gucci ever could, but with her minimum wage job at the rehab center she was going nowhere fast. With genetics like hers life wasn't easy. She inherited an empty head disguised by a beautiful exterior. Her body and face were magnificent, but they were of no value to her. She was simply living, trying to get by as best as she could. Her looks attracted men left and right, but the ones who caught her only took advantage of her. Although she wasn't labeled mentally challenged she knew that she wasn't ever the smartest girl in the room. She knew other girls who looked like she did. They used their assets to get what they wanted. They had established hustles, pulled capers, and put a price tag on their pussies—all of which made life a little easier. Gucci was afraid to grind it out because she knew that she was easily outwitted. So instead she played the back, her confidence too low to ever take the lead.

"Gucci! Gucci!" her mother shouted from her room. Gucci sighed as she closed her eyes, overwhelmed by the abundance of responsibility that was placed on her. *I can't wait to get out of here. This shit is just too much,* she thought. She grabbed her bag and rushed out of the door. She was desperate for a way out and when she finally did escape she would never look back.

"What is she doing? She never goes home with him," Raegan exclaimed as they watched Gucci get back in Jamie's car. "She would pick today of all days." Raegan looked at Chanel and said, "Let's just do it another day."

"We're doing it today," Chanel concluded.

"Chanel, I work with her everyday. She's cool people. I don't want—"

"Nobody's gonna get hurt Raegan. We're just after the money. It'll be fine," Chanel said.

They followed Jamie until he arrived home. He wasn't smart enough to have a separate stash spot. He broke the number one rule: Don't shit where you eat; and although he hustled hard, he was accessible. Now Raegan and Chanel was about to test him. Gucci pulled out two .45s and handed one to Raegan.

"Where did you get these from?" she asked.

"A friend of mine hooked me up. I told him I needed them for protection. They're dirty so if we have to pop a nigga they can't be traced back to us," Chanel stated. "You ready?" she asked.

Raegan nodded as she eyed the house. Her eye never left it, not even for a moment. She hawked it, wanting to make sure she knew exactly what she was getting herself into. When night fell the girls got out of the car.

"Pop the hood to the car," Raegan said as they got out. "She'll recognize me. You take the front and I'll be at the back." The girls split and as Chanel approached the house she turned the doorknob to see if it were locked. When it didn't budge, she had no choice but to ring the doorbell. She wore a winter hat and a cashmere scarf that she had wrapped around her face. She looked harmless. Like an around the way girl who had gotten herself stranded and was wrapped up to stay warm, despite the Louboutin hooker heels and short designer dress she wore beneath her short trench coat.

"Who is it?" she heard him yell through the door.

"Hi . . . I was wondering if I could use your phone. My car broke down and I don't have any cell reception," she replied.

Just as she suspected, Jamie was soft on a bitch. If a man had come to his doorstep with the exact same problem he would have turned him away, but when he saw the pair of long legs glistening on his doorstep he opened up without hesitation.

"Thank you sooo much," she said as she stepped into the house. The only thing that they could see was her eyes.

Gucci came out from a back room to make her presence known. Scantily clad in her bra and panties she walked into the living room.

"Who is this?" she asked.

"Oh my car broke down I'm just using the phone," Chanel stated. "Oh yeah and can I ask one more thing? I promise, after this I'll be out of your hair," she said sweetly as she looked at Jamie seductively.

"What's that ma?"

"Where's the money?" Chanel asked as she aimed her gun directly at him.

Jamie grabbed Gucci and pushed her toward Chanel, then took off for his back door. Thinking he had gotten away he threw it open and ran right into Raegan's gun. "Get in the house," she ordered as she eased him back inside. He backed up slowly, his eyes searching the kitchen for something he could use to defend himself. "Don't even think about it," Raegan said. "By the time you make your move, your brains will be all over your kitchen floor."

Raegan walked him back into the living room.

"Fuck," he grimaced as he shook his head, realizing that it was a set up.

When Raegan saw Gucci sitting on the couch shaking in fear as Chanel held her at gunpoint she immediately felt bad. She was ready to get this over with.

"Where's the money?" she asked.

"I don't know what you talking about! What money?" he asked, feigning innocence.

"You don't know what we talking about huh?" Chanel asked. She bitch smacked him with the gun. "Don't play me Jamie. Where's the money?"

"Just tell them!" Gucci shouted.

Jamie spit blood from his mouth. "Fuck you bitch."

"Go search the house," Chanel said.

Raegan ran through the house searching for the bedroom. She tore it up from top to bottom and found nothing.

"I can't find it," Raegan mumbled to herself. She moved from room to room in less than five minutes, but came up short. "Think Raegan think," she said. She ran inside the kitchen and opened up his cabinets. Condiments and jars filled them. She pulled one of the cereal boxes down and opened it up. "Got it."

She didn't give a fuck. She grabbed every cereal box in sight, stuffing it into the empty black duffel bag she carried.

"Let's go," she told Chanel as she rushed back into the living room.

"Get your ass on the floor and turn around," Chanel ordered. Jamie didn't protest and did as he was told, all the while making threats.

"I'ma find you bitches," he stated bitterly.

"Yeah yeah," Chanel replied. She bound his wrists with zip ties and then his feet, hog-tying him so that he couldn't move. "Tie her up," she told Raegan.

Gucci watched in horror as Raegan approached her and when she saw the tattoo on her wrist her eyes bugged out in disbelief. She recognized it instantly and when she looked Raegan in the eyes they both knew that Gucci was aware of her identity.

"Let's go," Raegan said as she applied that last zip tie. The girls left out of the front door, ran to their car, and closed the hood before pulling off into the night.

Chapter Four

"Oh my God I can't believe we just did that," Chanel yelled in disbelief as she flew down the interstate.

Raegan laughed, but nervous jitters filled her stomach. She knew that she had a problem. Gucci knew that she was behind the robbery. Nervous butterflies filled her stomach. "I think she recognized me."

"What?" Chanel shot out.

"There was something about the way she looked at me. Like she couldn't believe it was me," Raegan said. "What if she goes to the police?"

"She won't," Chanel said.

"But what if she does," Raegan said. "What if she tells ol' boy it was me?"

"Now that she might do," Chanel responded.

"I have to cut her in," Raegan concluded.

"Fuck that. If you cut her in, it'll be from your own half," Chanel said seriously. "And there's no way she can prove it was you. She doesn't know anything. Don't get paranoid girl . . . just chill out and think about all that money in that bag. That'll take all your worries away."

The girls sat in the middle of the kitchen floor emptying the cereal boxes. By the time they were done they were $40,000 richer and had a quarter brick in their pockets.

"That's twenty each," Chanel said happily. Instead of scraping and stealing her dough a few hundred at a time, she had just come up nicely by putting in less than ten minutes worth of work. "This is chump change compared to the bigger dealers in town."

"I know. I think we need to keep it to a minimum though. I'm willing to do it again, but we have to be smart about it. We should only do one lick a month. The hood gets paid on the first and fifteenth of the month. That's when niggas get big money because all of the smokers have that government check in their pockets. We need to do it on those days from here on out. This money is good money, but I guarantee we would have come out a lot nicer if we had hit ol' boy on the right day," Raegan said.

"What do we do with the coke?" Chanel asked.

"We definitely can't sell that to anyone around here. That'll be a dead giveaway. You try to meet some out of town hustlers and make some connections with them. This little bit ain't worth selling right now, but I'm sure we'll come across more. When we get our weight up we will whole-sale it," Raegan said. "You just work on finding buyers for it."

The girls split the pot, but Raegan's money was already spent. After paying Micah the $10,000 she owed him she would only have $10,000 left. No matter what Chanel said, she knew that Gucci was a threat and she planned on paying her off to keep her silent.

Raegan picked up the phone to call Micah. She was eager to see her baby. She had his money and now all she wanted was for him to give her baby back and stay out of her life.

"We're sorry. The number you have dialed has been changed. No new number is listed."

When Raegan heard the operator's voice she was livid. *This nigga thinks I'm playing about my son,* she thought as she stood up. She grabbed the keys to Chanel's car and headed out the door. She was tired of the back and forth charade Micah was playing. It was tit for tat with him. As she sped over to Micah's house her blood pressure rose as she cussed him out in her head the entire way. She pulled up to the house and hopped out of the car. Everything in her was tired of him. His spiteful ways turned her off completely. Raegan would never regret her son, but she regretted the fact that she had made him with a man like Micah. Her fists pounded his door repeatedly, knocking so persistently that he didn't have a choice but to answer for her.

"Where's my son?" she asked as soon as he opened the door.

His face was bruised from the once over that Nahvid's goons had given him. She threw the stack of money she had for him directly in his face. His tall frame blocked the door so she was unable to enter his home. "Give me my baby. You got your money."

"You can have him back when I say you can have him back," Micah said.

Tears filled her eyes. "Micah!" she cried out in frustration. "What is this really about? How can you keep him from me? I'm his mother."

"And I'm his father. Get the fuck off my doorstep before I blow your fucking head off," Micah said hatefully. "Don't come back. You wanted to leave so stay the fuck gone, but my son is staying right here."

He pushed her away from his door and slammed the door shut in her face.

"Micah," she yelled as tears trailed her cheeks. She pleaded on his doorstep until she had nothing left in her. When the lights went out she peeled herself off of the ground. Feeling hopeless she left, not knowing what else to do.

Nahvid spotted Raegan from behind the bar at his soul food restaurant. *Everywhere I go I'm seeing this girl,* he thought. The two of them together were kismet in his eyes. He had never wanted to know more about a person. She sat in the corner of his bustling establishment, drinking a glass of wine as she stared out the window at the falling snowflakes. He thought that she was playing hard to get. He had no idea that she was preoccupied with other things. Starting something with him was the furthest thing from her mind. The fact that she didn't seem to want him, made him want her more. As if his energy had tapped her on the shoulder she turned her face toward his. The chandelier lights reflected off of the tears on her face and as he walked from behind his bar toward her, she gathered her things to leave.

"Sonny Rae," he said as he walked up behind her and whispered in her ear. "Let me find out that bum nigga of a baby daddy got you crying your eyes out."

"I'm sorry. I've gotta go," she said as she tried to leave. She couldn't focus on him right now. She was too distracted. Her emotions were all over the place. She was distraught and a little tipsy from the wine she had been sipping on.

"You can't drive like this. Stay for a while until you calm down. Have you eaten?" he asked.

She shook her head no and he snapped his finger to get one of the waitress' attention.

"Yes sir?"

"Please set up a private table on the second floor for me and my guest," he instructed.

He led her up to their table and than pulled out her chair as she sat down.

"Everything okay?" he asked.

"I'm fine, it's just been a long day for me," she replied. "I'm sorry I didn't call. Things have been crazy for me."

"I've been running into you a lot lately," he said.

"That's a good thing right?" she asked.

"I'm not sure just yet," he replied. "I find myself thinking a lot about you . . . wondering how you are and I don't even know you."

She looked up at him in surprise. A man like Nahvid could have anyone he wanted, but he was stuck on her. Flattered was an understatement.

"There's not much to know," she replied with a shy smile. "I'm like most girls."

"I highly doubt that," he responded. "What do you spend most of your time doing?"

Raegan thought about it and instantly became ashamed of her answer. She had been with Micah for three years and ever since meeting him her days and nights had revolved around him. "I've wasted a lot of time pleasing a man. I haven't taken much time for myself."

"We're going to have to change that," he responded. "A man is supposed to make you his center of gravity—not the other way around."

"So what do you do?" she asked.

"So she feigns ignorance huh?" he asked with a smirk, knowing that she was aware of his street status.

She shook her head and laughed slightly at his blunt nature. "No, I've heard about you, but I want to hear it from you. The streets say you are a scary guy, but the man I'm sitting across from seems so different."

"I'm a businessman. I like to involve myself in anything profitable. I don't like to take losses. I guess over the years I've had to make a few examples out of people, but that's not all that I am. I take care of the people I love," he admitted.

"I can tell. You seem very loyal," she said.

The two conversed over dinner and wine as if they had known each other their entire lives. Their chemistry was off the charts and as they learned a little bit about one another their attractions grew.

They talked and laughed for hours, the wine loosening lips that were usually so airtight. Raegan had never felt an attraction like this before. He had a way of making her feel better about life as if nothing could break her, not even Micah.

As the sun came up, she yawned. "I have to get back home. I have my roomate's car and I have to be somewhere in a few hours. I had a good time with you. You don't even know how you turned my night around."

"Can I see you again?" he asked.

"The way that our paths have been intertwined I'm sure that you will," she replied. She stood and he escorted her to her car. "Am I going to have to kidnap you in order to take you out on a formal date?" he asked. He put his hand behind her head and massaged the nape of her neck gently with his fingers. His touch electrocuted her body, making her eyes flutter and her clit throb. She was beautiful and sexy and classy and innocent and mischievous all at the same time.

"I don't want you to think I'm playing games," she whispered. "I'm just—"

"Playing games," he said, finishing her sentence. He stepped closer to her, trapping her against the car and whispering in her ear as his body pressed against hers. "It's okay though. I enjoy the chase ma. I'm just wondering if I'm ever going to catch you."

Her nipples stuck out at full attention as her pussy rained her wanting onto her thigh. Her clit bloomed like a springtime flower and she gasped because he was making her hurt in a good way. The sexual tension between them was high and a thousand sensations shot through her.

"I'm caught," she whispered as she took his lips into her mouth and kissed him seductively. His hands roamed her body until he reached her ass, squeezing tightly as he aligned his throbbing dick with her middle. He was hard and she could feel it through his jeans that he was thick and didn't come with any shorts below the waistline. They were in pure heat as he lifted one of her legs and slid his hand up her dress, ripping the thong she wore. The street was deserted but the possibility of being caught by a passerby made it even better for Raegan. It heightened her pleasure. She wanted to tell him to stop and that they barely knew each other, but he was making her feel too good and the only thing that came out was sighs of pleasure as he played with her clit. He rolled it, smashed it, tugged at it—pleasing her without ever sticking his dick inside of her.

"Let's go back inside," she whispered. She was feigning for the dick and could no longer contain herself.

Nahvid picked her up, holding her voluptuous ass in his palms as her legs wrapped around his waist and kissed all the way back to the door. He pressed her against the glass their grunts and moans filling the early morning streets. He would have made love to her right there but their moment was ruined when a car came down the street, the driver blaring his horn at them.

Raegan and Nahvid were on cloud nine, but quickly came back down to earth when reality set in. He put her down and rested his forehead against hers.

"You think I'm a ho now, right?" she asked insecurely as she fixed her dress. "I don't usually sleep with men on the—"

He put a finger to her lips to silence her nonsense. "I think that you're beautiful and I want to see you again."

Her embarrassment was evident by the shade her red cheeks had turned. She couldn't even look him in the eye. He put his finger underneath her chin and lifted her face. "Don't be embarrassed. I've smashed chicks that have made me wait forever and they still turned around and did me dirty. That means nothing to me Raegan. We're two grown individuals so whenever we decide to take it there, it will be because we made the decision together—responsibly. I don't have expectations of you, only standards of myself and you meet every one of them. I respect loyalty. I caught you, now I got to trap your heart ma. Spend tomorrow with me."

"I can't. I have community service at the rehab center tomorrow. I have to complete 250 hours so that I can go back to the judge and try to fight for custody of my son again," she said.

"The director owes me a favor. You're done with that. He'll let the judge know you fulfilled your time. Now what's your excuse?" he asked.

She shook her head, unable to hid her smile. She was smitten with Nahvid. Whatever she needed he could make happen and it felt good to be handled with such care for a change. "I guess I don't have one. Can you pick me up from the center? I have to stop in for a second in the morning to handle something," she said.

"Done. Just text me when you're ready," he replied.

Raegan nodded and he kissed her lips as he admired her beauty, noticing the way her eyes glistened with insecurity when she was unsure. He grabbed her hand and walked her back to the car, tucking her safely inside before she pulled away.

Chapter Five

Raegan walked into the rehab center paranoid that the police or better yet, Gucci's man, would come for her at any moment. Nahvid had made good on his promise by getting her out of the community service. *As soon as I clear the air with Gucci, I'm blowing this joint,* she thought. She quickly located Gucci and walked up behind her grabbing her hand to drag her into the ladies single stall bathroom. Raegan locked the door and took a deep breath as she turned around, preparing herself for a confrontation.

"Look Gucci . . . I know you recognized me last night, but I want you to know that we were never going to hurt you. You were never in any danger," Raegan stated honestly. She reached into her purse and pulled out five stacks, handing them to Gucci. "This is half of what I earned last night," she offered.

Gucci was hesitant to take it. She felt betrayed by Raegan. "What's this? Hush money?" Gucci asked.

"It's my way of saying I'm sorry," Raegan responded.

"So what? You pretended to be cool with me so you could get to Jamie? That was your plan all along?" she asked.

"No. It wasn't like that really," Raegan replied.

Gucci shook her head and said, "I don't want the money. I want in."

"What?" Raegan exclaimed in surprise. She hadn't pegged Gucci as a hustler. She didn't seem like the type. Gucci wasn't cut from the same cloth as Raegan; if she were, the two of them wouldn't even be having a conversation. If the shoe was on the other foot, Raegan would have popped off on sight. Gucci was too nice, too trusting, and too understanding. As Raegan thought about how naïve and innocent Gucci really was, a light bulb went off in her head. *She's perfect,* Raegan thought. *They will never see her coming.*

"I want in. I need a come-up Raegan. This job is a dead end for me. Me and my mom are barely making it at home. I have to put up with bullshit from dudes like Jamie because without them I would be starving. I'm tired of it and I want in. I just want to get enough to set my mom up and send me on the first thing smoking out of this city," Gucci stated.

"I'm not in this by myself. I'll have to run it by my girl. Can we meet you somewhere. Tomorrow night?" Raegan asked.

"We can meet at my place. Maybe then you will see why I need y'all to put me on," Gucci stated. Raegan was surprised that Gucci was singing this tale of poverty. She would have put her bottom dollar on it that Gucci was living the champagne life, but from the look of desperation in her eye, Raegan knew that this wasn't the case. Looks could be deceiving and Gucci had the world fooled. She was down bad and ready to climb her way to the top. Tired of watching other women get it—envying chicks who had the world in the palms of their hands, she wanted to become a part of the big girl club.

As Chanel sat in Gucci's driveway, anxiety filled her gut. "I don't know about this Raegan. We just robbed her boyfriend," Chanel said skeptically.

"I'm not advocating either way. If she's in that's cool and if she ain't that's fine too. Just meet her. See what type of vibe you get and then we'll decide from there."

When the three of them got together they clicked instantly. Their interactions were so natural that they appeared to be old friends. Gucci was so easygoing that she endeared herself to Chanel and Raegan. Her spirit was infectious and now that they had an additional set of eyes and ears, they were ready to take it to the next level.

Gucci sat inside the crack house; her eyes discreetly roamed the room as she counted the number of people in the room. She had become a regular over the past month. Playing her part and getting as much information on their victims as she possibly could. The dirty clothes she wore and her ruffled hair, made her almost fit in with the fiends around her. She stood and went to cop from one of the d-boys in the kitchen. Their operation was all the way sloppy. They allowed their customers to get high in the basement so that when their highs came down they didn't miss the second-helping sell. It was this tactic that allowed the girls to catch them slipping.

Gucci kept her head low as she approached one of the young hustlers, "Can I get two twinkies?" she asked. She handed him the twenty-dollar bill and took the beige colored rocks out of his hand before scrambling back into the basement. She carefully searched the room until she found a young girl sitting idly in the corner. Eyes wide and shaking she was in need of a hit. She had been lingering in the dope spot all day trying to hit a lick on one of the other fiends. With no luck, she had the shakes and was irritated beyond belief. So when Gucci approached her with a proposition she jumped at the opportunity.

"Hey, you trying to hit this with me," Gucci said as she sat down next to the girl.

The girl eyed her suspiciously but all doubt was erased when she saw the twinky sitting in the palm of Gucci's hand. She reached for it as if she were about to touch a precious art exhibit, but Gucci snapped her hand shut quickly—right before the girl got to it.

"What you playing games for? You not even a smoker," the girl snapped.

"You don't know what I am," Gucci responded harshly.

"Look I might be down bad but I'm not out. I've seen you in here trying to blend in but you never smoke nothing," the girl said.

"I've seen you in here too—too broke to smoke anything. Now you want this or not?" Gucci asked.

"What I got to do for it?" the girl asked.

The girl was so transfixed on Gucci's closed palm that she couldn't focus.

Gucci snapped her fingers. "Hey . . . you want it?" she asked.

"What I got to do?"

"I need you to go upstairs and cause a distraction," Gucci whispered as she looked around to make sure no one else was listening. Despite her convincing appearance she felt naked as if everybody in the room knew that she was present with ill intent.

"What kind of distraction?" the girl asked with a frown.

"I don't care what you do. Just distract the niggas upstairs. A girl is going to knock on the front door. When you hear the knock—you start," she said.

The girl couldn't have been a day older than eighteen. She had a bad addiction but hadn't put enough years in on the street to realize that this was a fool's mission. As Gucci watched her walk up the stairs she picked up her phone to let her girls know that her part of the plan had been fulfilled. Now it was up to them.

***

Ten smokers in basement and six guys upstairs cooking up. Guns all over the kitchen
table. Money under floorboard in kitchen. Girl
about to cause distraction. Come in now!

When Raegan read the text she relayed the
message to Chanel and with adrenaline on high,
they made their move. Their disguises never
changed. Trench coats and high-heeled Louboutins was the get up, that way if they ever had to
switch roles they could easily play the damsel in
distress card.

Gucci crept up the stairs and saw the girl
she had bribed, approach the hustlers. Out of
nowhere she fell out on the floor, knocking the
boiling pots off of the stove.

"Fuck is this fiended out bitch doing up here?
Get her ass out!" one of the hustlers said ir-
ritably. "I told y'all about letting these mu'fuckas
smoke in the spot anyway."

"I think the bitch dying or something," one of
them observed.

"I don't give a fuck—just get the seizing ass
bitch out the kitchen. Throw her ass back in
the basement and get up here and bag up this
batch," the block lieutenant ordered.

Gucci smirked knowing that the girl was putting on. She had gone all out. Gucci hurried to the back door and unlocked it, turning it quietly as she let Gucci and Raegan inside. They passed her a pistol and tied a scarf around her face.

"Don't blow this Guch. Just point your gun and get the money. Any nigga get stupid you pop off. We'll ask questions later," Raegan schooled before making her way up the landing that led to the kitchen.

"Nigga get that bitch out of here!" the dude said, losing his patience. Raegan and the girls met him on his way down the steps and she clicked off her safety, placing the chrome .45 dead center in his forehead.

"Back the fuck up," she ordered.

The young girl screamed out in surprise and raised her hands as Raegan and Chanel backpedaled them into the kitchen.

"Let me see them hands gentleman! You cooperate and we leave quietly!" Raegan shouted out as Chanel and Gucci came up behind her, guns pointed. They followed her lead as they quickly gained control of the room.

"Get on the floor," Raegan shouted.

"You know whose money you fucking with?" one of the hustlers asked as he complied, getting on his knees.

"Yeah . . . mine, now get your ass down," Raegan spat as she kicked him in the back, digging her heel into his neck as he lay helpless beneath her. She turned to the young fiend and nodded her head, "You too. Get down."

Chanel and Gucci let their girl star in the show; they alternated so that no one voice would become recognizable. Each one did things differently and it made them less predictable. Today was the Raegan show, her girls were just the guest stars.

Making the men lie belly down in a circle, Raegan watched them all at once. She wasn't stupid. She knew that their brute strength could easily overpower them. She had to depend on her pistol in order to give her the advantage. Gucci went around binding their feet and hands. Her nervous energy caused her hands to tremble, but she moved diligently, not wanting to misstep.

Chanel quickly located the floorboard and a smile spread across her face as she saw the pot. It was definitely bigger than their last hit and in her mind the money was already spent as she helped herself to their stash. She put the money and uncooked cocaine in the bag, then moved to the table and stuffed the guns inside as well.

In less than five minutes they were in and out. As they left, the young girl came running out of the house behind them. They hadn't tied her up because she didn't pose a threat, but as Chanel turned on her heels, her finger wrapped around the trigger.

"Yo!" she shouted.

When she saw Chanel's gun her hands went up in fear. "I just wanted my dope. She forgot to give me what she promised," the girl said.

Raegan reached into the bag and pulled out a stack of money then tossed it to the girl. "Let's go," she said, knowing that it was only a matter of time before the niggas figured out a way to get loose.

"Your fingernails weren't dirty!" the girl shouted as Reagan, Gucci, and Chanel climbed into the rental car. "That's how I knew you weren't a fiend! You're fingernails were too on point."

Chanel knew that the girl was right. They would have to pay more attention to detail next time. Luckily the hustlers they had just robbed hadn't noticed. The girls left the scene, thinking of the riches in the bag and the lovely capers to come.

***

"Nah hey baby it's me. It's mama."

Nahvid looked at the number that had appeared on his cell's caller ID when he recognized her voice.

"Where are you Nita?" he asked concerned.

"I'm staying with a friend in Baltimore," she said back. "Mama miss you baby. I'm ready to come home now Nah. I need help baby. I'm ready to get clean. I just need some money baby. I need a little bit of money so I can fix myself up before I see you."

As soon as she asked for it he knew that she wasn't serious. She was gaming him, trying to use him to get her next high. He didn't want her out their tricking and selling her soul to the devil in order to get high. "I'll give you some money Nita. Just come stay with me. We'll work on your habit Nita. Wean you off of that shit," he whispered.

The line was silent as if she was seriously thinking of his offer.

"I'm ready baby. I'ma come," she promised.

"I'll come get you," Nahvid stated. "Where exactly are you?"

"I don't want you coming here Nah . . . coming over here causing havoc to my friends . . . like they the ones got me hooked on this shit. I did this to myself baby. But I'ma come. I'll be there next week. As soon as I get back in town I'm coming to you," Nita promised.

"Is this the number I can reach you at?" he asked.

"Yeah this my cell phone Nah. Look at your mama with a cell phone," she bragged with a laugh.

"I see you old lady," he said as he chuckled. "I love you Nita. Keep this phone on so I can reach you. I'll pay the bill. Who's the carrier?" he asked. He knew that Nita would blow with the wind in a heartbeat and he wanted to be able to reach her, no matter what.

"Verizon," Nita replied.

"Promise me you're coming," Nahvid said seriously.

"I promise baby. I'll be there," she said.

Chapter Six

The first thing that Raegan did was hire her own lawyer to fight against Micah's pricey, experienced attorney in family court. She knew that if she wanted her son back she couldn't take any shorts so she contacted the best and then moved into her own place to prove to a judge that she could take care of the two of them. As she stood in her large three-bedroom luxury apartment she became sad. It was empty just like her heart and because she couldn't fill the void within her she decided to fill the space within the four walls.

Raegan laced her home with every comfort and modern design that she could find as she ordered exclusive furniture. Her tastes were exquisite and she didn't hold back. She purchased without thinking; without negotiating; without a budget. She threw caution to the wind, ignoring price tags—partly because she wanted to see what it felt like to be a rich bitch, but mostly because it was a lovely distraction from the absence of her son. As she chose things to fill her son's room she felt a pair of hands squeeze her shoulders. The touch was so comforting that it made the stress melt from her tense body. She spun on her heels and smiled when she saw Nahvid's face.

"Hey, how are you?" she asked as she reached up to hug him.

"How are you?" he asked. "You're the toughest woman in the world to keep in touch with. You making me feel like an ugly nigga."

She blushed, surprised that he hadn't given up on her yet. It had been a few weeks since their last encounter and even though he took her absence as disinterest she thought of him all the time. But the lifestyle she had picked up and the robberies she was committing left her with little free time. She was in grind mode and a man was the last of her concerns.

"Stop—you're making me feel so bad. I've just been busy that's all," she replied. "You shopping?"

"Yeah for a new bedroom set," he said. "Can you help me out? My mom is coming to stay with me for awhile and I need a woman's touch to make her feel at home."

"Of course," she agreed. Raegan thought that she was doing it big until she watched how Nahvid lived. She picked out things from store to store and he purchased without even looking up from his cell phone. He handled his business while she worked with his personal sales associates at each store. She picked out everything from furniture and clothing to toiletries, and jewelry sparing no expense. They ripped through the entire shopping center and when she was done, Nahvid whipped out a Black Card and totaled out the bill. Impressed by his status in the game but more importantly she was surprised by his legitimacy in the corporate world. She listened as he talked Wall Street language, speaking of stocks and shares. He was a dream man. He came from the hood; from nothing and had made quite the businessman of himself—all without losing his connections to the streets.

"Sorry about that," he said as he finally hung up the phone.

"That's okay. I live to shop. I haven't done it in a long time and I've never done it like that before. I didn't even notice," she replied.

"You should visit Paris then. If you like to shop you would love it there," he said nonchalantly as if he wasn't speaking of a place halfway around the world.

"I don't know what world you live in, but in mine, Paris might as well be another planet," she said, slightly offended.

"Let me take you," he said.

She scoffed and laughed.

"I'm serious," he concluded. "I need to get you all to myself. Show you my world. Maybe convince you to be a part of it for awhile."

"Are you for real?" she asked.

The dudes that she was used to dealing with thought dinner and a movie was the crème de la crème. Nahvid was on a completely different level.

"I don't put things out there that I don't mean. I can rent a private jet and have it waiting on the tarmac in a couple of hours," he said.

"A couple hours?" she exclaimed, overwhelmed at his generosity and hypnotized by his power. She shook her head in disbelief and said, "Okay. Let's do it. I have to go pack. I have so much to do."

"It's a shopping trip. Everything is on me. We'll buy it all when we get there," he said. Nahvid was really blowing her mind.

They dropped her car off at her place and then she stayed the night at hotel near the airport.

Raegan expected for Nahvid to push up on her that night. She was waiting for him to make his move, thinking that she had to reciprocate the trip with sexual favors. To her surprise he got her a separate room. The move was unexpected but she definitely appreciated it. After calling her girls and letting them know where she would be, she fell asleep, anxious and excited all at the same time.

Paris was beautiful in the wintertime. The crisp, clean, glittering city lent an ambiance for romance and Nahvid and Raegan seemed to get seduced by it all. They appeared to be a couple who had known each other for years as they shopped in designer stores, ate on snow clad terraces, and held each other from the top of the Eiffel Tower. They did everything that lovers do and spared each other of nothing. Nahvid lavished Raegan with all that her heart desired and while she couldn't afford to return that gesture, she ravished him without inhibitions in the bedroom each night. Their conversations were so deep that sometimes they became heated as they argued their points to one another. They never took it personally though. Make up sex was the remedy to everything and they enjoyed the fights because they knew the pleasure that was to follow them. Together they were incredible; their chemistry, amazing. Nahvid was glad that she had decided to come. Being so far away from home, they were in their own little world. Neither of them spoke French so they only conversed with one another. They were each other's friend, ally, and mate all at once. One week felt like one year to them and even they were surprised at how connected to one another they became. She told him everything about her, except for how she made her money. That was the one secret she kept because she knew it would change his perspective of her. Uninterrupted they were able to get to know each other. It had been a long time since Nahvid had given a woman so much attention, but with Raegan it felt right. It felt natural. It was inevitable that those three little words slipped out while they were there. Paris was the city of love and they had gotten drunk on it, night after night. The time flew by so quickly that they didn't want to leave, but as they sat on the international flight they both knew that they had to go back.

"I don't want things to change when we get back," she whispered in his ear as she kissed him repeatedly, gently.

"They won't. You're mine ma. Nothing in the world can change that. Not after everything we've done this week. I'm selfish and I want you to myself."

As soon as Raegan stepped foot inside her home her cell phone rang back to back, first with Gucci blowing her up, then with Chanel calling.

"Hey?" she answered. "What's up I just got home," she said.

"Look outside bitch," Chanel yelled excitedly.

Raegan went to her window and dropped the phone when she saw her girls lined up outside in a parade of foreign whips.

"No they didn't!" she yelled excitedly as she slipped into her UGGs and threw on a pea coat before rushing outside.

"Bitch!" she shouted.

"You like 'em?" Gucci asked.

"Of course. I'm about to cop me one today!" Raegan said. Lisa came up and shook her head. She tossed her a Benz key to the car that she had driven over there.

"No need to," Lisa said. "You know I can't afford a Benz. It's yours." She laughed as Raegan jumped up and down like a kid on Christmas.

They all hopped into their cars, Lisa riding shotgun with Raegan as they skirted out with no destination, stunting around the city.

***

When Nahvid returned home he called Nita repeatedly but she wouldn't answer his call. He looked at the room full of new furniture and clothes that he had purchased for her, shaking his head. He had known that she would disappoint him; but one day, when she was ready, he knew she would come home—and that room would be waiting for her.

Chapter Seven

The girls popped bottles in the club. Cristal and Louis XIII flowed freely at their table as Raegan, Gucci, and Chanel partied like social-ites. Everything about them rang new money. Lisa couldn't believe the way that her friends had grinded to the top. As she sat partying at their expense she silently wished that she had gotten down from the beginning. They had come up in a major way. Well into their sixth heist, the girls were getting paid. Raegan had $250,000 put up on her own and she barely touched it thanks to Nahvid's generosity.

Easy money.

Dirty money.

More money.

. . . was their thought process. Now that they had taken their first hit of the fast life they had be-come indulged in it. Mega shopping sprees filled their days and they spent frivolously because they knew that it could be easily replenished. The girls were in a circle on the dance floor, dancing their asses off, feeling like rock stars for the night. As Nahvid and his crew sat back, he admired his lady from afar. She was definitely the bell of the ball and he loved how she stole the show. Raegan blew him a kiss and smiled sexily as she winded her body while staring him in the eyes. He was completely satisfied with Raegan.

Reason leaned into his man's ear and whispered, "Yo, I'm not feeling your girl Nah. Her and her girls are flossing a whole lot of paper. You know them bitches that been going around robbing stash spots? From the looks of it, that's them, and your girl is shining like the ring leader."

Nahvid shot Reason a look that would have bodied him where he stood, if looks could kill. "She don't got to rob nobody fam. I'm taking care of that. Don't come out your mouth reckless about her," Nahvid said in a low controlled tone. The last thing he wanted to do was beef out with his man over Raegan, but he had to make it known that she belonged to him now.

Reason's temple throbbed in anger. *This ol' pussy whipped ass nigga. I'ma have to watch that bitch—closely,* Reason thought. He didn't think Nahvid could see through the trance of a beautiful woman, but nothing was more attractive than his paper and Reason wasn't about to let Raegan or anyone else eat off his plate.

"No disrespect Nah. You my man a hundred grand. I just don't want some broad to interrupt the paper flow, nah mean?" Reason asked.

"Have anything ever stopped me from getting money? Nigga, have I ever stopped you from eating? Everybody eats, but let me tell you something fam—it's nothing if you don't have somebody to share it with. All them square feet I'm living in is pointless if I'm in it by myself. I want a wife and some kids fam. It's time and she's it," Nahvid stated seriously.

Reason nodded and tapped his Rémy glass against his man's to show support, but in the back of his head his skepticism ate away at him. He didn't trust Raegan—point blank and would keep an eye on her. It took more than a happy face and a magnificent ass to catch him slipping.

The girls finally made their way off the dance floor and returned to their table. Raegan and Nahvid had been on each other all night. Their eyes never left one another as they flirted across the room. He nodded to her, summoning her to him and as she was arose from her seat, Chanel leaned into her ear to whisper over the music.

"Gucci and I need to talk to you," she said to Raegan as she grabbed her hand, pulling her through the crowd.

"Guch!" Raegan shouted and nodded her head toward the bathroom to tell her to follow. The three girls left Lisa at their table to watch their hand bags as they made their way to the back of the club. Lisa knew how they got down, but they never cut her in on any of the details. She didn't need to know the when's and where's. It was better for all of them that she remained untainted.

Nahvid stopped her just before she entered the restroom.

"You coming home with me tonight ma?" he asked as he pinned her body against the wall.

"I've barely slept one night in my place since we got back," she whispered. She wanted to tell him no, but they both knew whose bed she would end up in tonight. He trapped her words in a kiss and grabbed her aggressively behind the neck to devour her tongue, teasing her and making her love button pulse.

"I've got a surprise for you ma. Let's bounce," he said.

She grabbed the hand that caressed her face and kissed his wrist. "Okay. Meet me at the car in fifteen minutes. I need to talk to my girls real fast and settle our bar bill," she said.

He gave her a knowing look and said, "You know I already took care of you. Just holler at your people and meet me outside."

As soon as she walked inside Raegan could see that Chanel and Gucci had a lot on their minds. They stopped talking as soon as she stepped foot inside the restroom. "What's up?" Raegan asked.

"Gucci and I think it's time to hit another lick," Chanel said.

"You and Gucci? Or just you, Chanel?" Raegan asked.

"B . . . both of us think it's time," Gucci spoke up.

Raegan shook her head in disbelief. They were lucky to have kept a low profile this long. Hustlers all over the city were talking about the group of chicks that were sticking up dope houses. They had a schedule and Raegan was sticking to it.

"I'm not for it. We need to lay low and take a month off," Raegan advised. "Niggas are on edge all over the city. It's best if we just fall back and then start up again in thirty days," Raegan said.

"I don't know about you but I can't wait thirty days Raegan," Chanel said.

"Me neither," Gucci added.

"Fuck is you bitches playing broke for? I know how much y'all getting cuz I'm getting it the same way, the same amount. We're falling back. That's the smartest thing to do right now," Raegan said.

"Smart for who Raegan?" Chanel countered. "Everybody ain't fucking with a rich nigga like you. These diamonds, the clothes, the shoes, the cars—it all costs and it's coming out of my pocket. Homeboy out there got your head in the clouds. We need to hit a lick—like tomorrow."

"I'm strapped right now too Raegan. It is time. Putting my mama in that home is a big expense. I can't miss no money. Thirty days is too long," Gucci stated.

"I'm out of here. Y'all tripping and you're getting risky," Raegan said as she headed for the door. Chanel rushed and pushed the door closed, then grabbed Raegan's hand to make her face them.

"We're doing it—tomorrow," Chanel said sternly.

"Don't get fucking greedy bitch, just stick to the plan. We hit one spot every month. That's how we been doing it. That's how we should keep doing it," Raegan whispered harshly as she snapped at her friends as they stood inside of the marble tiled bathroom in the plush, upscale nightclub. The three ladies were dressed to kill as they discussed business in an unconventional setting. They heard the toilet flush behind one of the stall doors and Raegan's eyes bugged out in disbelief. "You bitches didn't clear this mu'fucka out?" she asked incredulously. "You must want to get caught the fuck up?" She stormed over to the stall and banged on the door with a flat hand. "Hurry the hell up bitch. Time's up."

The stall door opened and a girl frowned as she stared Raegan down. "Excuse me?" she asked.

"You deaf or something? Get out!" she shouted harshly as she pushed the girl toward the door. There wasn't a scary bone in Raegan's body and it was nothing for her to strong arm the girl out of the restroom. Once they were alone Raegan pushed open the other stall doors to make sure there was no one else inside. The last thing she needed was some ear hustling ass bitch blowing up her spot.

"Why are you so paranoid? I know Sonny Rae ain't scared?" Chanel asked with an accusing stare.

"Ain't a damn thing about me scared bitch. I'm smart and I'm not down for hitting another spot a few days after we just wrapped up the last job. That's what we agreed to. Hit one stash house a month. If we do it right we don't need to go back in every other week looking for more. That's just greedy. Our luck is sure to run out if we play this thing the wrong way. Shit has been lovely. I don't know about y'all but I'm sitting on more cash than I can spend. Why press our luck?" Raegan argued.

"Look Raegan you're lucky. You get to stack your paper because you have a good man who takes care of business. We gotta live the best way we know how and this is how we eat. You're going soft Raegan," Gucci stated. She pulled a small compact mirror out of her Hermes bag and removed a small bag filled with white powder. The substance was so pure that it sparkled slightly under the dim bathroom light. She quickly set herself up and hit two fat lines of cocaine. It was a habit she picked up by being around so much coke. The girls hadn't found any buyers for the product they stole, so Gucci sampled it from time to time—a recreation high.

"I'm not going *soft* Gucci. I just don't want to change things up. If it ain't broke why fix it?" Raegan argued.

"Because I'm broke and my pocketbook needs fixing," Chanel shot back as she stared challengingly at Raegan.

Their friendship was new, but they were extremely loyal to each other. They had become thick as thieves. Coming up in the trenches of DC, they each had been groomed for the game. Treachery was bred within them; larceny their religion; money their motivation.

"I'm out. This is not a negotiation. We are not doing this," Raegan concluded.

"We are doing it. I've already scoped the spot and everything. It's out in Trinidad. You're acting real brand new but it's fine—we'll do it without you," Chanel spat as she walked past Raegan, her Louboutin stiletto boots stabbing the floor as she walked out.

Raegan looked at Gucci desperately for support, but Gucci just shook her head in disappointment. "We would never leave you hanging like that Raegan. You know we need you out there," she said before following after Chanel. Raegan went back to the table and air kissed Lisa good-bye before grabbing her handbag and leaving the club.

Chapter Eight

Lying underneath the crumpled satin sheets Raegan's head spun out of guilt. She tossed and turned, feeling guilty for not riding with her girls. Restless, she crawled out of bed and wrapped Nahvid's robe around her shoulders. The moon was full and although it was freezing outside, she needed to clear her head. She stepped out onto his balcony and stared up at the night sky. The crisp air hit her instantly, refreshing her as she stared out onto the sparkling snow.

She heard the sliding door open behind her and she closed her eyes as she felt Nahvid's lips grace her neck.

"It's freezing out here ma," he whispered. "Come back to bed."

"It's beautiful though. It's so still at night," she said.

"You wanna talk about it?" he asked, thinking that she missed her son. He hated to see her sad. He could tell by her tense shoulder and the heaviness in her tone that her heart was burdened.

She shook her head and turned around to kiss his lips. "No . . . not really. I just want to be with you. When I'm with you everything in my world seems right. I forget all of the bad," she whispered.

"Me too ma. Me too," he whispered. "You're my get right."

He led her back inside and lay down in his bed, wrapping his arms around her. "I feel like I want to take things to the next level with you. You're my Sonny Rae. I'd like you to meet somebody," he said.

"Who?" she asked.

"My mother," Nahvid answered. "You're the only woman that I have ever cared for besides my moms. I would like for the two of you to meet. I called her when you fell asleep to see if she was available." Nahvid waited for her to respond. "I've arranged a dinner at the restaurant tomorrow night. Is that okay?" he asked. He wanted Raegan to know where he came from and to meet the woman who had birthed him and the one who he had let break his heart repeatedly.

"Of course," she answered. "I'd love to meet her baby." As she thought about her girls she feared that they may be right. She didn't want to let them down just because Nahvid had chosen to upgrade her lifestyle. *I have to be there for them. I have to do this,* she thought. She turned to Nahvid and added, "I just have to go get pampered in the morning. I'll have to meet you there. I want to make a good impression on her."

Raegan had the best Brazilian blowout in town and she was always well maintained. Pampering herself was the last thing on her mind, but using it as an excuse was the perfect lie to give herself enough time to hit the lick with her girls before the dinner. She cared about Nahvid and she gave herself to him like no other man before, but she owed this to her girls. *When he wasn't in the picture they were all that I had. I can't let them down.*

Raegan hesitantly came out of her sleep, wishing that she could live in her dreams forever. Her son was always available to her in her dreams and as she opened her eyes she could still hear his coos in her head. She crawled out of bed and did her morning beauty regimen before making her way downstairs.

"Nahvid!" she called as she descended the stairs. He met her at the bottom and lifted her off of her feet as he kissed her lips.

"Good morning beautiful," he complimented. "I need you to be quiet though. My homeboy is asleep in there on the couch."

"What?" she questioned in confusion.

"Go take a look. I'm about to make breakfast. Wake him and see if he's hungry for me?" Nahvid asked.

Raegan frowned in confusion as she made her way into the living area. She stopped mid-step and her hand shot over her mouth as tears came to her eyes. Her son lay comfortably on the couch with his thumb in his mouth. It had been so long since she had seen him. He was seven months old. "How did you? When did? Oh my God," she whispered in disbelief. "How long do I have with him?"

"A lifetime ma. Your baby's father and I had a talk. He sees things much clearer now and he sends his sincere apologies," Nahvid stated seriously as he wiped the tears from her face. "He's all yours."

Raegan ran to her baby and woke him up with hugs and kisses. Her heart swelled so much that it hurt. It was the greatest gift that Nahvid could have ever given her. It was one that she would never forget.

She played with her son for hours, wearing him out with laughter and love. She was relieved that he seemed to recognize her and she did all that she could to make sure that she showed him how much she had missed him. As time slowly ticked by she wished that she didn't have to leave him, but she had to take care of one thing—one lick with her girls. Nahvid came over and took her son, cradling him as if it were his own child. "Let's put your mommy out so she can get ready for tonight li'l homey," Nahvid said. Baby Micah seemed to take to Nahvid and as Raegan looked up at the two of them, she realized that she loved Nahvid. He was her man; they were built for one another. *After today I'm done with this. I have enough money put up to last at least a couple years if I live modestly,* she thought. As she stood, sadness filled her eyes.

"He'll be here when you get back. Go ahead. Take whatever you need out of the knot on the kitchen counter. Enjoy yourself and li'l man and I will meet you here at 8 p.m."

Raegan nodded and then kissed her son before heading out to meet Gucci and Raegan. Whether they liked it or not, this would be the last time she put her life on the line.

***

"Hurry up before I put your brains on the floor," Gucci shouted as she pointed her gun at the guy.

"He thinks we're playing with his ass," Chanel stated harshly. The guy was moving extremely slow. They had already been in the stash house too long. She hated to admit it, but things were much harder without Raegan. There were just too many niggas in the room to watch. She felt out of control and frantic without the extra security that Raegan contributed. Uneasy and a bit fearful Chanel was ready to shake, but she wasn't leaving there without the money she had come for.

Chanel felt completely unprepared. In her rush to come up on some new paper, she hadn't done her homework well enough. She had scoped the spot briefly, but had been far from thorough. If she had done her job she would have known that the five hustlers in the room was one man short. So as the dude stuffed the money in the duffel bag, he moved molasses slow, purposely trying to give his man time to return to the spot.

The situation was out of control. A smoker who had come to cop lay quivering in the corner of the room and as she tried to stand Chanel almost lost her cool.

"Sit the fuck back down!" she shouted as she applied pressure to her trigger. "All of you sit! On your hands!" The various fiends in the room sat down on top of their hands wishing that they had kept their promises to God to kick crack. Maybe this was their punishment for living life addicted to the devil's smoke. Chanel was overwhelmed. There were simply too many people in the room and not enough firepower to keep things looking favorable for the girls. Feeling as though they had gotten in over their heads, Chanel decided to get what they could and retreat. "Get the bag," she told Gucci.

As she hit the back door she was met with a Beretta to the face. "Bitch, get your ass back inside," the guy said as he snatched the gun from her hand, catching her off guard.

"Put your gun down!" Gucci stated as she immediately placed her pistol to the head of the man that had been bagging the money.

"Bitch you put your gun down," the dude shot back.

Boom!

Without warning a shot let off and the dude was met with a slug to the back of the head as Raegan stepped into the room.

"You already know what time it is. Move faster or don't move at all," Raegan threatened.

Distracted by Raegan's presence Gucci never saw the guy reach for the pistol he had taped beneath the table. He popped off, his bullshit aim causing him to miss, but inciting a shootout. Gucci grabbed the money and shot out the front door as Raegan and Chanel held it down inside. Bullets flew and when Chanel's clip ejected itself empty, Raegan kept firing—relentlessly. She had to toe tag that nigga before he left her son without a mom. Raegan dumped on him until she heard him stop firing and when Chanel went to check the body; her eyes bugged as she announced, "He's dead."

The men on the floor trembled. Their hands and feet were bound and they anticipated being executed one by one, but Raegan wasn't cold-blooded. When she saw the woman dead in the corner, blood trailing from a dot in her forehead, her stomach turned. Things had gone bad—fast, and there was no turning back. "Get the rest of that money and let's go," she said harshly as she walked out of the house dazed from all of the carnage she left behind inside.

"You came," Gucci mumbled as she drove away from what was now a crime scene.

"I wish I hadn't," Raegan shot back. "I told you bitches—I told you! We were supposed to play it smart, not reckless. Now three people are dead—dead! You couldn't see that that nigga was stalling?"

Chanel and Gucci thought it wise not to argue back. Raegan was livid and they knew she was right. They had overestimated their game and now it had backfired. Chanel drove back to her house and they quickly went inside. Blood covered Raegan and she trembled as she rushed upstairs.

"Count the money and put it in Lisa's room. Nobody touch it. Nobody. I have to get cleaned up and get out of here. I have to meet Nahvid somewhere. Just don't get to spending this money right away. Lay low for a couple weeks until things die down," Raegan stated.

Chanel and Gucci nodded while looking guiltily at each other. When Raegan stepped into the shower she broke down. She cried good and long. Her soul hurt. Her conscience heavy. They had been greedy. After the first hit they should have stopped, but their insatiable love of material things had led them straight to the breaking point.

***

Raegan walked into the room looking as beautiful as ever. A borrowed Badgley Mischka dress out of Chanel's closet helped cover up the sins she had committed just moments before. As she walked over to Nahvid, she hoped her eyes weren't red. He held her little man in his strong arms and embraced her gently.

"We missed you ma," he whispered into her ear.

She blushed and took her seat. Her heart melted when he passed her baby Micah. He was her joy. He instantly distracted her from the events that had just taken place.

"Where's your mom?" she asked.

Disappointment filled his face as he replied, "I don't know." They waited for an hour before deciding to order and midway through the waiter approached their table.

"Sir, I have an important phone call for you. They say it's urgent," he said.

"Excuse me for a minute Raegan," he said as he arose from the table. When he returned he helped her out of her seat. "We need to go. I have something important I need to handle."

They drove in silence until they pulled up in front of the very house that Raegan had just robbed. Her chest became tight as she fidgeted nervously. "Why are we here?" she asked.

"Just stay in the car ma. This is one of my spots. Somebody robbed me," he stated. "Lock the doors." He got out of the car and walked up to the door where Reason was waiting for him.

Raegan watched in horror. She didn't know if she should get in the driver's seat and peel out or if she should stay put. *There is no way he knows it's me,* she thought as her breathing became deep—panicked.

She saw him emerge from the house grief stricken as blood covered his shirt. She got out of the car, running to him as worry filled her. The look on his face was one of pure heartbreak. "What's wrong? Nahvid talk to me," she begged as she cupped his face in her hands. She could see the pain seeping from within him, but he refused to cry. *It's just money. He can't be this broke up about money,* she thought.

"My mother was in the house when it was robbed. They killed her," he said. "It's been a long time since I've put my murder game down . . . but the bitches that did this is gonna see me."

"Bitches?" she said.

"One of my li'l niggas . . . they left him alive. He said it was three bitches . . . red bottom heels, trench coats, and winter scarves wrapped around their face," he stated.

As he spoke she dug her heels into plush grass. She was wearing the exact pumps she had worn during the robbery and she discreetly hid them, not wanting him to put two and two together. He knew that she owned many pair. Hell he had purchased most of them, but suspecting her was the last thing on his mind.

"Let's go home baby," she said. "I'm so sorry."

He had no idea that there was more to her apology than sympathy. Her mind spun as she got into the driver's seat and made her way back to his house. He stayed up half the night drinking his guilt away as Raegan sat on the couch rubbing his back to ease his tension.

"I should have pulled her out of them streets," he said regretfully.

"You didn't know this would happen Nah," she soothed, all the while fighting her inner turmoil. Everything in her wanted to tell the truth but feared the repercussions. She knew of his power in the streets and had heard of the things that he had done to those who crossed him. She hadn't known him long enough to be the exception to the rule. He wouldn't hesitate to end her life. The doorbell rang loudly throughout the house and she stood to answer it.

"It's four o'clock in the morning," Raegan noticed, wondering who it could be.

"It's Reason," Nahvid stated as he stood too. He went to answer the door and Reason walked in with a badly beaten young boy at his side.

"Take him to the garage," Nahvid stated. Raegan watched timidly as Reason pushed the boy toward the garage door.

"I didn't have shit to do with it fam. Nah! Please man. I was at home with my sister fam! I swear on everything!"

Reason dragged him kicking and screaming all the way out of the house.

Nahvid walked over to Raegan and noticed that she was shaking.

"Nah please don't hurt that boy," she pleaded.

"Don't worry about that ma," he said. He kissed her forehead. "Go upstairs and get some rest. I'll be up after awhile."

The sound proof garage masked the torture that was going on inside but Raegan wasn't naïve. When Reason left dragging a heavy-duty bag behind him, she knew what lie inside. She closed her eyes knowing that she was responsible for all of this. She had to go talk to Gucci and Chanel. They had no idea what was going on and she needed help, figuring out what to do next. She loved Nahvid and was positive that he adored her . . . but that line between love and hate was so thin that she knew if he ever found out what she did, things would never be the same.

Raegan awoke first to find that Nahvid hadn't been to sleep. The stress in his brow was evident and she stood on her tip toes to kiss his ails away.

"Li'l man is still sleeping. I just checked in on him," Nahvid said.

"Thank you. Why are you so good to me? I don't even deserve you," she whispered.

"You and baby Micah are all I have right now. I see you in my future. I want you and your son to be a part of my life for a long time," he said.

"Me too," she said. "But if something ever happens to make you feel otherwise . . . know that I always loved you and that I would never do anything intentionally to hurt you."

He pulled her close and inhaled her scent.

"Are you hungry? You have to take care of yourself," she said.

He nodded and placed his forehead against hers.

"I'm going to go grab a few things from the grocer. It'll give you some space to think. We'll be back," she said as she went to get her son dressed.

"Leave li'l man here. It's too cold to take him out there. I don't want him to get sick," Nahvid stated.

Raegan nodded and then dressed. She always dressed as if she were going to a fashion show. She couldn't help it. She was a bad bitch and as she walked out of the house an eerie feeling came over her. She looked back, feeling as if she would never come home again. Shaking off the feeling she got into her car and sped to see Chanel and Gucci.

When she arrived the front door was wide open and the house was in shambles.

"Guch! Lisa! Chanel!" she called out. She made her way upstairs and ran from room to room looking for her girls. When she saw Lisa bound to her bed, tongue lying on the pillow beside her, eyes gouged out of their sockets she hurled on sight. She rushed to the closet to re-trieve the cash and when she saw the empty safe open on the ground her entire body went numb. She rushed out of the house, so frantic that she could barely dial the numbers on her iPhone.

"Hello?" Gucci finally answered.

"Where are you? Where's Chanel?"

"We went to breakfast. What's wrong? Where are you?" Gucci asked.

"I'm at your house staring at Lisa's dead body. The stash house we took was Nahvid's!"

"What?" Gucci slipped. Raegan got their location and raced to meet them. She was pissed. She could tell by the way that Gucci reacted that she hadn't known they were hitting Nahvid's spot, but it was a little too coincidental for Raegan. Her girl's were waiting in the parking lot of the restaurant and when Raegan pulled up, she got out of her car and ran up on Chanel. Her fist connected with Chanel's lip, bursting it on impact.

"You bitch. You knew that was his spot. Why would you target him?" she asked.

Chanel knew that Raegan would be in her feelings when she finally found out so she held her composure as she wiped her mouth with the back of her hand. She spit blood onto the pavement and replied, "Because the nigga is loaded and I knew you would never agree to it if you knew. Robbing him was the only way we would hit it big. Nobody was supposed to get hurt."

"Yeah well somebody did. His mama! She was in the house Chanel! She died and now Lisa's dead too. The money's gone!"

"What?" she asked. "We just saw Lisa two hours ago."

"Yeah well she's dead and Reason killed her. There is no telling what she told him before she died. They tortured her. Cut out her tongue. I know she talked," Raegan said. "He knows it was me—he knows." She frantically paced back and forth.

"We have to skip town," Gucci said. "We have to get out of here."

"And go where? Huh? We don't have any money. Besides, Nahvid has my son! He's there with him. I left him there!" she shouted as tears welled in her eyes. Raegan remembered the feeling that had passed over her before she had left Nahvid's house and she shook her head, knowing that she couldn't go back there. "He has my son."

"He's not going to hurt Micah. You know that," Chanel said.

"I'm going back," Raegan stated.

"You can't Raegan. You have to leave him there, at least for now," Chanel said. "Whoever murdered Lisa, the jokes on them. The security system tapes the property around the clock. I can upload the tape online and we can use that as leverage to get Micah back. But right now we need to let things cool down. We have to skip town."

"And go where?" Gucci asked.

"A friend of mine owns a boat in Florida. If we can make it there, he'll take us wherever we want to go. He's powerful. He can get us passports—whatever we need. I know that he will help," Chanel stated. "I stopped talking to him awhile back, once we started our hustle. His number isn't the same but I know where he lives. If we can make it down there, we'll be okay."

"I can't believe this," Raegan cried. "I don't even have any money on me right now? We can't make it too far on broke and this fucking credit card is going to give Nahvid a damn GPS to come find my ass."

"We've got to take a bank," Chanel whispered.

"What?" both Gucci and Raegan exclaimed looking at her as if she had lost it.

"Stop talking stupid," Raegan shouted. "I should slap the shit out of you for even saying some stupid shit like that."

"What's the other option Raegan?" Chanel countered. "Go back to Nahvid and hope he doesn't dead you on sight? We need money and this is the only way."

"A stash house," Gucci spoke up and said. "We could hit another one."

"Every hood nigga in the city is on to us now. A bank . . . we have to hit a bank . . ."

Chapter Nine

Back to Present Day

In the news today a group of three young women robbed the downtown branch of First National Bank today. The three unidentified suspects held up the bank at gunpoint. The branch manager was able to flip the alarm and alert police, which caused the ladies to flee with only $10,000 in unmarked bills. Three people were injured in the robbery and police have labeled these women as the Red Bottom Bandits due to their oddly fashionable disguises. If you have any information that will aid in the arrest of these perpetrators please contact your local police . . .

"What you think? You think I should contact the police Raegan?" Reason asked her as he nodded for the driver to turn off the radio. He sat beside her menacingly as the car pulled off. He was too calm and the smirk on his face taunted her. She knew that it was over. She was caught and a murderous goon like Reason only had one fate in mind for her. "I knew you were a snake bitch the first time I lay eyes on you. You're too fucking pretty. It's the ones like you that hide ugly motives. My man trusted you . . . I never did," he stated.

"I didn't know it was Nahvid's spot," she defended as tears fell down her face.

Reason cackled in her ear as he unbuckled his pants. "I'ma fuck the dog shit out of you before I blow your head off." He grabbed himself mannishly as he loomed over her. She kicked him off, letting her legs fly at full speed but he was too strong for her. He wrestled her down onto the seat and spread her legs forcefully.

"You fucking bastard," she screamed. "Stop!"

He hit her so hard that stars appeared before her eyes and everything went dark. It wasn't until she felt the cold water dripping on her forehead did she come-to. She knew that she had been raped. She could still feel his semen dripping out of her and onto the chair that she was tied to. A leaky pipe tortured her as it rained one drop at a time onto her forehead. The water rolled down her face, resembling tears so closely that they mixed with her own.

She wanted to scream for help but who could she call? The only person who could save her was the very same man that she had crossed. She wasn't a gangster, a killer, or even a hood chick. She never proclaimed to be tough. She was just greedy. Money had been her motivation and she had used her quest to see her son as an excuse to do bad things. The locks to the basement door clicked and Reason descended the steps. He stood in front of her—his pistol aimed, ready to take her life . . .

The Takedown

by Amaleka McCall

Prologue

"If niggas think you snitchin'
they ain't tryin'a listen"

"We call state's witness Javona Blakely to the stand," the prosecutor announced loudly. His words garnered hushed murmurs and deep grumbles from some of the people that were squeezed tightly into the jam-packed courtroom. A cold chill shot down Javona's spine as she heard herself referred to as the state's witness, which in the hood equaled snitch. Javona would have rather been known as a terrorist than a snitch. Javona's legs felt like lead pipes and her feet like cinder blocks as she walked slowly toward the boxed-in wooden sitting area to the left of the judge's bench. She could feel the heat from all of the eyes on her, burning holes into her. She wouldn't dare look out into the crowd. Where she came from, snitching of any kind—especially testifying in court—was like a cardinal sin. Javona looked down at her hands as she finally took her seat.

"Ms. Blakely, please raise your right hand," a tall, slender court officer told her. Javona raised her right hand and answered yes when he asked her if she swore to tell the truth. "Would you state your entire name for the record," the prosecutor said. Javona mumbled her name, barely wanting to speak out loud. She felt like she had eaten an entire jar of paste, her tongue was heavy and stuck to the roof of her mouth. Her throat also felt dry as a desert. "Ms. Blakely, you will have to speak up," the judge announced.

"Snitch bitch!"

Before Javona could say her name for the record a loud scream erupted from some place in the back of the courtroom. Javona jumped, her heart thundering fiercely. She looked out into the crowd for the first time. Damn! There was more than one scowling face staring back at her. She recognized the faces of a few dudes; one put two fingers up to his head mimicking a gun and acted like he was pulling the trigger.

"Order!" the judge screamed as the court officers raced to the back of the room to find the troublemaker. A few guys and girls were shuffled out of the courtroom doors.

Javona finally sat down in the snitch box as it was referred to in the hood. She had to place her hands under her thighs in order to keep her nerves at bay. The prosecutor asked her a few questions about things she knew first hand.

"Ms. Blakely, is the person responsible for the murder in this courtroom today?" the prosecutor asked her. Javona shook her head in the affirmative. "Can you point to that person for the court? He followed up. Javona's eyes grew wide. This wasn't what she had rehearsed with the prosecutor. He had promised her that she would be able to focus her attention on him and she wouldn't have to look into the familiar face of the person she was ultimately betraying. Javona froze. She couldn't move. Her instincts were telling her to bolt out of the chair and run far away, but she was actually frozen, catatonic.

"Ms. Blakely you need to follow the instructions," the judge said jolting Javona into action.

Javona lifted her arm slowly and extended her pointer finger toward the defense table.

"There," she whispered. "That's the person who did it."

"You fuckin' snitch bitch! You fuckin' traitor ass bitch! After all I did for you! I fuckin' made you! I saved you! You ain't hear about what they did to Sammy the Bull—ain't no such thing as witness protection! The fuckin' feds can't protect you!" the defendant jumped up and screamed. Javona was finally forced to look into the familiar eyes. They were cold and unforgiving, a far cry from the way they used to greet her.

"Order! Order!" the judge screamed. "Counselor you will control your client or I will impose a contempt of court sanction that will send both of you to jail even if you get an acquittal!" the judge yelled out.

Javona was shaking all over as the pandemonium that had erupted in the courtroom started to die down. She thought the judge would ask for a recess, but no such luck. The prosecutor just kept right at it. Making her look more and more like the biggest turncoat in the world. He was throwing questions at her like hard, fast balls. None of this shit was her fault. They all had forced her into this shit. Javona was pissed. She would be living the rest of her life in witness protection.

"Ms. Blakely. Why don't you recount for the court what you remember about how this all came about," the prosecutor said.

Javona opened her mouth to speak as a flood of memories came rushing back into her mind. Even she didn't know where to start.

Chapter 1

"It's that Brooklyn Bullshit We On"

Spring 2009

Javona sat on the barstool inside of Houlihan's on Wall Street sipping on a cosmopolitan. The white guy next to her was blabbing on and on about how he hated his wife and kids and his job. Javona smiled and nodded. The white Wall Street executive was fucked up out of his mind. His words were slurring and his instincts were slipping. From where Javona sat, that was a good combination. She eyed his Rolex, his Charriol cuff links and his Gucci tie and knew she had certainly picked the right one tonight. Javona made small talk with him, when she could get a word in edgewise.

"You want another drink baby?" he asked Javona as he stared down into her cleavage.

"Sure, why not daddy?" she cooed, puffing up her chest to give him something to stare at. The man was drunk and looking for a good time. He thought he was getting Javona, the nice black girl he wanted to fuck, all liquored up; but she was really the one kicking the game. "A drink it is," he slurred and he felt around in his inside suit jacket pocket for his wallet. The man pulled out his very pregnant wallet and sat it on the bar. A pang of excitement came over Javona like a kid at Christmas. *Jackpot!* Javona said to herself, her eyes lighting up as she stared at the little leather beauty he had pulled out. The man peeled off a few bills from the stack he had in the back compartment of his wallet and just as he was about to place the wallet back in his pocket, Javona went into action. She started coughing frantically. "Help!" she rasped, grabbing her neck with one hand and flailing the other one. The man's eyes stretched open, but he couldn't get his equilibrium together fast enough. "Geez, she's choking!" the man blurted, stumbling off of his barstool to help Javona. She was definitely blowing his high right now. "Aww shit, what can I do," he slurred some more. He could barely stand steady on his own two feet but he sure as hell was trying. He grabbed Javona around the waist and made a poor attempt at the Heimlich maneuver.

Javona had one eye on her partner; the choking was their signal. She just needed to feign choking for a couple more minutes and it would be a done deal. The man pushed his balled up fists into Javona's stomach again. She rolled her eyes, not from choking like everyone that was watching thought; but from him almost breaking her damn rib cage. The man was thrusting her from behind. It looked more like he was trying to fuck her from behind than save her from choking. He pushed again and then he started patting her on the back roughly. She couldn't wait for this shit to be over with. "Get it out," he slurred, unable to help the fact that his dick had become erect from her ass rubbing on it while he tried saving her. While the drunken Wall Street stock broker was—in his assessment—saving a life; Lissette had smoothly passed by and snatched up his wallet. There was so much going on she was sure that no one had seen her, but Javona definitely had.

"Oh my goodness. I thought I was gonna die," Javona huffed, holding her throat and ending her charade once she noticed Lissette heading for the door. "Thank you for saving my life," she said, kissing the man on the cheek and wiping her head like she was relieved by his heroic act. The little crowd that had gathered around them started clapping once they saw she was ok. By then, the bartender had put new drinks down on the bar for Javona and her new hero savior. Javona had no plans on drinking another thing. She had a few more minutes and then she was trying to bounce. She put the next phase of her plan into motion right away. She knew the window of time between the wallet going missing and the drunk looking for it was slim.

"I'm so selfish. Choking and shit just when you were telling me about your kids . . . how many do you have? How old are they?" Javona continued talking to the man like nothing had just happened. He smiled at her. In his inebriated state he thought it so nice that the black girl wanted to know things about him—more than he could say for his selfish wife. "Six, three, and two," the man slurred, raising his glass to his mouth.

"I'm so into kids. I love them. When are their birthdays?" she asked, rubbing the top of his hand. The touch told the drunk that he could trust her. The man told her that all of his kids were born in the spring—two in April and one in May. Even his wife's birthday was in May. *Shit that makes it easy,* she thought. Javona made a mental note of the dates. She listened a bit longer as the drunken man started more complaining about how his wife was so fat now that he hardly wanted to fuck her, but Javona was only half listening. She had gotten the signal from Lissette that it was time to go. Javona's heart fluttered. This was always the part she hated, the getaway. She knew it had to be smooth, yet swift; so as not to attract any unwanted attention.

"I have to pee. I'll be right back," Javona lied, hopping down off the barstool before the man could even get a word out. "Wai . . ." he started, but Javona was already on the move. "I'll be back baby," she called back to him as her legs moved with the fast precision of a gazelle. She zigzagged through all the stuffy rich white dudes that crowded their after work haven. Lissette had already hit the door. They knew once the air hit their asses they would have to run to Lissette's car, which was all the way down near Broadway and Nassau Streets.

"You got the numbers?" Lissette huffed as they started out running.

"Yeah," Javona told her. That was all Lissette needed to hear. They would figure out the number combinations later. Javona had the jump on Lissette as she glided her long legs down the Manhattan streets. "C'mon bitch you tryin'a get caught!" Javona wolfed as she looked back at her struggling friend. After they ran for a few blocks, Lissette started walking as they got closer to where her car was parked up. Her chest was rising and falling rapidly. "Bitch this running shit ain't for me no more. Damn, I used to be able to hang with the best of them," she wolfed, her words strained.

"That's 'cause your ass keep eating all those rice and beans and you keep gaining weight in the ass," Javona laughed.

"Shut up just cuz you wanna be a skinny ass stick figure, with those long giraffe-ass legs . . . shit I'm Puerto Rican we fuckin' eat. Y'all little half this and half that bird ass chicks wanna-be model chicks better get with the program," Lissette replied, still huffing and puffing. They both busted out laughing and got into Lissette's car. Lissette bent down with her hands on her knees as she fought to catch her breath.

"Gimme the fuckin' keys . . . actin' like a old ass lady out here," Javona scolded, snatching Lissette's car keys and unlocking the car doors. After a few seconds, Lissette climbed in behind the steering wheel. "I ain't gon' be too many old ass ladies and shit. I told you before . . . we need some licks where we ain't gotta run all the fuckin' time," she said, still breathing a little hard through her nose but not huffing and puffing anymore.

"Get a gym membership! We stealin' how we not gon' have to run—you sound stupid," Javona said jokingly, shaking her head at her friend.

"Shut the hell up 'bout a gym membership. Let's get the fuck back to Brooklyn so we can boo this bastard's debit cards out. He got like four or five different shits in there—we gon' fuck his cards up!" Lissette said excitedly.

"Yeah. Let me write down these birthdays before I fuck around with you and forget the numbers I have in my head," Javona told her. Javona reached down and pulled open the glove box. Peering inside, she flipped through a stack of junk and located their infamous steno writing pad. She started jotting down the dates the drunken victim had told her. "This dude shit might be the easiest I've ever done . . . everybody born in May which is five or April which is four, kids all a year apart so the last two digits ain't gon' be that hard either," Javona said as she scribbled down a few possible PIN code combinations. It was never hard for them to figure out the PIN numbers of the Wall Street cats they pick pocketed and juxed. It was almost always the men's eldest children's birthday or a combination of the months and years of their kids' birthdays. Javona usually took a few tries, but most of the time she got it before the third time lockout at the ATM machines.

"I'm so glad these dumb muthafuckas think they so smart that two little hood bitches can't figure their shit out," Lissette commented. "It makes the jux so much more satisfying."

"Word. I know if I had big paper in the bank like that I wouldn't be using no fuckin' birthdays as my PIN number and then telling strange bitches all my business at that. But see they underestimate me because I'm black and because I'm pretty—to them that combination equals dumb bitch only good enough to fuck," Javona replied. Although she was serious about what she was saying, they laughed some more and lightened up the mood. The girls were professionals at their scams by now. They had it down to a science. The men would be so drunk the first night that Lissette and Javona took their wallets and would be able to take out the bank's minimum; which was usually $800 or $1,000 the very first night they got hold of the cards.

Then they would wait until midnight and take out more of the maximum amount all over again. Most of the time these men had four or more bank cards for different accounts in their wallets, so the girls usually walked away with a good bit of cash before their victims even woke up hung over the next afternoon realizing their wallets were gone. By the time those cats called to report their cards lost or stolen, they had definitely been set back a couple of stacks.

"A'ight . . . here goes nothing," Javona said, sliding on her purple Nikki Minaj wig, dark oversized shades and a hoodie. She inhaled deeply right before she hopped out of the car in front of the first Bank of America they spotted as soon as they crossed back into Brooklyn. Lissette watched the surroundings and kept the car running, she had put on her wig, glasses, and hoodie too. Just in case the surveillance cameras picked up her car. Lissette had already done the bamboozle with her license plates. She would change them back after they pulled far enough away from the bank. When Javona turned around smiling, Lissette knew it was a done deal. *This chick is a super brain!*

"Yeah bitch! Ching-ching!" Lissette sang out as Javona scurried back in her direction.

Javona raced back to the car waving the cash. She was clearly excited and Lissette couldn't front that was the fastest she had ever cracked a PIN since they'd been doing the shit. "On the first fucking try I got it!" Javona said, kicking her legs as she planted her ass in the passenger seat.

"That's cuz you a smart ass bitch. You knew your nerdy-ass math skills was gonna come in handy one of these days. I'm such a lucky girl to have the biggest nerd in Brooklyn as my bestie!" Lissette said cracking up. "Now let's get back to the bat cave and count up our hard day's work. These licks get easier and easier. Especially with you on deck," Lissette said proudly. Javona had to agree with her friend, they'd come a long way.

"Yeah . . . easier than back in the days when we was fucking stealing shit out of Macy's and snatching bitches earrings off on the train," Javona replied, exhaling. She was really relieved that they had found alternate ways to make money as they got older. Javona had to admit to herself, when she and Lissette were younger they were more reckless. They didn't have a fear of shit—well she did, but to be down with Lissette, Javona played it off like she wasn't scared every time they did some straight reckless shit. She never liked when they did real risky stuff like the things they did when they first started out on their get money "licks" as they called them. Javona had always been too scared of Lissette to tell her no when they started doing strong arm type of shit, like snatching other chick's earrings and boldly walking out of sneaker stores with the new kicks on when they had put their old ones in the shoe box and left it on the floor of the store. They would also go into department stores, line their shopping bags with aluminum foil to prevent the alarms from going off, and they'd fill the bags with all sorts of high-priced stolen merchandise. They would return to their hood and sell most of the stuff, what all they didn't keep for themselves. Lissette and Javona were the most fashionable fourteen year olds on their block when they first started boosting. Javona was rambling on about the stuff they used to do.

"Yooo! You ain't lying 'bout that. We used to hit Macy's, Bloomy's, *L & T*, all those big ass stores. Then when we started getting dressed up and goin' into Saks we was killin' them. Remember you used to talk like you was from England and shit—like a rich model bitch. Hilarious! They wasn't ready for us. But you can't front, we used to come off love, love with that boosting shit. Remember all those Polo shirts we had the hood open off of—we was the only bitches pushing those big horsey shits, niggas was flocking to us like bees to flowers!" Lissette reminisced.

"For real and all the Seven For All Mankind jeans when they first hit big in the streets in like 2004, we were definitely innovators on those shits around the way," Javona added. She was smiling from ear to ear just thinking about the good ol' days.

"Here you go . . . using big words . . . innovators," Lissette said mockingly. "Bitch—speak ebonics for me. You know I ain't no fuckin' walking baby genius like your ass," Lissette replied jokingly, but she was serious. She knew Javona was much smarter than she was book-wise, but Lissette still felt she had the street smarts jump on her friend. Sometimes it was a sore spot for her though, Lissette knew there was no way she would make smart moves without Javona. She had already slipped a couple of times and did a few licks without Javona's thorough planning and that had gotten Lissette into some hot water. "First of all, 'innovators' is not a big word! Second of all, I'm far from a baby genius," Javona joked.

"Yeah a'ight Ms. Hacker-Ass-Bust-A-Nigga-PIN-Number ass bitch," Lissette said laughing so hard she had tears coming out of her eyes.

Both girls were laughing hysterically at Lissette's joke. Javona was definitely the brains and Lissette the brawn of their two-woman operation. They had stories for days. They had long since left the stealing behind and moved on to bigger and better things. Boosting got too hot and after Lissette got picked up inside Bloomingdale's, it seemed like the girls' luck started running dry on that lick. It was all good, they were just on to the next one and that's how they had been rolling ever since. When one hustle dried up, they moved on and on. With no real plans for their future, Lissette and Javona depended on each other and just hoped for the best each time they set out to make some fast money.

Lissette pulled her Honda Accord up to her new building in Ocean Hill Houses in Brownsville. She had got a crackhead name Daisy to sublet the apartment to her for $400 a month. Lissette wasn't worried about Daisy running off with her loot and not paying the rent because the welfare was still paying for the crib. Lissette immediately noticed how crowded it was outside. The spring was just starting to show up, which was all a sign for Brooklyn residents to come crawling out of their winter hiding spots. "The hood is out tonight. One hot day and niggas come out like roaches when the lights go off!" Lissette said as she passed by and ogled a line of dudes on motorcycles posted up on her corner and the hand-to-hand corner boys kicking it with them.

"You thought moving to the ville was better than East New York? I beg to differ. From the looks of it, it's the same shit, different hood," Javona told Lissette as she eyed the same dudes.

"You act like I wanted to move out of East New York . . . those crazy niggas that I robbed wasn't gon' let a bitch rest easy so I had to go . . . shit you lucky you can still rest ya head there. I guess they knew your ass wasn't down with me that day," Lissette replied. She had definitely gotten out of East New York in the nick of time. Lissette had pulled a snatch a stash scam on a hustler name Rori and he was looking for her ass. Word had it that he wasn't fuckin' around. Lissette was definitely hiding in plain sight though, because Brooklyn was a big, small place. She would run into his ass or some of his workers one day sooner or later.

"One good thing about a fresh new spot, I see some of our future vics out here right now though—they just don't know it yet," Javona said focusing on all of the new bikes and cars and their owners. Javona and Lissette didn't discriminate at all when it came to moneymakers to pull their licks on. Their motto was "Eight to eighty, dumb, rich, poor, or crazy—they got money, we gettin' at 'em." They scammed and robbed from executives on Wall Street to the hustlers on Mother Gaston Boulevard. To Lissette and Javona money was money, it all could be stolen and spent the same.

Lissette parked her car and they got out. "Hurry up. We holding too much paper to be lollygagging with all these heads hanging out here," Lissette told Javona as Lissette watched her surroundings carefully. She never trusted a soul. It was how she was raised. Although she wasn't from Brownsville, Lissette knew the streets anywhere were always talking and definitely always watching. It wasn't lost on her that mad people in the hood knew that she and Javona were known for getting and having money; what people couldn't figure out was

exactly how the girls got their paper, especially
when they were no longer boosting and selling
stuff. "Walk faster chica. I don't wanna have
to blast on a nigga before I count my dough,"
Lissette told Javona. Javona had a habit of doing
her model walk stroll. Lissette always teased her.
"C'mon on pretty bitch—ain't no time for Tyra
Banking it," Lissette quipped. Javona put pep
in her step. It wasn't very often that she didn't
listen to Lissette's advice.

Lissette was the protector and watchdog of
the two girls. Standing five feet three inches and
weighing in at close to two hundred pounds, Lissette was a husky roughneck that would fight any
dude in the street. She had a pretty butterscotch
complexion, but her face was marred remnants
of old bruises, cuts, and scratches. Lissette had
been in many fights in her twenty-one years of
life. She had truly lived the hard knock life in
every sense. Lissette had been shot, stabbed, and
sliced all by the time she was fourteen-years-
old. Lissette had come from rough beginnings.
From birth, her life was filled with turmoil and
instability. Born to very young parents, Lissette
wasn't afforded what most would think of as

a traditional family setting. Her mother and father were more interested in the streets than being parents. Lissette didn't have the benefit of having grandparents like most of her peers that were born to teenage parents. So she grew up as if her mother and father were like her brother and sister. That was exactly how they treated her too. Both of Lissette's parents were into the drug game by the time she was conceived. They worked for Tito Munoz, a big time Puerto Rican heroin pusher that reigned supreme in the drug trade in Spanish Harlem in the eighties and nineties. Tito was ruthless and everybody knew not to cross him. Her parent's lifestyle was crazy and all over the place. They worked all night, slept all day, and when they weren't doing that they got high and fought like a cats and dogs. It was never apparent that they worked for a rich hustler. Their house was dirty, had little or no food most of the time, and the furniture was raggedy. Lissette never had a bed until she was much older. She slept on the floor, sometimes barely with a blanket. Her parents spent money as fast as they made it. As a child, Lissette was never cuddled, kissed, or treated with love. In fact, she had never heard the words "I love you" until she was seventeen and Javona had said to her, "I love your crazy-ass chica," after they had pulled off a dope-on-a rope lick in Atlantic City where they had slipped a rich Asian dude a roofie, took him back to his room and robbed his ass blind.

In Lissette's house when she was a kid there was always some kind of drama. It was never a minute of peace and she grew up so used to screaming, cursing, fighting, and bloodshed that even as she got older too much silence made her uneasy. Lissette was often referred to as "bitch" and her brother as "dumb fuck" when her mother and father spoke to them. It was like her parents resented the kids for being born. Both kids had gotten so used to being called out their names that they didn't even flinch when their parents called them by the derogatory monikers.

Lissette's mother, a drug mule for Tito, often got her ass beat by Lissette's father for little things. Lissette's father had given his mother two black eyes one time for not putting enough salt in the rice and beans. He would also fuck her anywhere he felt like in the house at any time. Lissette and her brother got so used to her father banging out their mother right in front of them that they would just leave the room. Lissette learned first hand how to suck a dick when she was about six years old too—one night her father was too high and horny to wait for her mother to get back from running Tito's packages.

Lissette's father ran his home with more than iron fists, to say the least. He would beat her mother mercilessly. One time Lissette witnessed her mother get beaten so bad, her mother had pissed and shit on herself as a result. Lissette had taken a few beatings at the hands of her father as well. He had knocked out her front tooth when she was four for changing the channel on the TV. Because it was before the tooth's time to fall out, it took forever for her adult tooth to fill in the missing space, so Lissette walked around like snaggle-tooth until she was almost eight-years-old.

Although Lissette's father sold drugs for Tito, he also used just as much as he sold, so in turn he stole just almost as much as he sold too. Everything came to a head one night when some of Tito's men busted into Lissette's house after they found out her father had been stealing drugs and money to support his ever-growing heroin addiction. Lissette didn't remember much about that night, but when she had come into consciousness in the hospital days later; she did find out that she had been shot and stabbed. Tito's men thought Lissette was dead like the rest of her family, but surprisingly the shot they meant for her head had just grazed the side of her face and caused enough bleeding to make them think it was a good shot. They had stabbed her for good measure too, but the knife had missed her lungs by less than half an inch. Maybe she had a guardian angel watching over her. Probably not, it was just sheer stupidity on the part of Tito's sloppy hit men.

Lissette was the lone survivor of Tito's ordered hit. She was placed in foster care in Brooklyn with an old Dominican lady named Ms. Ruiz. Everybody knew Dominicans hated Puerto Ricans so Ms. Ruiz never really treated Lissette nicely. Ms. Ruiz had made it clear she only took Lissette in for the check. Lissette was angry and she fought everybody she came into contact with. She gave Ms. Ruiz hell up until the lady finally told Lissette she had to leave her home. Lissette had never been given the right amount of therapy to deal with the deaths of her family; so she acted out, often violently, everywhere she went and everywhere she lived until she aged out of foster care. She hardly ever went to school and if she did she terrorized the teachers and other kids so much that she would get thrown right out. Everywhere Lissette went most girls and even boys feared her. That reputation never bothered her.

Javona on the other hand was the polar opposite of Lissette. Javona stood five feet seven inches tall and she was rail thin. As skinny as she was, Javona had large breasts that stood out so much they looked as if she had purchased them from a top notch plastic surgeon. Javona's skin was the color of coffee beans and her hair was long, even longer than Lissette's and Javona wasn't even Spanish. Javona was often mistaken for Middle Eastern or Indian, but in actuality her family was just what they called mutts—mixed with a little of this and a little of that. Javona simply referred to herself as an African American, fuck all the "I'm half this or I got Indian in my family." She didn't feed into none of that.

She was soft spoken and hated confrontation. Her childhood was pretty stable and not filled with much drama. She came from a two-parent household and although her mother's husband wasn't her biological father, he treated her like he was. Her mother worked as a receptionist for H&R Block part-time during the tax season and her stepfather was a sanitation worker. They both made a decent living and did the best they could for their kids. Although they didn't make a hell of a lot of money, you would've never been able to tell by looking at their kids. Javona and her three siblings were given what they needed and then some. They never missed a meal and they wore decent clothes. Christmas and Easter in their house was made to be extra special too. Javona definitely couldn't complain about her early years at all.

Javona was always smart in school and she especially excelled in math. She had dreams of becoming a pediatrician when she grew up. She'd always loved playing with and holding babies. That is until something tragic changed her life forever that dashed her dreams and sent her spiraling down into the pitfalls of depression. When Javona was thirteen years old, she was raped and sodomized by her stepfather's brother, who she had known half her life as Uncle Ron. Javona kept reliving the moment that he had come into her bedroom, held her down and forced himself into her virginal opening. When she'd started to bleed, he had dragged her into the bathroom, made her sit in a hot tub of water while he stood at the side of the tub and forced his dirty dick between her lips. Javona was never the same after that. That evening when her mother came home from her job at H&R Block, Javona didn't speak much and she didn't eat at all.

Uncle Rob had threatened to kill Javona, her mother, and her siblings if she told on him. For some reason, as smart as Javona was, Uncle Rob was able to convince her that he could and would kill her entire family if she ever said anything. Her silence backfired on her. Because she hadn't told, he continued to victimize her every chance he got. Javona never told her mother what had happened, but she became even more introverted than she'd been before the rapes.

Javona barely spoke at home after the incidents and she didn't let any man hug or touch her. Her mother was oblivious to what was going on with her. Soon Javona's grades began to suffer. Her mother would put her on punishment, but that didn't improve her grades, it just drew Javona further away from her family. As a kid, Javona never spoke up for herself. But when her stepfather had announced that Uncle Rob was moving in with them; that had been the last straw for Javona. She had turned to the streets for comfort.

Growing up, Javona knew of Lissette—everybody and their mother who lived in East New York knew of Lissette's loud mouthed, bad ass, at the time. Javona had always steered clear of Lissette and they had never been real close friends until they got to high school. The day she really met Lissette had changed Javona's life forever and she never turned back. The day always stuck out in her mind as clear as crystal.

Freshman Day 2003

"Slap that bitch and take her fuckin' sneakers! It's open season on all this fresh meat! These freshman bitches is ducks and they gettin' got! Free Jordans over here!" A tall Alice the Goon looking chick screamed out rallying her little posse of followers. Javona heard the words but she didn't think they were referring to her. She wasn't bothering nobody. She had been quiet the entire first day of high school; therefore, she never dreamed that anyone would bother her. She was sadly mistaken. "Let's get that lanky freshman right there!" the same tall girl called out.

Suddenly, a group of high school upper class-man girls advanced on Javona like a pack of wolves. She didn't know whether to run, scream, or just stand there. She was frozen with fear. Her heart was pounding painfully against her sternum as she backed up until she was finally caught cowering in a corner up against the school's brick building.

Javona froze with fear dancing in her eyes. She shifted her gaze from from one scowling face to another. "Look at that skinny bitch, she scared as hell. Let's take her sneakers and cut that long pretty hair off," another girl announced pulling back her fist like she was going to punch Javona. This caused Javona to jump so hard she dropped her book bag on the ground.

"Nobody ain't warn you about freshman day? Now run those fuckin' sneakers pretty bitch! I should slice ya pretty face just on GP too," the first big bully growled her hot breath on Javona's face. Javona felt like she would shit on herself when she saw the girl clicking the little black lever on her orange box cutter. Javona had heard about these wild Bed-Stuy girls coming up to schools slicing other girls faces out of jealousy.

"Please don't take my sneakers or cut my face. My mother don't got money like that and she—"

Javona stammered, but her words were cut short. "Oww!" She crumpled to the ground holding her cheek after receiving an open handed slap to her face. Javona looked at her own hand to make sure they hadn't sliced her. The slap had happened so fast that she didn't even know who had administered the stinging hit. All of the girls converged on her and started pulling her long hair and trying to forcefully take her sneakers off her feet. One of them had already picked up Javona's pink and purple Jansport book bag she had saved up all summer to buy. Finally, one of her Jordans came off of her foot; all of the girls were going after it like a pride of hungry lions.

"Help!" Javona screamed as she tried to kick the girls off of her. Her attempts were all for nothing. All of the blows to her face and head made it hard for her to stay consistent with her kicking and fighting back. Aside from that, being on the concrete, she was suffering scratches and scrapes that stung like hell. Javona felt her shirt rip in the front and she could tell that one of her breasts had jumped free of her bra. "Ahhh, haahah! Her titty is hanging out," someone in the crowd yelled seemingly very amused at the damage being done to Javona. Javona finally felt her other sneaker come off. That was it; they had all of her shit. Javona was crying now, but she was grateful they hadn't sliced her face.

"I got the other sneaker!" somebody else in the crowd of bullies announced.

"C'mon! Let's get the fuck outta here!" another one of the assailants called out. They all turned to run, but they didn't get too far. They ran smack dab into somebody they all feared.

"Give that girl back her fuckin' sneakers Tabitha," a voice boomed. All of the girls' eyes grew wide when they saw Lissette standing there blocking their exit out of the school yard. They all started trying to disperse. None of them wanted to take ownership of what they'd done to Javona. They didn't need to, Lissette already knew the deal and although she fought a lot when people made her mad, she fucking despised coward-ass bullies.

Nobody fucked with Lissette because everybody knew she could and would fight a bitch in a heartbeat. "Yo, y'all fuckin' speak English! Give that fuckin' girl back all of her shit!" Lissette barked. Lissette was flanked by four dudes. She was fourteen, but she resembled a twenty-year-old woman in size. "I said give that little girl back her fuckin' sneakers right now," Lissette gritted through clenched teeth. Lissette and her dudes moved in on the bullies now. Lissette never hung out with other girls, it was always her and dudes at that time. The big bully who had been the instigator of the attack on Javona turned around to Javona and handed her back her sneakers. Javona stood wide-eyed and in shock. She thought for sure she would be explaining to her mother why her brand new sneakers were gone. Javona started putting her sneakers back on and trying her best to cover up her exposed ample breasts.

"Say sorry to her and help her brush off her clothes," Lissette instructed the same Alice the Goon chick. All of the girls rushed over to Javona and started assisting her with pulling herself back together. Javona brushed them off, she didn't want their help after what they had just put her through. Lissette walked over to one of the girls and snuffed her just for GP. "Ahhh," the girl screamed as blood gushed out of her nose.

"How you like somebody bigger and better than you to fuckin' hit on you for no reason? Take off your fuckin' shirt and give it to shorty!" Lissette hissed. The girl did as she was told for fear of another blow to the face from Lissette. The girl reluctantly handed Javona her shirt. Javona snatched it and pulled it over her head to cover herself up.

"Now all y'all get the fuck from around here. Y'all bet'not let me see y'all messin' with shorty again either. This is the East, take y'all dirty, bum-asses back to begging-ass Bed-Stuy," Lissette boomed. The group of bullies split up so fast their departure resembled the Red Sea parting. Javona didn't know whether to say thank you to Lissette or run away herself. She recognized Lissette from her fourth and fifth grade classes as the girl who caused a lot of trouble in school and had all of the teachers shook as hell.

"Javona right?" Lissette asked. She remembered Javona from her classes too.

"Yeah," Javona whispered. Although Lissette had just saved her ass, Javona was still leery about her.

"I remember you helped me cheat one time on a math test. Shit, that was the first time I ever got an *A* on anything in my life. That was good looking out. I never forgot that shit either. So count what just happened as repayment for a long time owed debt," Lissette told her. Javona just stared at Lissette in awe. Javona thought Lissette spoke like an adult and was more powerful than some men she knew. She instantly had an overwhelming sense of respect for Lissette.

"I'ma be around here e'ry day, so if those bitches fuck with you again you let me know. Consider me your friend," Lissette told Javona. Javona smiled. She was overjoyed to have a friend like Lissette. Javona was never scared to come to school again, freshman or not.

From that day forward the girls forged an unbreakable bond and friendship that just grew tighter as the years went by. Seven years later, they had grown closer than sisters.

Chapter 2

"Big Up, Big Up It's a Stick up, Stick up"

Winter 2010

"Hurry up before we miss our fuckin' flight!" Lissette barked at Javona impatiently, leaning on her car horn. Javona rolled her eyes and smacked her lips as she dropped her bags and headed back toward Lissette's building. "What the fuck you forgot now?!" Lissette hollered. "You know damn well we gotta park up and all that. Plus this weather is suspect," Lissette continued complaining.

"I'm coming . . . damn. You know I gotta make sure I don't forget my hot shit to wear. All this shit would be a big waste of time if I don't step up my game. How the fuck I'm supposed to catch a big money cat if I don't look good?" Javona snapped, as she flopped down into the passenger seat of the car.

"Bitch you ain't tryin'a find a husband. You tryin'a find a vic to make a lick," Lissette quipped, chuckling at her rhyme. Javona rolled her eyes at her friend.

"Maybe I can do both . . . shit I'm a hot bitch, I think I can snag a husband," Javona rolled her eyes playfully.

"Yeah, meet the man of your dreams at the all-star game after party, after you rob his ass blind he will marry you . . . right," Lissette said, twisting her lips.

They pulled up into JFK airport's premium parking lot and Lissette began roving for a spot. She didn't have to look long since that was the expensive lot which most people didn't use. Javona sucked her teeth and rolled her eyes when she noticed what lot they had pulled into. Javona and Lissette definitely had a different take on money. Javona knew her best friend probably didn't have a dollar saved from all of the licks they pulled. She hated when Lissette acted like she was a huge baller. They were out there hustling and risking their lives to scam, rob, and cheat; and Javona just hated the way her friend spent money like it came easy.

"Why aren't you parking in economy?" Javona finally asked with a motherly attitude.

"Because I can afford premium. Problem?" Lissette asked with just as much attitude.

"I just think you can save money. It just don't make sense to pay like fifty dollars a day when you can pay ten dollars a day . . . I'm just sayin'," Javona started. Lissette cut off Javona's lecture before it could get fully underway. "Don't just say shit. I'm good. You count your pockets and I'll count mine. I ain't ask you for no money for parking, did I? Now get ya skinny ass out and let's go snag us some balling out of control ass vics," Lissette replied, ending their almost argument with a joke. Javona smiled. Lissette was truly her road dog. She knew how to end some shit between them before it even started.

When the girls landed in Dallas they were excited. It was February and it was cold but the sun in Texas was shining bright. The trip had a few setbacks at first because they'd gotten a buddy pass hook up on their tickets, which meant they were flying standby, which also meant they kept getting bumped from their flights. It had taken forever for them to finally get seats on a flight and when they did, they had to sit apart. But what was important was that they'd finally gotten on a flight. Lissette complained the entire time about how she should've just thrown down the paper for the flight and how next time she was flying first class, blah, blah, blah. Javona put her iPod on and tuned her friend out. In Javona's book, free was free. All they had paid for was the taxes and 9/11 fees for the tickets, which was right up Javona's alley. Javona was all about stashing most and spending some. Lissette was definitely the complete opposite. It showed in everything they did. When they shopped, if Javona purchased a Michael Kors bag, Lissette had to purchase a more expensive Marc Jacobs bag. Lissette was definitely living from moment to moment. She and Javona had clearly gotten into their line of business for different reasons. While Javona wanted to make money to pay her bills and stay above water, Lissette wanted to make money to floss and show off.

Landing in Dallas made all of the stress of getting there go out the window. Both girls had money on their minds. "Whew hoo! Look at this baby right here!" Lissette screamed when she got the keys to the 2008 Bentley they had rented for the weekend. The airport shuttle had dropped them off at the luxury rental car place that was a couple of miles outside of downtown Dallas.

"This shit is kinda sweet," Javona had to admit, as she examined the beauty of a car. Although Javona didn't fully agree with the exorbitant price they'd paid to rent it, she wasn't gonna lie, that shit was sweet. Lissette had told her that in order to fit the part, they had to look the part. Seeing the car now, Javona couldn't have agreed more.

The girls were in heaven inside the supremely luxurious vehicle. "This shit hugs the road—you hear me . . . I mean, hugs the road and feels as smooth as a baby's ass to drive!" Lissette had announced excitedly. All Javona could do was laugh. She could care less if that shit squeezed the road and felt as smooth as an old man's ass, she hated driving so she didn't care if that Bentley drove like a spaceship—she wasn't trying to drive it.

Lissette and Javona checked into the Omni Mandalay Hotel on East Las Colinas Boulevard, which was very close to the new Cowboys stadium which was close to where all of the All-Star events were happening. Although they didn't have tickets to the games or the events, Javona and Lissette didn't need them to have a good time. Being in the midst of it all was enough. All Lissette and Javona needed was any kind of access to some fresh meat that they could victimize. They were in Dallas for one big lick that would finance their trip, plus send them home with a profit. If they had fun in the meantime, so be it. Javona had warned Lissette that they had to be careful though. She had warned that they wanted to pick their vic correctly so they could avoid wasting their time. Both girls were fully aware that the types of dudes that came to the NBA All-Star games ran the gamut from broke wanna-be-ballers all the way to balling-out-of-control-ass niggas. Lissette and Javona were looking for the latter.

They rushed and got dressed for their night out. Their hotel room resembled the back dressing room of a runway fashion show. There were pieces of clothes put together as outfits with shoes and accessories laid out, thrown across the bed and chairs. The girls had gone through several different changes until they were confident that they had on the right outfit for their night out. Javona did Lissette's makeup, which made her look like a totally different person. It didn't matter how chubby she was, with makeup covering her blemishes, Lissette was unquestionably pretty. Javona wasn't a slouch herself. With her huge breasts, slim legs, and her long natural hair; she often got mistaken for a model. Sometimes people even mistook her for Kim Porter, P. Diddy's baby mother. Javona's shape and looks often played to their advantage because one thing was for sure, dudes that had money, loved to have eye candy to flaunt. Lissette and Javona surveyed each other's gear, paid each other compliments, and headed out. "Promise me something," Javona said to Lissette as they boarded the hotel's elevator headed to the lobby.

"Oh boyee, here the fuck we go," Lissette rolled her eyes. She knew her friend was a worry wart all of the time. Sometimes it drove Lissette crazy. "What is it?" she asked, tapping her foot and folding her arms.

"Promise we'll just get one big hit and get the fuck out of Dallas. I don't have a good feeling about this city and we both know that being greedy is how you get got," Javona said ominously. Lissette let out a long sigh and twisted her lips to the side. She sometimes grew wary of Javona's negative outlook.

"A'ight bad luck Chuck. One lick and we can be out," Lissette promised giving Javona a sideways glance. Lissette secretly had her fingers crossed in her pocket. "Do me one favor too," Lissette came back. Javona looked at her inquisitively. "Stop being a damn *traer mala fortuna*," Lissette said in Spanish. Javona screwed her face up.

"English muthafucka . . . English . . . in my Radio Raheem voice," Javona responded, busting out laughing.

"Bitch what the fuck I said was stop being a fucking jinx!" Lissette translated. She laughed too, but she couldn't shake the feeling she had about Dallas either. It wasn't good.

"Yo you sure this nigga ain't lying about being Shaq's brother," Javona huffed as she looked down at the six foot seven inch tall man sprawled out on his hotel room bed drooling like a dope fiend in his deep sleep. Lissette shrugged her shoulders.

"I can only go off what the nigga said when he pushed up on me. He ain't have no bodyguards or none of that bullshit, but we did fly over here in a Range so the nigga seem like he got long paper.

I mean, he ain't seven foot tall like Shaq but shit he got big lips like Shaq. To me, he look like he could pass for a NBA baller's brother. What you want me to say? I don't know." Lissette replied, looking from the man to Javona and back again. Lissette had caught the man's attention and they had begun to talk. When she offered up the goods real fast the man was down immediately. Lissette didn't bother wasting time with fronting; she wanted to make some money. When the dude fell for it that fast, Lissette thought the shit was too easy, but she went with it anyway. Lissette had used the bathroom, texted Javona where they were going to be, and told her she would send her the hotel room number after she had dude knocked out. That's exactly how it had gone down. It was risky, but it had definitely worked—so far.

"Yo, just get his shit, search it, and let's go," Lissette told Javona as she held her newly purchased hunting knife tightly. Lissette had bought the knife in Dallas since she couldn't fly with any weapons. She told Javona they had to be prepared just in case the extra dose of sleeping pills she had to give the huge hunk of man started to wear off. "If this nigga wakes up his ass is gettin' stuck," Lissette had said. Javona riffled though the man's pants and finally found what she was looking for. "A'ight maybe we did luck up," she said as she pulled a rubber banded knot of money out of the man's pants pocket and smiled. She tossed it to Lissette. Lissette smiled too. "Maybe he is Shaq's brother," Lissette said, her eyes lighting up as she caught the wad of cash against her chest. Javona continued to search through the man's wallet for his credit cards, debit cards, and anything else of value they might be interested in taking. To her disappointment, there wasn't much else to find. "He don't have one damn credit card or bank card. Looks like his ass is just a hood rich nigga carrying his life savings around in his pockets. I mean shit . . . nowadays even broke muthafuckas carry bank cards," Javona said disappointedly.

"Yeah and this shit here is only two, one hundred dollar bills on the outside, for fronting purposes, but nothing but single dollars on the inside. Ain't this a bitch," Lissette complained as she flipped through the man's knot of cash. "Damn!" Javona huffed. She felt deflated. She knew that meant this wasn't going to be enough for what they had planned; which was, get in, get the money, and get out.

"Let me see his wallet," Lissette demanded. The small vein against her temple was throbbing. She was pissed because she would never hear the end of it from Javona. It seemed like when Javona picked dudes, they really had money, but whenever Lissette snagged a nigga, he was always faking like he was balling.

"What you don't believe we been tricked by this fat ass nigga?" Javona snapped. "Plus, you shouldn't be touching this nigga's shit, you don't have no gloves on," Javona continued angrily. She wasn't touching anything in that fucking hotel room without her little black gloves on, it had been her practice since they'd started out taking dudes money.

"Fuck this broke bastard and his wallet. He gon' wake up and he won't remember shit no way. I wanna see the fuckin' name on his ID," Lissette snapped. There was heavy tension in the room as both girls let their frustration and disappointment take over. The mood surrounding them was palpable.

"Suit yourself," Javona relented tossing the wallet to Lissette. *She wanna touch some shit without gloves that's her fuckin' business* Javona thought. Javona looked at the guy as Lissette gave his wallet one more fine toothed once over.

Lissette sucked her teeth when she didn't find what she was looking for.

"Yo why he look like he ain't even breathing and shit," Javona said, crinkling her eyebrows as she dipped her head at different angles trying to see if the man's chest and stomach were actually moving so she could tell if he was really breathing.

"This nigga is gon' be a'ight. His ass is just fine. He is simply knocked the fuck out from those pills. I'm tellin' you when he wake up he won't remember shit . . . e'rything gon' be a'ight. Let's get the fuck outta here and find a real nigga to get," Lissette instructed, throwing the man's wallet on the hotel nightstand. Javona sighed. Her friend was hardheaded. When they got outside, it was suddenly freezing cold in Dallas. "I know this can't be fucking snow I'm seeing in Dallas!" Lissette said, raising her hand to look at the small, perfect flakes that had landed on it.

"Snow in the south? In fuckin' Texas? We leave New York only to bring fuckin' snow to Dallas with us . . . what the fuck! " Javona said amazed. "You still think I'm a jinx?" she mumbled to Lissette. Lissette was quiet. Shit just wasn't right all the way around.

***

Javona sauntered into Ghostbar at the top of the W Hotel in Dallas. She was wearing a close fitting sequined mini dress, a classic little number that garnered more than a few looks as she walked by. Between the dress and her pretty face, she had managed to talk herself and Lissette's way into the exclusive party, although security was more than White House tight. Lissette had found out about the party before they'd gotten to Dallas, but she wasn't able to get them any tickets. They had just taken a chance and decided they'd go see if they could game their way inside. Sure enough, it was all good, Lissette was overjoyed by Javona and her pretty model ass.

"This shit right here is sweet as hell," Javona whispered to herself, looking all around as she walked through the inside of the club. Lissette wasn't with her, but Javona wanted to share her excitement with somebody. Javona scanned around for Lissette, but she had gone to the bathroom as soon as they stepped inside. Javona found a seat and examined her surroundings some more. She thought the club looked like the set of a rapper's music video. Everything inside was ultra modern, with sleek chairs, and beautiful shiny table tops. A huge neon sign was suspended from the ceiling reading "Live 2010." There was a champagne fountain illuminated by dark purple and fluorescent pink lights. The club was definitely inviting and the surroundings were screaming money, money, money! But, when Javona saw the little folded signs lined up on the bar that advertised "Open Bar All Night" she almost fainted. That's what she was talking about. Javona always thought she belonged in settings just like this one. In her opinion, this party was not only exclusive, it was the shit! She was so glad Lissette had heard about it and they'd decided to come. Javona was sure they'd find a vic in there, or so she hoped.

Lissette finally returned and took her place next to Javona. Lissette had a huge smile on her face. "Didn't I tell you this was going to be the shit. Yo', how about I just saw fuckin' Kevin Durant and Russell Simmons up in this piece," Lissette rasped loudly over the music in what she thought was a whisper. Javona's heart was pounding with excitement. She too had noticed more than one hip hop heavy hitter and NBA baller in the party. She could only dream of the credit cards and cash those dudes must've been holding down in their pockets. Shit, she was hoping she saw that little boxer that walked around with knapsacks filled with money. Javona wanted to get at his ass so badly. The more she looked at the celebrities up in the club with their entourages, she wasn't sure she was ready to fuck with somebody who might have a bodyguard or some shit, but snagging a rich man to call her own was surely something she was considering. Javona was daydreaming about the possibilities of being a celeb wife.

"Oh shit! Look to my left, blue Yankee fitted, chinchilla fur on," Lissette mumbled in Javona's ear excitedly. Without trying to be too obvious Javona turned her head slowly to find the person Lissette was describing. After a few seconds, she noticed a dude fitting the description sitting with like ten other dudes and a gang of females around them. "And?" Javona asked Lissette once she noticed all of those people surrounding the dude. From what Javona could see, the dude was fine, but he looked like the typical black celebrity with an entourage. She wondered what type of business he was into, but before she could ask, Lissette started filling her in.

"That cat right there is from straight from BK. A major weight player, I'm talking fish scale type of dude. His name is Armon. A muthafucka is official. Word is, he got the game on lock in Roosevelt and Sumner and a few other hot spots," Lissette said, her heart fluttering at the sight of him.

"How you know him?" Javona asked eyeing her best friend strangely. Lissette had never talked about this dude to her before.

"Remember the cats I used to run with when we first met? Before we got close and I cut them niggas off?" Lissette asked. Javona nodded her head in understanding. "Well they had been scoping this nigga out to take him, but your boy right there got his security game down tight. That muthafucka don't let no outside niggas in his world so it was hard for those cats to get up close and personal enough to know his moves. This nigga keeps the same few niggas around him and his circle is like airtight. But as niggas watched him they started noticing something about him—a weakness. The cat Armon likes chicks and he goes hard for a pretty bitch any day," Lissette continued yelling over the music, not even realizing how loud she was screaming in Javona's ear. "I'm telling you, this dude Armon got a real thing for chicks . . . like on another level type of thing for chicks. They call him a sucka for love ass dude. He would like you Javona . . . you know, since you're one of those so-called exotic chicks," Lissette said with a raised eyebrow. Javona took the not so subtle message, but she wasn't going for it. There was no way with all those pretty-ass chicks surrounding him and not to mention the dudes, that Lissette could've seriously thought this dude was a good vic. "If it was impossible for your so-called boys back in the day, what makes you think me and you can pull off a caper against somebody like that," Javona said skeptically. She didn't even give Lissette a chance to answer. Javona turned to the bar and ordered an apple martini. She was going to definitely need a drink to deal with Lissette when she told her she wasn't with this set up of the BK cat Armon.

"You gotta at least walk by. I'm telling you Javona . . . he's gonna try to holla. I'm sayin' he is predictable on that note. I know his steelo, trust me on this one, please. Those dudes back then said that they could never find a chick they could get this nigga interested in, to set him up.

You might be just the pretty bitch for the job. Even if this Dallas trip just serves as a meet and greet and we get at him when we get back to NY, it's all good. I'm tellin' you Voni, this nigga got long, long paper. I'm talkin' about Al Pacino in Scarface type paper so it would be worth the wait," Lissette said, staring over at Armon and his crew. Lissette definitely had a way with words. The more she pressed, the more Javona started leaning toward making it happen. All Javona was thinking about was money, money, and more money. Javona couldn't front, Armon was fine as hell from what she could see. He was one of those dudes that just looked like he had swagger. Kind of like Jay-Z, he didn't have to wear anything or try that hard to exude a confident air about him. Javona also noticed that he didn't seem to put it on display that he had money. She kept glancing and turning away so she wouldn't be obvious and from what she could tell, aside from the obviously expensive chinchilla fur, he wasn't flashing a big chunky chain or the obligatory diamond Jesus piece laying in the center of his chest. Javona didn't notice any big bling sparkling from Armon's ears either. In other words, she got the sense that he must've always had money. He wasn't acting like a new money nigga, like those that wear clothes and jewelry just to send the message that they have money. In Javona's assessment, the dudes who didn't brag or put it out there that they had money were usually the cats with the most money. They were the ones that didn't feel the need to flaunt it. The more she assessed the situation, the more onboard she got.

"Fuck it. We ain't come all the way to All-Star Weekend to leave without at least the prospect of a new lick," Javona told Lissette. Javona told herself she would just walk by and see what happened. If it led to something it did, if not, they would just move on. Besides, something about Armon intrigued Javona—there was just something about him.

"That's what I'm talkin' about bitch. Work those stick figure legs and that Cherokee hair," Lissette joked. "This dude gonna be the lick of the year. We ain't never gon' have to work again if we get at his ass, trust," Lissette assured her. Javona threw back the rest of her apple martini and did just what her friend advised. With a little liquid courage in her system, she hopped off the bar stool and sauntered slowly past Armon's table. Javona walked real close and real slow like she was going to speak to him, but she just caught eye contact with him and made a beeline toward the bathroom. All she wanted to do was get him to notice her. Javona didn't turn around, but she felt like his eyes were on her. She was right. Lissette watched with excitement welling up inside of her. Armon had turned to follow Javona with his eyes. Then he leaned into one of his boys and nodded his head in the direction that Javona had walked. *It worked! This nigga is still weak for pussy! Some things never change. First time we couldn't get you, but the second time gonna be the muthafuckin' charm,* Lissette said in her head as her plan started to unfold perfectly right before her eyes. She wanted to call her boys back in Brooklyn, that's how excited she was, but that would've been too risky right now. Lissette couldn't let Javona know she had just used her like a worm on a fish hook.

When Javona came out of the bathroom she felt someone touch her arm. She jumped and got ready to start swinging when she saw that it was a man she didn't recognize that had grabbed her. Javona looked at him like he was crazy and balled up her fists at her sides. She was thinking he better have a good explanation for touching her. She hated to be touched by strange men. Javona cocked her head to the side as if to say, *what the fuck you want.*

"What up ma? How you?" the man asked, licking his lips like she was a meal and he wanted to eat her.

"Do I know you?" Javona hissed yanking her arm away from him as she started to walk away.

"Hold on shorty . . . I came back here with a message so don't shoot the messenger," he said, putting his hands up in front of his chest to calm her down. "My manz wanna get to know you n'shit—that's all. He's the big boss nigga you see in the Yankee fitted over there," the man said, shifting his head in Armon's general direction. Javona could tell he was definitely a BK nigga; there was no mistaking his accent or his swagger.

"Why ya manz sent you if he wanna get to know me? He ain't got a tongue? He gonna get to know me if he come talk to me—not you," Javona retorted with a sassy attitude. She was being a bitch and she knew it, but that was her game.

"Nah. That nigga got a shorty here with him. I'm sayin' he ain't tryin'a be disrespectful to shorty n'shit, but he is interested in you though. He said he can get rid of her if you willing to give him the time of day, nah mean," the man explained.

"If he here with a shorty he need to stay with her. I'm not no home wrecker and I'm definitely not no second fiddle type of chick. So tell him I'm not interested if he can't come to the bar and tell me himself that he wanna holla, then no dice. I don't do the second hand rapping. This ain't the game of telephone and we damn sure ain't in high school," Javona replied, switching her ass away from the stranger. She could tell the man was awestruck at how she had shot Armon down. Javona knew with the money Lissette said he had, Armon was probably used to bitches flocking to him with no problems. She had different plans for his ass. Playing hard to get was a game Lissette had taught Javona a long time ago. When they had first started hanging hard and getting close, Lissette had explained to her that being too available made dudes get bored easy. "All men want a challenge. The thrill of the chase is the point of this whole shit," Lissette had explained. Javona remembered that lesson as she walked passed Armon's table again and gave him an evil sideways glance. She wanted him to believe she was offended by him sending his friend to speak for him. Javona wanted to send the message that she wasn't like all the groupie chicks hanging at his table. Lissette watched as

Armon followed Javona with his eyes. It was a done deal. He had let his weakness get the best of him just like she thought he would.

Javona slid back onto the bar seat Lissette had been holding for her. She had her back to the crowd, the club was packed now and the dance floor was bumping. The DJ was playing old school hip hop. Biggie's *Hypnotize* was blaring through the speakers and the bodies on the dance floor were swaying, arms in the air and all.

"Bitch don't turn around now, but that nigga Armon is walking this way. You did it with that famous model walk! I betchu he is coming straight for you," Lissette warned before she prepared to jump up. She didn't mind giving up her seat or her spot at the bar for a good cause like this one. As soon as Armon got close, Lissette walked away. She wanted to give him a spot to get close to her partner. Armon walked right into that one. He didn't even notice Lissette, he was too focused on the beautiful prize he was after. He slid into the space right next to Javona.

"Bartender, let me get a Henny and whatever the beautiful lady right here is drinking," Armon called out, then turned toward Javona, and smiled. Javona didn't even blink. She was acting like he wasn't even standing there. She was frontin' hard though, because her insides were fluttering with huge bat sized butterflies. Javona was extremely excited that Armon was actually taking the time to holla at her.

"So you gonna act like I'm not even here huh?" Armon commented, smiling. Javona turned toward him, her face like stone.

"Excuse me? Are you referring your question to me?" she asked him, her lips pursed.

"C'mon ma . . . let's keep one'hunned. I know you know it was me that sent my boy to holla at you. I also know you know I was on my way over here to holla at ya fine ass, but what you don't know is that I never do this; so consider yourself special baby girl," Armon replied, his words sounding as smooth as a lullaby. Javona was loving his sexy voice, but she would never let him know it. Just then, the bartender slid his drink in front of him and placed another apple martini in front of Javona. Armon placed a hundred dollar bill on the bar. Javona definitely took notice. That was going to be the bartender's tip, because the drinks were free since it was an open bar all night. *If the nigga thinks that hundred dollar tip impressed me, his ass is absolutely right!* She thought.

"Wassup bruh," somebody called out from behind Javona. She turned slightly just in time to see Dwayne Wade slapping fives with Armon. Javona's stomach muscles tightened at the sight of the celeb. *Damn he is cool with ballers for real* Javona thought. She believed Lissette now. Armon was some kind of heavy hitter and the fact that he was from Brooklyn made her slightly proud to be from there too.

Armon exchanged pleasantries with the top NBA star and then he quickly turned his attention back to her. "So what's your name pretty?" Armon asked flashing a winning smile. Although he had a gap in his teeth, his teeth were still bright white and straight.

"Javona," she said dryly, still acting like she wasn't interested.

"I can tell you from NY. No other place got the ladies with that accent and that unmistakable attitude. You're definitely not a southern girl," he said. "So you just out here for All-Star Weekend? You here with your man or with your girls? Where you from in Brooklyn?" he asked her his questions coming in rapid succession.

"Damn you ask a lot of questions. You sure you ain't down with the feds?" she replied snidely. He started laughing like she had just told him the

funniest joke ever. She looked at him strangely.
She was dead ass serious with her question.

"Nah. Me down with the feds? That would
be like Superman laying on a bed of kryptonite
on purpose. I'm Armon. It's nice to meet you
Javona," he said, extending his hand for a shake.
No nigga its nice to meet you! She said to herself
when she noticed his iced out watch. He wasn't
showing off anything else, but that watch alone
said enough for Javona. They began talking and
before long, cell phone numbers were exchanged.
Armon promised to reach out to Javona when he
got back to New York. That was just what she
wanted to hear. Maybe the fucked up feeling she
had about coming to Dallas was wrong after all.

Chapter 3

"Let's Get This Money Baby, They Shady, We Get Shady . . ."

Javona rushed through the airport gate waiting area with the Dallas daily newspaper in her trembling hands. She had just come from the snack shop when she noticed the words on the paper. A cold feeling had come over her body like someone had pumped ice water into her veins. Huffing and puffing, she rushed to the row of chairs and kicked Lissette's foot to wake her up. Javona was one step from all out panic. "What . . . what you want?" Lissette groaned. They had been sitting in the airport all morning trying to get on one of the flights back to New York.

"Get the fuck up," Javona whispered harshly, her hands were shaking so bad she couldn't control her nerves. She dropped the newspaper in Lissette's lap. Lissette sat up annoyed, her face folded into an evil frown. "What the fuck?" she groaned, wiping drool off her mouth. She looked up at Javona for an explanation.

"Look at that shit," Javona instructed through clenched teeth as she looked around paranoid. Lissette picked up the paper and tried to get her tired eyes to focus. She sat perfectly erect when she finally realized what the newspaper headline was about.

Brother of NBA Basketball Star Found Dead in Hotel Room, Police Suspect Foul Play

"Ok, so you was wrong. He was Shaq's brother—see I told you," Lissette said nonchalantly.

"What the fuck? Are you serious!" Javona growled as she watched Lissette read the entire article. "How many fuckin' sleeping pills did you give his ass," Javona whispered, her breath hot on Lissette's ear.

"Shhh. Bitch is you crazy. Be the fuck quiet," Lissette whispered back. Javona shrunk down in the chair. Her nerves were really on end now. Her best friend had involuntarily killed a man and not just any man. Javona felt like everybody in the airport knew what they had done. She kept replaying in her mind if she had ever slipped up while they were in the hotel room with the now dead man.

"Ain't no way they can connect the dots to us. Hell no! C'mon now—think about that shit. This dude got money, he was partying all night. That nigga coulda gotten those shits from anywhere. Now what's done is done . . . we'll be back in New York, so who gonna know anything. Just be quiet," Lissette scolded. "They gonna end up ruling that shit an accidental overdose anyway . . . you watch," she continued, crumpling up the newspaper article, standing up and throwing it in the garbage. In her assessment there was no way the police could trace anything back to her and Javona, or so she sure as hell hoped. "Damn we ain't on a flight yet," Lissette said calmly, trying to change the subject. She folded her arms, slumped back down in the airport chair and tried to fall back asleep. Javona folded her arms around her torso and hugged herself trying to get her nerves to calm down. In all the years they were pulling juxes and scams they had never killed anyone. Whether intentional or accidental, murder was murder in Javona's book. From Lissette's reaction, Javona was seeing just how ruthless her friend could really be. *This bitch killed somebody but she's telling me to calm down!* Javona screamed in her head. She was mad as hell at Lissette. Javona was sure that this shit would come back to haunt them in some way, even if it was just a karmic consequence.

When they got back to Brooklyn, Javona and Lissette didn't speak much during their ride from the airport. "Yo, you know I can't step foot in the East so I'ma put you near Broadway junction and get you a cab," Lissette said. Javona nodded, but she didn't say anything. When Lissette pulled up to the train station Javona prepared to get out of the car, but Lissette stopped her by touching her on her arm. "Yo Voni, listen, I didn't know that nigga was gonna die a'ight. I didn't even give him that many pills . . . he must've had a weak ass system or something. I figured as big as he was, it was gon' take more to knock him out for longer so we could get his shit. I mean I thought about it and I can take four of those shits and sleep two days, I only gave his ass about six and he was big as hell. I thought the most that would happen is he would sleep a few hours. I didn't do that shit on purpose. I would never put us out there like that . . . I'm not stupid. But we gotta move on from that shit. It's the past, you hear me? We gotta stick together even more now. Your attitude got me kind of worried . . . you seem like you wanna tell somebody about that shit," Lissette rambled, her tone apologetic and her voice shaky like she may have even wanted to cry. She needed to be sure the old weakest link Javona didn't show up right now. All Lissette needed was her friend feeling the guilt bug and telling somebody about the dead dude in Dallas.

Javona shook her head from side to side signaling the negative on that. "Picture me telling somebody. That would put my own ass on the chopping block," Javona replied. That gave Lissette a sense of relief. She quickly changed the subject. "As soon as that nigga Armon calls you, hit me up . . . I'm telling you girl this is gonna be that real lick that gets us up outta the hood. This shit gonna take some planning though and we need to be on the same page so it can go down smoothly," Lissette told her. Javona just nodded her head. She wasn't even thinking about another lick right now. That's how she knew, no matter how much they hung together and did dirt together, she and Lissette were definitely cut from a different cloth.

Lissette didn't have love for anybody but herself. Javona grabbed her bags out of Lissette's trunk and without another word she walked off. Once Javona disappeared into her cab, Lissette couldn't get her cell phone out of her cup holder fast enough. She dialed the familiar number. "Bam, it's me Lissette. I just got back from Dallas. All of your intel was on point. I mean, from what you told me about going to the party to how Armon would react to Javona was all right on point. He bit just like we knew he would. Now I just gotta get Javona onboard with this shit . . . it might take me a minute to convince her that we can't do this one alone. She listens to me all the time so I know she gonna be down. Yeah, I'm sure," Lissette said, but her words didn't have much confidence behind them.

It had been three days since their return from Dallas and Lissette and Javona had finally buried their little beef. Javona had decided that making money superseded having an attitude with her best friend in the whole world. They had made up and they'd even done two small get-money jobs together. During one of the jobs, they had just straight robbed a little corner boy near Lafayette Gardens Projects. Javona thought they were way out of their league and that it was dangerous, but they were kind of desperate for money since things hadn't worked out so well in Dallas. The robbery was Lissette's idea and Javona protested at first, but when Lissette told her she just had to drive the car away Javona just went along with it. If it meant she wasn't going to have to actually do the stick up, Javona agreed to drive although she hated to. Lissette had just simply got out of her car, put a gun to the kid's back and took all of the money he was holding. Just that simple.

For the next one, Javona had stood outside on Fountain Avenue like she was a working girl. Javona had strolled the street and of course a bunch of tricks had tried to pick her up. Javona had turned away a lot of them and she waited until she thought she had the right vic. Javona based her assessment on who she thought she could fuck up if shit didn't go as she and Lissette had planned. When the little white man pulled up, Javona had slid into the man's car, promised him a fuck and a suck, and instructed him on where to drive to and park his car. When Javona and the trick arrived at the designated location, the man prepared to pull his dick out for some fun, but his party was broken right up right away. The act was over. Javona wasn't even trying to be in the same car with some nasty bastard and his exposed penis. "Put that puny shit the fuck away," Javona snapped, pointing a small revolver Lissette had given her at the man's head. The gig was up. The man started crying immediately making Javona want to laugh at his perverted ass. He wasn't crying when he thought he was about to get his scrawny, stinky, little dick sucked. Lissette was waiting in the shadows and after a few seconds she sprang into action. She rushed over to the car and yanked open the man's driver's side door. "Aghhh!" the man screeched like a bitch. Lissette had scared the shit out of him, literally. Lissette yanked him out of the car, his dick still dangling through his zipper hole. "Give me all your shit, watch, rings, wallet, everything," she barked. The man did as he was told. His hands were shaking so bad it took him about six tries to get his ring off. Javona shut the man's car off, locked all of the doors and threw his keys off into the darkened woods of the deserted area near the Brooklyn dump where they had parked. It had become a game now and they were laughing at the man. Lissette yanked his pants down around his ankles, making it hard for him to get up. Satisfied that he wouldn't be able to get it together for a while, both girls raced to Lissette's car and peeled out. With his pants down around his ankles, the man was left in the dark struggling to locate his car keys so he could get some help or just get the fuck back to Long Island where he lived with his wife and kids.

Between those two jobs, the girls had come off with about three stacks each, enough to get through the week or maybe even two weeks, but they still had that one big job looming over them like a black cloud that just wouldn't rain. It had become a waiting game.

"Did you call that nigga Armon?" Lissette asked for the fifteenth time that day.

Javona let out a long puff of air as soon as Lissette formulated the question.

"I told you I left him a voice mail but he hasn't returned my call yet!" Javona barked. Lissette was annoying the shit out of her with the constant tabs on Armon. It seemed to Javona like Lissette was totally obsessed with carrying out this lick more than any other. Javona was lying to Lissette though. She hadn't called Armon and left a voice mail at all. She didn't have any plans on calling him either. Javona wanted to wait and see if he would call her first. She really didn't think a dude like him, that could have any chick he wanted, would actually be interested in her, so she wanted to test the waters and see if he called first. Besides, he was probably used to bitches flocking and stalking as soon as they got his number. That wasn't the type of vibe she wanted to send if she was going to get close to him. Javona didn't want to seem desperate and make Armon suspicious or have him thinking she was the same run of the mill type chick.

Lissette and Javona rode in silence for a few minutes, each of their minds racing about their next move and each secretly hoping for different reasons that their next move would be Armon. Ironically, Javona's cell phone started ringing and broke up the eerie silence inside the car. Javona looked down at the small screen on her phone. It was Armon! Javona picked up the phone. "Hello," she said in a soft, seductive voice. Just from the tone of her conversation Lissette could tell who it was on the phone. She turned down her music and listened as Javona got to know their next vic. Lissette could barely contain her excitement as she eavesdropped on Javona's entire conversation. Javona finally hung up and looked over at her friend. "He wants to take me to dinner tonight," she said calmly. "Bitch that's great! This is going to be the fuckin' start of something big!" Lissette sang out. She just didn't know how true her words would turn out to be.

Chapter 4

"You Must Be Used To Me Spending . . ."

Javona placed her Gucci boot down on the concrete as she stepped out of Armon's Mercedes G500 in front of Tao in the city. Armon held the door for her and then he leaned inside to speak to his driver, a guy named Blade. "Yo' son, never more than a phone call away, a'ight? Mad places to park up around here so do that. I'll see you in about two hours," Armon said. Blade nodded his understanding. Javona made a quick mental note—*this nigga is never alone. Damn!* There was a crowd outside of Tao as usual, but Armon had told Javona that they didn't have to wait. He didn't lie about that either. They weaved through the crowd and went inside. They got a few glares and snarls from the crowd of hungry patrons waiting for a table. Armon walked straight up to the host podium without waiting in the line of people standing in front of it already waiting to put their names down for a table. The little skinny gay male host behind the wooden stand looked up from his little list and smiled when he noticed Armon.

"Mr. A . . . so good to see you again. Thanks for calling us this time so we could have your table reserved and waiting for you. You know we hate to keep our most valuable customer waiting," the man sang in an effeminate voice, smiling like a real chick. Javona smirked to herself, it felt good to get the VIP treatment, she damn sure wasn't used to that. Armon gave the man a handshake and grabbed Javona's arm softly signaling her to go in front of him. Javona followed the switching hips of the male host and Armon was right behind her. They were led to a nice table for two that was positioned right in front of the huge Asian statue that was the centerpiece of the restaurant. "Thanks Doug," Armon said, slapping the host five. Javona was too astute for them to think she'd missed the money passing during their hand slap. Armon pulled out the chair for Javona and she sat down. "Thank you," she said smiling. She was impressed . . . really impressed. Javona couldn't wait to share all of this with Lissette.

As Javona sat across from Armon, she really got a good look at him for the first time. He was finer than she really thought. His swagger gave him sex appeal; made him look even better too. Armon was slim, with a baby face. He had a neatly trimmed mustache and goatee and smooth skin the color of a toffee. Javona thought he looked mixed with something and she had been right. He told her he was half black and half Puerto Rican. Javona thought Lissette would be amused by that fact.

Armon didn't wear clothes that screamed name brands across the pockets or chest. He rocked a simple pair of jeans, a button down shirt, and a blazer. Javona reasoned that all of his clothes were probably some expensive designers that didn't feel the need to display their name all over their products. She also noticed again that Armon didn't wear a lot of jewelry, with the exception of the classic, diamond bezel Breitling that graced his wrist. Armon looked relaxed, not one sign of stress or strife on his face. He didn't watch over his shoulder or act paranoid either. Javona had already witnessed that he had people looking over his shoulder for him. One thing was for sure, Javona sure didn't think that Armon looked like the ruthless drug kingpin Lissette had made him out to be. Armon didn't look at all like he had been through a lot like most big time hustlers, Javona knew that had clawed their way to the top of the drug game. That was something that made Javona wonder as she stared at him trying to figure him out and admiring him at the same time. She could only think of two reasons he'd be so put together with not so much as an old scratch on his face or hands—he was either a straight murderer that took what he wanted without any fights or he was the son of a hustler and had taken over the helm of an empire already built so he didn't have to fight. Javona figured she'd find out sooner or later if she was right about either of her theories.

"So Javona, tell me about yourself, ma. I wanna know everything there is to know about you—down to where you were born and raised," Armon said, as they prepared to order their drinks. Javona thought about his question and she started to tell him the truth about herself, but she thought that would bring them too close, so she opted on making up an alter ego. She just figured it would be easier to break away from him when the time came to rob him. But, his question alone was much different than what she was used to being asked by dudes. Men were usually asking her questions pertaining to sex or how they could get her pussy faster. Javona hadn't had any real luck with men over the years. Partly because she kept on attracting the same hood rat type of dudes and the other part because she had a thing about letting dudes get close to her heart.

That night Armon and Javona had a great time together. They talked about everything under the sun, even politics. Armon told Javona that with his type of money he thought he should be a Republican, but because he didn't pay taxes, he would stick to being a Democrat and supporting the first black president. Javona felt a sense of relief when he said he was a Democrat; hood nigga or not, she wasn't fucking with any Republicans. She had gotten so comfortable with him that she almost forgot that she was only there to find out as much information about him so she could set him up.

At the restaurant Armon bought the best of everything on the menu and he and Javona shared

the food family style, where they ate out of the
same dishes of food. Javona thought that was
so romantic. Armon knew how to treat a woman
and Javona was enjoying it. When he pulled out
his wallet to pay, Javona forced herself to look
away. She was so used to scoping out the wallet
of any vic she was with that it was hard as hell for
her to play it off. Damn, she wanted to look at his
wallet so bad to see if she could spot what he was
holding, but she didn't want to seem like a gold
digger or worse—a thief. He was being so nice to
her that guilt trampled on her mood when she
remembered what she was really doing there
and what she was really setting Armon up for. As
he was closing up his Louis Vuitton billfold wallet, Javona did get a chance to see that Armon
had credit cards and bank cards in his wallet.
She felt relieved that he wasn't living totally
hood rich. After what they ate and drank, Javona
figured that Armon must've spent at least close
to $500 between the dinner and the top-shelf
champagne he purchased. Javona could also tell
that Armon was used to spending like that. He
hadn't balked, flinched, or even blinked—not
even a little bit when he opened the little leather
billfold and examined the bill. As she stood up
to leave, Javona noticed that Armon had left

another hundred dollar bill on the table as a tip, same as he did at the bar the night she met him in Dallas. *Lissette was right; Armon had long, long paper*.

When Armon dropped Javona home he had asked her for a kiss. "You always ask for kisses on the first date?" she said to him playfully. "Strangely enough, I don't. But something about your lips makes me want to kiss them," he answered, smoothly. He was so damn hot in her eyes. Armon was laying it on thick; a sign that he liked Javona. *Damn this nigga is so good with his*, she said to herself. She smiled and gave him a peck on his full lips. The scent of cinnamon Altoids on his breath and the feel of his lips had sent heated stabs down her spine. Javona was kicking herself inside because catching sexual feelings like that was a first for her. Javona knew right away that she was sexually attracted to Armon. From the look and feel of things she figured she would be having a lot of firsts with Armon, one of which was making a victim out of—someone she was really feeling.

***

Lissette pulled back her apartment door to let Javona inside. They nodded at each other instead of speaking. Javona rushed inside and past Lissette. Lissette followed Javona with her eyes like she was crazy. "Did you fuck the nigga yet?" Lissette asked her question straight with no chaser. Javona flopped down on Lissette's couch and crumpled up her face at her friend's immediate barrage of questioning.

"No! We've only been to dinner three times. He hasn't even been upstairs in my house and he hasn't taken me to his house yet. Damn—give a bitch a minute to get acquainted with the nigga," Javona answered, picking up an Essence Magazine from Lissette's coffee table.

"Well the faster you give that pussy up, the faster we can get this shit underway. I see you got a few new pieces of jewelry out of the deal though," Lissette said, eyeing her friend enviously. "The only bitch I know get gifts from a nigga you about to set up for the downfall. I would be scared of a snake-ass bitch like that . . ." Lissette snapped like a jealous kid.

"Yeah, whatever. I can't help it," Javona said smiling wide. "Whenever he picks me up to go out, he gives me a gift. And not just any gift at that . . . I'm talkin' about nice shit," Javona said moving her left hand back and forth, rubbing in the fact that she was sporting a new diamond cocktail ring.

"This nigga is really laying it on thick," Javona said, smiling. Lissette was seething inside but she had to front like she wasn't fazed. Javona was so into her own lala dreamy world that she hadn't even caught on that Lissette was a little jealous.

"You need to push the issue with going to his house, fuck a bullshit piece of jewelry. Knowing where this nigga rest at is gon' be very necessary to pull off this lick. He ain't your average cat and from what it seems like, he don't roll solo. There's only gonna be one way to do this shit—the ski mask, tie a nigga up, maybe mirk a nigga way," Lissette said pointedly. Javona nodded her understanding, but she wasn't too happy about what her friend was yapping about. She knew Lissette was right though. If they were going to rob Armon it wasn't going to be simple. Armon didn't go anywhere solo, so the only place she would be able to get him alone would be in bed. They would have to run up in his shit while Javona had him in a compromising position; it would be the only way to do the jux. Javona couldn't front, she was having second thoughts about the whole thing. She couldn't tell Lissette, but she really liked Armon—a lot.

"Fuck all this small talk. You need to get up in this nigga's crib like yesterday. I'm sayin', throw the pussy, tie a nigga up, make him think you love him, and lets get it in. I'm ready to tie that bitch nigga up like a hog and get at his ass," a deep male voice filtered in from some place in Lissette's apartment. Javona whipped her head around in shock. She had been caught off guard since she thought she was there alone with Lissette. The sound of the voice started coming closer to where Javona was sitting. She dropped the magazine and scrunched her face up in confusion and shock. Javona looked at Lissette as if to say, bitch you had somebody hiding in here the entire time! Javona's face said it all. Lissette laughed nervously.

"Damn nigga you ain't smooth at all. I told you to stay in the bedroom until I was ready for you. Damn, I was gon' introduce you . . . to my girl here . . . and you . . . you . . . just," Lissette stammered, her voice cracking a little. Javona squinted her eyes into little dashes and looked at Lissette evilly. Javona couldn't believe this shit! If she didn't know better she would think Lissette was losing her fucking touch. First the so-called accidental murder in Dallas . . . now this! Javona cocked her head to the side waiting for an explanation.

"I ain't got no time to be hiding in no fuckin' bedrooms. I'm about my paper and gettin' this money. I'm ready to start living like this nigga livin'," the man said. Javona shot him an evil look. If eyes could kill the man would've turned into a pile of dust the way Javona's eyes were burning holes in him.

"Voni I was gon' tell you that we needed a strong dude in on this shit so I let my dude Bam know what we was gon' be doing and he said he was down. I think this dude Armon is too strong a cat for us to try to set this shit up by ourselves . . . you understand right Voni? I mean . . . its still our lick though . . . " Lissette rambled, her words coming out all jumbled together, rushed and garbled. Javona knew Lissette very well. It hadn't been too many times Javona had witnessed Lissette display nervousness, but right then Javona knew Lissette was nervous as hell. That fact coupled with this grimy-ass dude standing in front of her sent a real fucked up, uneasy feeling over Javona.

"Do we ever involve anybody else in our licks? Did this nigga here ever put in work on the streets with us and split the paper? I ain't never lay eyes on this grimy-ass dude. You gotta fuckin' be kidding me here Lissette!" Javona boomed, she wasn't going to bite her tongue on this one. She stood up and grabbed her purse.

"Yo who this bitch calling grimy. She know me? You sure this emotional bitch can handle this assignment. She acting a little salty if you fuckin' ask me," Bam interjected smacking his purple-almost-black lips, the weed smoke reeking from his clothes.

"Who you callin' a bitch?! I got ya bitch you bum ass nigga!" Javona retorted. She never used to stick up for herself and she usually hated confrontation but right then she felt caught up, she was experiencing a whirl of emotions that was as fast and furious as a tornado. Javona was angry and felt kind of betrayed by her best friend.

"What?! I'm calling you a bitch . . . bitch!" Bam replied advancing toward Javona menacingly. A pang of fear flitted through Javona's stomach for a quick minute, but she stood her ground. She was so angry that if she had to fight a nigga right now that was what she was going to do.

"Whoa, whoa! Both of y'all niggas trippin' right now with all this back and forth bullshit. Stop the fuckin' madness! Javona sit the fuck down! Bam you too! This shit ain't goin' down like this in my crib. Y'all both my peoples and I'm the mastermind behind this whole shit. Now we gon' all get along because all of us need each other here. Javona your fuckin' job is to get that nigga Armon to trust you, find out where he rest at, make him fuckin' love you for all I care. We need to know as much about him as possible. If that nigga like red Kool-Aid bitch I wanna know about it. Bam . . . when the fuckin' time comes your role is gon' be executing the shit. We still in the set up phase and I don't want to hear no bullshit. If this shit don't work out like it's supposed to y'all ain't gon' have to worry about fuckin' each other up. I'ma fuck both of y'all up myself," Lissette barked, making her point loud and clear. Javona jumped back up, grabbed her bag and stalked toward the door. *This bitch was the one who always told me when you include outsiders shit always goes wrong and look at her,* Javona thought as she let Lissette's apartment door slam behind her.

Chapter 5

"But You Was My Bitch, The One Who'd Never Snitch"

Spring 2010

Armon's hands on her breasts made Javona let out a soft moan. "Ohhh," she cooed. But when he lowered his mouth onto her areola she nearly screamed. Her body was on fire like he had lit her with a match. Armon sucked her nipples gently at first, but he started sucking them hard the hotter she got. Javona's breathing was labored and her pussy was soaking wet. "You like that?" he whispered. Javona didn't want to say no, but she couldn't even speak to say yes. She was in ecstasy. "Mmm, hmm," she groaned. She didn't even realize she was grinding her hips; she wanted him so badly. Armon lowered his mouth from her breast, trailing his tongue down her chest and stomach. He stopped at her naval and kissed it gently. Javona's legs trembled in anticipation of what was coming next. Armon seductively licked the insides of her thighs, teasing her. "Ahh," she whimpered. He smiled. "You ready?" he asked her in a soft murmur. "Yes!" she replied. Javona didn't know if she really was ready or not. Armon moved for a minute. But he came right back. Javona opened her eyes just in time to see him put a piece of ice between his teeth. He was too fast for her to react. He dropped down between her legs placed his ice cold lips and mouth on her clitoris. "Oh shit!" she screamed out. So much for trying to keep her cool, Javona had lost it now. Armon started devouring her pussy like it was his last supper. He flicked his tongue over her clit and then lowered his tongue and buried it into her wanting, hot box. "Fuck!" she huffed, holding onto his head.

Javona had let all of her inhibitions go now. She wasn't thinking about the times she had been molested as a child; instead for the first time, she was having a sexual experience on her terms and she loved it. Armon pushed his tongue into her pussy hole and pulled it back out drawing out her salty juices. He fucked her over and over with his tongue. She was breathing so hard she felt like she would hyperventilate. Javona couldn't take it anymore. Her body shuddered and quaked as the strongest orgasm she'd ever felt ripped through her loins. "Aghhh" she belted out as her walls pulsated like a volcano erupting. "I'm cumming!" she screamed, grabbing onto Armon's head. Finally the waves subsided, but her thighs still trembled. Javona's head lolled to the side as her body relaxed. Armon started laughing as he looked down at her and admired the work he had put in to get her to that state.

"You not finished are you?" Armon asked her as he stood up and took off his pants. It was time for round two for him.

"Nope, I'm not done. It's my turn to put it on you," she said. Javona sat up and tugged on his Gucci monogram belt until it was loose. He smiled and followed her lead. Armon definitely didn't mind a chick that could take over. She pulled him closer to her until his lower half was positioned right in front of her face. "You sure you ready," she purred. She was definitely out of her element. Javona had never gone there with a dude in her life. Something had taken over her and she just couldn't explain it.

"I was born ready baby girl," Armon huffed. Javona helped him pull his jeans down. She looked up at him seductively, then she pulled his boxers off. His thick, long meat jumped free from its cotton captivity.

"Mmm," Javona moaned as she grabbed Armon's thick, dick in her hand. His flesh was warm and it was pulsating with each excited beat of his heart. She licked her lips wetting them so she could pleasure him. Before she did, she looked up into Armon's face again; she wanted to watch his reaction as she pulled his dick into her mouth. He rolled his eyes up into his head and placed his hands gently on the top of her head. At first a dirty feeling came over Javona like when her uncle would do that to her, but she quickly dismissed the feeling. She couldn't let her past fuck this up. She wanted this right now. Armon guided her head up and down on his dick. His legs trembled slightly with each rotation of her head. Seeing his reaction made her want to work harder. Javona opened her mouth wider letting some of her spit fall from her mouth. A long string of it hung from her lips while Armon moved in and out of her lips.

"Oh shit! That shit looks so nasty and freaky. I love that shit," Armon whispered as she watched her lips go to work on his meat. Javona pushed her mouth so far down on his swollen flesh that when it hit the back of her throat she gagged at first. The pulsing in her throat squeezing on his dick head threatened to send Armon into overdrive. Javona started moving rapidly now. She squeezed her cheeks together as she went up and down, up and down, over and over again. The two actions together caused a good bit of suction from her mouth. The squeezing and suction was making it hard for Armon to keep his composure. "Damn your head game is serious!" Armon growled in seventh heaven. His compliment made Javona work her jaws even harder. She wanted to impress him. "I'm right there! I'm right fuckin' there! Urgghhh!" Armon growled as his waist bucked and thrust with a racking orgasm. Javona snatched his dick out of her mouth and jerked his cum onto her huge titties. "Shit that was good baby girl," he wolfed. Armon's legs were weak, but his dick was still hard. That shit always baffled Javona. They had been fucking for three months now and she didn't know how he stayed hard after he busted his nuts. Not that she was complaining, a hard dick always made shit better, but sometimes it made her wonder if she could ever please him to the point of a limp dick. Javona dried Armon's dick off with a Kleenex from his nightstand. She pushed him down on the bed and straddled him. Once again he turned over the action to her. He followed her lead. Javona lowered her sopping wet pussy down onto his dick. "Gotdamn . . . I think I'm starting to love your ass," Armon gasped. Javona smiled as she buried her face into his neck. *That's what I want you to do. That's what I need you to do.* She thought.

They fucked for hours that night until they both finally collapsed from exhaustion. Javona was almost where she needed to be with him.

Javona jumped up from her sleep and whirled around. The surroundings were strange at first glance. After a few minutes, she regained her bearings and realized she was still at Armon's house. She flopped back on the pillow and looked over at his side of the bed. He had already gotten up and out of the bed. Javona could hear him talking downstairs. It sounded like he was giving instructions to someone over the phone. She crept out of the bed and stood by his bedroom door and listened for a minute. "I don't really care what his excuse is . . . lost or stolen my shit is still missing and he is responsible. Tell him he's got twenty four hours to find it," Armon was saying, his tone gruff and abrasive. Javona could tell he was engrossed in his conversation and whoever he was referring to was in big trouble. As long as she could hear him talking she knew she had time to take a quick look around. With her heart thumping wildly, she crept back into the bedroom and started frantically looking around. She didn't see any immediate signs of a safe, but there was a stack of money on the dresser along with yet another of Armon's high priced watches, this time is was an Audemars Piguet. Javona picked up the watch and she could tell by the weight it was expensive. She walked lightly over to his side of the bed and carefully opened Armon's nightstand drawer. Peering inside she saw that it was empty. *Damn* she cursed to herself. She listened again. Armon sounded like he was getting even more fed up and he was yelling louder at the person on the phone now. "Fuck that nigga! If I gotta see him myself he ain't gon' like the result! Niggas must think I'm scared to get my hands dirty . . . I can show him better than I can tell his ass," Armon barked.

Good! Javona thought. As long as Armon
was still talking, she had a little more time to
look around and through his shit. She scanned
the room with her eyes like she thought she
was being watched. Shaking off the paranoid
feeling, she opened the door to his closet. The
wood from the door made a little creaking noise
that unnerved her. "Shit," she mouthed silently.
She listened again to make sure Armon was still
talking. He was still on the phone. She peered
into his closet, which she didn't expect to be so
big inside. She raced into his walk-in closet and
she stood in awe at first. "This nigga is doin' it,"
she mumbled. The inside of Armon's closet was
off the hook in her assessment. Javona didn't
think she had ever seen so many jeans, hats, furs,
clothes, sneakers, and shoes. It was definitely
like some *MTV Cribs* type of shit. Armon had
what appeared to be a million pairs of sneakers.
Everything was in place by color. His clothes
were hung so neatly Javona was afraid to touch
anything for fear that she wouldn't be able to
get them back as perfect as he had them and he
would know she had been in there.

Javona looked around for a few minutes and
she finally noticed a safe that was built into the
wall. "Jackpot," she mouthed to herself. She

made a mental note of where the safe was and she examined the combination dial. It was a cipher lock dial which was more difficult to crack than regular safe locks. Javona immediately started thinking about things Armon had told her that she might be able to associate with numbers—his birthday, how many sisters he had, how close he was with his mother, her birthday, all things that would help her figure out his safe combination.

After she spotted the safe, Javona's mind raced with thoughts about the other things she needed to know to execute her and Lissette's plan. Javona knew she just needed to have a good enough of picture of the layout inside the house to be able to draw it out for Lissette. They had already decided that a strong arm robbery, complete with binding and gagging or possibly knocking Armon out was the only way to get him. It would also have to be when he was at his most vulnerable and when most of his bodyguards were not around, which wasn't often. The plan Javona and Lissette had come up with was Javona would get Armon in bed and Lissette and Bam would then bang up in his crib, tie him up, and get his shit. That was the plan, but it still needed some perfecting. That's where Javona was supposed to come in at.

***

Javona came back out of the closet and carefully pulled the door shut being careful not to make too much noise. Just as she made it back to the side of the bed she had slept on, Armon walked into the room and scared the living daylights out of her. "Good morning baby girl" he said excitedly. Javona almost jumped clear out of her skin. She let a halfhearted smile come across her face and she flopped down on the bed. "Hey! You scared me" she huffed, placing her hand up against her chest, trying to force her trembling lips to be still and racing heart to calm down. Her nerves were definitely rattled. Inside she breathed a sigh of relief as she realized that she had made it out of the closet just in the nick of time. "You should never be scared of me baby girl," Armon said, smiling and coming back over to her for some more of her good loving. Javona had his ass open. That was part of her plan too. She laid back down to give him what he wanted. The more she gave him, the closer she got to her goal.

It was the first time Armon had brought Javona to his house in the three months they had been dealing. It was a beautiful brownstone in Park Slope situated on a block where doctors and lawyers lived; not exactly where she would expect a drug dealer that was rumored to have trap houses in some of the worst parts of Brooklyn to live. Armon told Javona that he also had a condo up in Harlem as well. She had already figured out that he probably had a few places to stay. Javona knew that Lissette would be expecting an entire layout of the inside of the house. Just thinking about it had made Javona feel sick inside. She realized that she had feelings for Armon and they were just getting stronger with each moment she spent with him. Over the past three months, she had gotten so many beautiful gifts from him, including, a damn banging ass diamond bezel Rolex with the mother of pearl face. When Javona had showed Lissette, she could tell Lissette was hating on her. Lissette had insisted that Javona pawn the watch and they split the money. Javona had told her, "hell no!" Javona had convinced Lissette that she would need to wear the watch around Armon to keep his trust and that after the lick went down she would pawn the watch. That was the only reason Lissette didn't fight Javona any further about pawning the watch. Although she didn't protest after that, Lissette kept the incident in the back of her mind. She started putting much more pressure on Javona. Lissette thought it was taking way too long, although she kept telling herself that the payoff would be much greater. In Lissette's assessment they would walk away with enough money to get out of Brooklyn for good after they robbed Armon. Lissette planned on going to Puerto Rico to live. Javona hadn't even anticipated leaving Brooklyn. Lissette had been doing small licks on her own, mostly sneaky pickpocket type shit in the time it was taking Javona to set Armon up. Lissette was growing restless and so were the dudes she had asked to help them rob Armon.

Javona turned around and smiled and waved at Armon one more time before she headed into her building. She felt like she was walking on air when he had dropped her off. The more time she spent with him, the less she felt like she could go through with the set up. As she fished around in her purse for her keys, her cell phone started ringing . . . again. It was Lissette of course. Lissette had been blowing Javona's phone up the entire time she was with Armon. She had been hounding Javona to get the house layout . . . to find out where Armon kept his trap . . . to find out his coming and going patterns . . . to find out if his boys stood guard outside his house at night . . . to find out what types of guns he carried . . . if he had a stash house. It was too much! Lissette was relentless with this lick for some reason. Javona had never seen Lissette so hell bent on one job in the years they had been pulling them. Something about Lissette's urgency didn't sit right with Javona. It had been a while and it was difficult for Javona to get enough information on Armon to set the plan into real motion, by now if it were anybody else, Lissette would've given up on this one, but no, she was kind of relentless with going after Armon.

"Damn this bitch won't give me a break," Javona huffed, pressing ignore on her cell phone. She located her keys and used them to open the building's two inside doors. With her head down and not paying attention, Javona walked inside of her building. As soon as she stepped through the doorway somebody grabbed her roughly and placed a hand over her mouth. "Mmm," she muffled a scream, her full bladder threatening to release right there. She had almost jumped out of her skin and her knees were actually knocking against each other. Javona started to flail thinking someone was trying to rob her.

"Shhh, Javona. We're not going to hurt you." a man breathed into her ear, his breath feeling like a torch on the side of her face. "You're Javona right?" the tall, white man in a dark suit asked her as he slowly released her. Javona whirled around wildly, her eyes stretched into huge circles and her arms moving wildly with no direction. She noticed that the man that had accosted her was with a female. The female who appeared to be of some sort of Hispanic descent, held a gun out in front of Javona. The woman signaled Javona to be quiet by putting her free hand's pointer finger against her lips. The female was in a dark suit as well. Javona felt like her heart would come through her chest cavity, but at least she could tell it wasn't a hood stickup.

"Who are you? What do you want?" Javona stammered nervously, looking from the man to the woman and back again. She already knew they were some kind of cops or detectives. White people didn't just show up in East New York wearing suits and pointing guns for a social visit.

"You need to come with us," the man said, moving closer to her and grabbing onto her elbow like he was escorting her somewhere voluntarily. Javona tried to wriggle her arm from his grasp.

"I . . . I . . . didn't do anything . . . I know my rights," Javona replied, her voice cracking. This unplanned visit from these strangers totally had her thrown off. She started thinking about all of the white dudes she and Lissette had juxed. She started thinking about all of the dirt she had been involved in and wondered which deed had drawn the cops to her. Javona immediately thought about Lissette and their promise to each other. *If we ever get bagged don't snitch. Take the L and do the time. Don't talk to the cops if they don't have you under arrest and read you your rights and always ask for a lawyer.* Javona and Lissette had pledged it to each other years ago.

"I don't have to talk to you. I know my rights," Javona reiterated.

"We can arrange to have your rights read to you if you want . . . but that would mean you would be under arrest. You're not under arrest *yet* . . . but trust us it can be arranged. We know you've been real busy lately. We know a lot more about you than you think. So like we said, we just want to talk to you for now. You can come the easy way—or we can do it the hard way," the white man growled. He had already started pushing her out of the first door of her building. They couldn't take a chance with someone coming in and giving her a chance to flee. Javona still tried to wrestle her arm away from him, but he was holding on to her with a death grip. "I can walk," she said with an attitude, deciding that talking and being under arrest was a big difference as the devil looking white man had pointed out. As they all stepped out of her building Javona looked around nervously. *These muthafuckas tryin'a get me killed*, she thought, knowing that if anybody saw her going with cops, she would be labeled a snitch.

Javona was pushed into the back of a black Chevy Impala with smoke dark tints. The female drove, while the male sat next to Javona in the back seat. There was a heavy, eerie silence inside of the car until Javona finally broke the silence and spoke. "I don't understand what y'all want with me . . . I haven't done anything. Y'all are not identifying yourselves or anything . . . I know my rights," Javona said as she rocked her legs in and out nervously. Neither of them answered her. She kept looking out of the windows apprehensively trying to figure out where she was and where the hell they were taking her. In the meantime, her cell phone was ringing every ten minutes off the hook. "Turn that thing off," the man instructed. Javona scrunched up her face. "If I do that my friends and family will be looking for me and worried," Javona snapped at him. She was getting tired of him barking orders at her. It was bad enough she was with them in the first place. "Turn it off," the man demanded, shifting in his seat. She looked over at his gun holster which he had so conveniently pushed his jacket back to display. She rolled her eyes and reluctantly turned her phone off.

Finally, they pulled up to a non-descript brick building in the city. It was some place off of the West Side Highway, that much Javona could tell. She was ushered inside the building. When she walked in that's when she saw the huge gold shield with blue lettering on the wall that read DRUG ENFORCEMENT AGENCY. *Fuck!* She screamed inside of her head. Javona's heart dropped. She was really confused now, but she figured this unexpected visit had to have something to do with Armon because she

and Lissette were thieves, but they had never
sold drugs. Javona was taken through a series
of coded doors where the white man and the
lady punched in codes, had their fingerprints
scanned and swiped key cards to get in. The
security measures in the building were like Fort
Knox. The female took Javona into a small room
that resembled a utility closet and patted her
down for weapons or contraband. The entire
time Javona complained and kept asking what
was going on, but the female refused to answer
her questions. Afterwards, Javona was led to
another small room with nothing in it but a
rickety metal table and three chairs.

"Sit down Ms. Blakely," the same man who
had practically kidnapped her said, pulling out
a small, silver metal chair for Javona. With her
eyebrows furrowed, Javona took a seat. *How do
they know my whole government.*

"I'm agent Mason and this is agent Giovani . . . as
you can see we're DEA agents," Agent Mason
introduced himself finally. Javona stared at him
blankly. *I don't give a fuck if you're Inspector
Gadget and that's your niece Penny!* Javona
thought as she squinted her eyes evilly at the man.

"We brought you here because we need your help and we trust that we won't have a problem convincing you to help us," he continued, stopping for a minute to gauge her reaction. Javona's face was stony. "We've noticed you've been keeping company with Mr. Armon Munoz . . ." Mason started talking again. Javona's shoulders slumped. She knew it had to have something to do with Armon. She wasn't trying to tell them shit because she honestly didn't know shit.

"I just met him. I don't know him that well. I can stop seeing him. Y'all got the wrong person . . . I don't know nothing about him . . ." Javona interrupted, her words coming out rapid and choppy as her nerves kicked into high gear again. She was thinking that they must be crazy if they thought she would help them, little did they know she was already betraying Armon in the worst way. Javona kept pleading her case. Agent Mason put his hands up in a halting fashion. "You didn't just meet Mr. Munoz. You've been dating him for a couple of months. We've been watching you and him. You seem to be the only one he's kept around this long lately," Agent Mason said, busting Javona's bubble. His words about Armon having her around for the longest out of any other chicks kind of made

Javona feel good for a fleeting second, but she quickly remembered the predicament she was in right then. "That's why you're here Ms. Blakely. I know you didn't think this was a fuckin' happy social call. We need you to work with us to gather some inside information on Mr. Munoz. You will work as our insider . . . since Mr. Munoz thinks he is untouchable right now," Mason said as he leaned back in the chair like he had just got something big off his chest.

Agent Mason sounded more like a woman scorned and out for revenge than a federal agent with society's best interest in mind. His words exploded in Javona's ears like loud firecrackers. The mission they had in mind for her was the bomb Javona was waiting for them to drop. *I fuckin' knew it!* Her mind raced. She felt like someone had slapped the shit out of her when agent Mason said that bullshit. It took a minute to settle into her mind, but when it did Javona jumped up out of her seat in a delayed reaction. "I'm not a fuckin' snitch! He doesn't tell me shit and if he did what the fuck makes you think I would tell you! Like I keep telling y'all, I know my fucking rights so if you are not arresting me you can't make me do shit," she yelled indignantly. Agent Mason smiled like Javona wasn't even yelling at them. He was clearly unfazed by her outburst. That wasn't the reaction Javona was hoping for.

"Sit down Ms. Blakely. Let us tell you why you *will* help us or else . . . " Agent Giovani interjected calmly, her attitude was snide and snobby. She was amused by Javona's protest. Agent Giovani thought Javona's little tirade just made the process of turning her into a federal informant much more interesting.

"Sit down or else what? Y'all gonna fill me with bullets? Y'all gonna frame me for some shit I didn't do . . . I mean what? What can y'all possibly do to me because I won't be a fuckin' snitch for y'all?!" Javona snapped, the large vein in her neck pulsing fiercely against her skin. She was so angry she didn't even realize she had her fists balled up by her side. She was not about to be a snitch for the feds. There was no fucking way she was getting down with them. They couldn't make her. Javona folded her arms in a rude display now, waiting for them to tell her she was free to go.

"Ms. Blakely sit the fuck down," Agent Giovani boomed. All of her calm composure had gone out of the window. Javona was a little taken aback by her forceful words. Javona didn't sit though.

"I know how to get you to sit the fuck down. Let me just tell you this . . . we know all about you, your scams, your breaking into people's bank accounts . . . which by the way is a federal crime that we happen to *know* you've been doing down on Wall Street and some other places . . ." Agent Giovani said evilly as she placed her hand on a stack of VHS tapes that were neatly stacked on the end of the table and labeled "surveillance video evidence." Javona felt like she'd been gut punched, her legs got a little weak but she still didn't sit down. "There's more Ms. Blakely . . . oh there is a lot more," Agent Giovani said. Javona's pulse quickened now. She felt a wave of nausea and small beads of sweat formulated on her hair line.

"Yeah a lot more. Let's not forget that little thing called murder or at least accessory to murder . . . you know about murder right? The crime you could get life in prison for?" Agent Mason interjected. They were playing bad cop/ bad cop now. Javona's eyes stretched as wide as dinner plates and her stomach muscles seized now when Agent Mason brought up the topic of murder. She wondered now how much they really knew about her and Lissette's lifestyle. Javona's face told the story; her eyebrows were arched and her mouth involuntarily hung open.

"Surprised? Hmph, yeah we know what you did in Dallas . . . there is a certain NBA star willing to pay big money to put away the people responsible for killing his not so little, little brother," Agent Mason announced, then he placed his locked fingers behind his head and smiled. He and Giovani were enjoying torturing Javona.

Javona slid way down into the chair. She didn't know whether to cry or scream. The pledge she and Lissette had made went right out of the window. All Javona could picture was herself in prison garb being cornered by a bunch of butches in prison. She felt lightheaded and dizzy. The entire room began to spin in her eyes.

"So if you help us we can help you with those little situations. Maybe even make them disappear forever. I don't think you want to take your little pretty face to jail for life do you?" Agent Giovani said. Javona put her hand over her mouth; partly to muffle and scream. "I didn't think you would," he continued.

"We thought you'd change your mind about refusing to help us . . . so I guess that settles it . . . you'll be our new informant in the takedown of Armon Munoz. What do they call informants in the hood . . . oh yeah . . . snitches," Agent

Giovani said laughing cruelly. Javona had no idea how they knew about the murder in Dallas. She also would rather be shot than become an informant. Javona's cheeks welled up and her face crinkled into a frown. Her stomach swirled and the sick feeling she had was too overpowering. With both hands over her mouth now she couldn't hold it. She opened her mouth as vomit spewed from her lips all over the DEA agents' table.

"Fuck!" Agent Mason jumped up as flecks of vomit flew onto his freshly pressed French cuffed shirt. Agent Giovani pushed away from the table before she could get hit with any.

"Didn't this same shit happen in an episode of the Sopranos," Giovani said, laughing wickedly.

Chapter 6

"DEA Federal Agents Mad Cause I'm Flagrant, Tapped My Cell and The Phone In The Basement"

Lissette was pacing outside of Javona's apartment door when Javona arrived home. As soon as Javona stepped off the elevator onto her floor she was greeted by a scowling, raging mad Lissette. Javona smiled but it was short lived. "Yo bitch! You tryin'a play me or something!" Lissette boomed, rushing into Javona so hard Javona stumbled backward bracing herself up against the hallway wall. Javona was caught off guard once again. She didn't know how much more of these violent pop up visits she could take. "I never took you for a traitor-ass bitch! I guess I was fuckin' wrong!" Lissette growled. She was in Javona's face now pinning her up against the wall.

"What are you talking about?" Javona rasped out as Lissette forcefully pushed her forearm against her throat. "Get off me!" Javona groaned, barely able to breathe as she felt like her friend was going to crush her windpipe. Javona didn't even bother to try to fight Lissette, she knew she was no match for her husky friend.

"Bitch I've been calling you and calling you for almost two fuckin' days! No fuckin' answer?! You couldn't even holla back! What if it was a fuckin' emergency or something? You actin' like I'm not important no more. You dissing me for a nigga? Huh? The dick that good!" Lissette barked, causing little sprinkles of spit to fly into Javona's face. Lissette was pushing on Javona's throat harder and harder with each question. Javona could see fire flashing in Lissette's eyes, but at the same time she could hear hurt behind Lissette's words.

"No . . . I . . . I . . . was gon' call you," Javona said, forcing her words through the pressure on her throat. Javona was mad at Lissette for being in her face, but on the same token she could fully understand why her friend was leery and thinking that she might be turning on her . . . everybody in the hood knew there was no real honor amongst thieves.

***

"Where you been Javona? You turning your fuckin' back on me . . . I made you! How you gon' fuckin' leave me out!" Lissette gritted through clenched teeth. She was relentless, but she also sounded like a jealous lover. In Javona's mind, her not answering Lissette's calls was not that serious.

"You are buggin' the fuck out! Let's go inside and talk about this. I'm not dissing you Lissette!" Javona screeched, pushing Lissette's arm away from her neck, still trying to breathe. Lissette eased up off of her for a minute. She knew Javona was right, they needed to go behind closed doors to discuss their problem before they started drawing a peephole crowd.

"Open the fuckin' door! Yo', I'm tellin' you . . . you better have a good fuckin' explanation," Lissette hissed, standing over Javona menacingly. Javona's hands were trembling fiercely as she retrieved her keys. *What the fuck I'ma tell her now!* Javona didn't know if she was going to be able to keep the story together that the feds had told her to tell to explain away her disappearing act to her family and friends. She also didn't know if she would be able to lie to Lissette with a straight face without breaking down. They never really lied to each other from what Javona could tell. Javona wondered if Lissette would be able to see right through her lies. She knew she couldn't tell Lissette the truth though. The feds had already warned her that if she told Lissette anything about her new mission to takedown Armon, they would definitely kill Lissette. Of course, Javona was shocked when they had made such a blatant threat but that didn't change the fact that she believed them. Javona had to protect her friend who over the years always protected her.

Javona and Lissette spilled into Javona's apartment. Lissette was right up on her so close that she had stepped on the back of Javona's shoe as they moved inside. Lissette wasn't going to let Javona get a minute to make up a story. "Start talkin' right fuckin' now!" Lissette barked, up in Javona's face once again. Javona's mind was racing a mile a minute. She couldn't even look Lissette in her eyes.

"I was with Armon, Lissette! Where do you think I was? How is that dissing you or betraying you?" Javona yelled, turning on her Lissette like she was prepared to defend herself now. Javona was tired of this bullshit now.

"I finally got into his house and when he asked me to stay longer I said yes so I could get a good layout for our plan. Why the fuck are you trippin'? What would make you think I would betray you Lissette?" Javona said bordering on tears. She wanted to cry for so many reasons; half of what she was saying was the truth, but some of it was just what she knew Lissette wanted to hear. This was all too much. The secrets, the lies, the future as a snitch. Javona felt like she was drowning.

Lissette looked at her best friend suspiciously. She wanted to believe Javona, but she had been paranoid. Things with setting up Armon were taking too long and she was afraid that Javona was falling in love, which would fuck up their plan.

"So why the fuck you had to ignore my calls?" I could tell you was ignoring my shit, then your shit started going straight to voice mail . . . yo, you got me fed right now . . . word life, I'm steamin' fuckin' mad, I can't even calm down," Lissette huffed as she started pacing the floor with her hands on her hips. It was something she did when she was contemplating her next move. "Something about this disappearing act you did ain't fuckin' right Javona . . . I'm not stupid.

Something stinks like shit here?" Lissette huffed, still pacing. Javona's stomach cramped up. She had to be convincing right now and she knew it.

"I'm telling you Lissette . . . my word is my bond, I wouldn't fuck you over like that. Look, I even got the nigga's shit written down right here for you . . . I even know where the safe is at inside the house and I wrote down some possible safe combos from shit he told me over the last couple of months," Javona said with a shaky voice as she pulled a piece of paper out of her pocketbook. She didn't know what she was getting herself into. She had just given the same information about the inside of the house to the feds. It was like double jeopardy for her. She was playing both side of the fence and she knew it was a dangerous game. "I mean we knew this shit wasn't going to happen over night with Armon so I'm not understanding why you are buggin' all of a sudden," Javona said holding the paper out in front of her.

Lissette snatched the paper from Javona's hand. It was a perfect diagram of the inside of a house. There was a star where the safe was located. A huge sense of relief washed over Lissette. Then it turned into all out excitement welling up inside of her. She was starting to believe that Javona was still on course for their plan. Javona could see Lissette's face ease from a scowl into a partial smile. She smiled too, relieved that Lissette was buying her story.

"See . . . why would I play you?" Javona assured, balling her toes up in her shoes at the same time.

"Whew bitch, I thought I was gonna have to fuck you up! Word up! I was about to get it in on that ass," Lissette sighed, holding on her chest. She sat down with the paper Javona had just handed her and examined it carefully.

"Is this his main crib?" Lissette asked. Javona had gone into the kitchen where Lissette couldn't see her behind the wall. She put her head up against the kitchen wall and rocked it back and forth, she wanted to bang her head so badly. For a minute Javona ignored all of the questions Lissette was throwing out at her from the other room. "Yeah that's his main crib. "You have no idea how tired I am. I need a shower and some rest," Javona said coming out of the kitchen with a glass of soda.

"Shit, I bet all that fucking and sneaking around his crib done wore you out. I'ma call you double o' seven," Lissette said snidely. Javona wanted to tell Lissette to shut the fuck up and tell her she had no idea what she had been through in the past couple of hours. But, Javona kept quiet. All she wanted was some alone time with her thoughts.

"Damn. I was so mad at your ass I stormed up in the East knowing damn well that nigga Rori looking for my ass big time. See what you made me do? Now a bitch gotta get the hell out of here before a hood stool pigeon spots my ass and carries a message," Lissette said, folding Javona's paper and sliding it into her pocket. Javona wanted to ask for the paper back but she decided not for fear that it would just raise another red flag with her already paranoid friend.

"You better be careful. I heard Rori is out for blood from your ass. I don't know why you brought your ass over here, you know I woulda got right back," Javona scolded seriously. They both knew Rori was a dangerous dude.

"Nah . . . you don't understand. I was on a mission. Bam and them niggas is ready for this lick to go down and I thought your soft ass was all falling in love and getting cold feet on me," Lissette explained. Javona shuddered at the mention of Bam and she had caught on that Lissette had slipped a "and them" into the mix but Javona was too exhausted to argue about it right now. She just wanted Lissette to leave.

"Me, get cold feet? Never that," Javona said in a low whisper.

Lissette finally talked enough shit and got ready to leave. She had already peeked out of Javona's front windows about ten times to make sure she didn't see any signs of Rori or his people. Lissette knew she should have never had her ass in East New York.

"You sure you gon' be a'ight? You scaring me with all that peeking shit. I'm sayin' what the fuck you did to Rori that he would want to be on your ass like that?" Javona asked.

"I'm good son . . . don't you worry about me. You keep your mind on that nigga Armon . . . we gon' need to do this shit soon and when we do you know we gotta get gone . . . far gone," Lissette said with her hand on the doorknob.

"I hear you," Javona replied. "Don't ever think I would turn on you. I will always look out for what's best for you, even if you may not agree," Javona told her. She meant it too. Shit was about to get critical and if Javona wasn't careful she would be pulling her best friend into a deadly game of cat and mouse.

"I know you my bitch. Just don't scare me like that no more. Let a nigga know what you got goin' on n'shit," Lissette said, grabbing Javona roughly into an embrace. Both girls smiled.

"I'm out," Lissette said, stepping out in the hallway.

"Call me when you get home," Javona said, closing the door behind her.

Javona's phone started buzzing on her coffee table almost immediately after Lissette left her house. She walked over and looked down at the caller ID It was them. "Hello," she whispered closing her eyes.

"I hope you didn't tell her anything that would get her killed. We're not playing a game with you Ms. Blakely . . . we're watching you," Agent Mason said. Before Javona could reply he had hung up. She clutched the phone tightly in her hands and it started vibrating again. Jolted, she jumped. When she looked at the phone her heart sank into the pit of her stomach. It was Armon. According to what she had been instructed to do by the feds, Javona had no choice but to answer the call.

Lissette rushed into her car and peeled out of East New York in a hurry. She felt relieved that her friend hadn't betrayed her, but now she was regretting the fact that she had showed her face back in the East, she knew how much of a chance she had taken.

Lissette picked up her cell phone and dialed Bam's number. He picked up on the first ring. Bam had been waiting for Lissette's call.

"Yo nigga . . . I got the info! She fell right into the trap on this one. We're good, fuck it I'm not waiting no longer to do it," Lissette said excitedly. "Yeah, she got the inside of the house, the safe spot, she even sat down with me to figure out some possible safe combos. She did so good, I might even consider really giving her ass some of this trap when we get it," Lissette continued sounding like a grimy snake. "I knew you was gonna say don't give her ass shit," Lissette laughed at whatever Bam was saying on the other end of the phone. Bam was excited on the other end of the line too. He was notorious for being a backstabber so the fact that Lissette was about to do her best friend dirty didn't even bother him in the least. Bam pressed Lissette for more details.

He wanted to know when he could put on his black ski mask, get his Glock and run up in Armon's crib. They had already gathered that whenever Armon was with a chick, his boys kind of fell back and Armon's security was kind of lax during those times. At least that's what Bam and Lissette thought from what Javona had told them.

"I say we do this shit as soon as possible. She is supposed to be with him tonight, I'm sure we can probably get that nigga while he running up in that pussy. Nah, she don't know we comin'. She thinks we gonna give her more time. Yeah, fuck it if we gotta tie her ass up too we just gon' do that," Lissette said.

"A'ight its all gravy then. I'ma go home and wait until nightfall. We about to make some major paper and be out," Lissette said selfishly. She never once thought about leaving Javona behind once the lick went down. Lissette was too focused on revenge and getting the money to even care about her friend.

Javona looked at herself in the mirror again. Her eyes were sad. She couldn't stop staring at herself, thinking how easily she had become a snitch. Javona wished she had the guts to blow her own head off, she felt like she'd be better off rather than betraying a man she was growing to love. As she continued to stare at herself, Javona touched her neck and ran her fingers over the platinum, ruby and diamond necklace that lay flat on her collar bone. She closed her eyes. Guilt trampled her mood like an invading army. Armon had been so good to her . . . too good to her. Now she would betray him in more ways than one. Javona was serving him up on a platter to everybody and he had no clue she was the biggest Judas around.

Her phone buzzed on the wood of her dresser, startling her. She was so jumpy lately. "Hey," she sang, feeling tears burning at the backs of her eyes. She swallowed. "Ahem, yeah I'm ready. I'll be down when you get here," she said softly. She crinkled her face. "Oh, you can't come get me? Ok . . . you're sending the driver? Um . . . ok," she stammered. That was something different than he'd ever done. Armon usually came with the driver to pick her up. Her heart began racing. Mason and Giovani had given her specific instructions on what they wanted her to do when Armon picked her up again. She was supposed to stick something . . . a GPS device in his car. It was in the mirror compact they'd given her. She was supposed to drop it down in the seat. "Fuck!" she cursed nervously after she hung up.

Her first assignment and she had failed before it even started. Javona didn't know what to expect in return from the feds as a consequence.

Blade, the guy Javona had come to know as Armon's driver came and picked her up. He was in a different car, it was a low key Buick Enclave, one Javona didn't recognize at all. "Hey Blade," Javona said as she slid into the back seat. "Wassup ma?" he replied giving her a small smile.

"Where's Armon at? Why he send you by yourself to get me?" she asked. Blade looked through the rearview mirror and Javona thought he was looking at her, but she noticed he was looking past her. Then she noticed that he checked his side mirrors and he did the same rotation again. It was like he was looking for somebody.

"I'ount really know where he is, he just told me to get you and take you to the house to wait for him so that's what I'm doing," Blade replied as he continued to check the rearview and side mirrors. It was like he was looking for someone. Javona's heart started racing. *What if he knows something? What if he saw me going with those agents?* Her mind raced a million miles a minute.

"These muthafuckas think I don't fuckin' see them!" Blade cursed as he made a sharp turn. Not expecting the sudden movement of the car, Javona fell over in the backseat unable to brace herself. She got up from the seat and clutched the door handles. She was really nervous now because Blade could clearly tell they were being followed.

"I'm sorry ma . . . we got a little visitor," Blade told her, then he whipped the car into an abrupt U-turn. Javona almost died inside her nerves were so rattled. She held on as Blade whipped the car this way and that way. Javona was being given a crash course in hood defensive driving 101. Blade had noticed someone following them and Javona knew just who it was.

"What's going on?" she croaked, her mouth as dry as the desert. She had to play it off.

"I don't really know. Maybe the narcos or the feds . . . seems like somebody in our airtight camp done turned Judas. Shit just ain't been right the past few days. Armon gon' handle it though. You just sit tight and look pretty. My man is really feelin' you that's all you need to worry about," Blade said, as he whipped the car down a one way street and drove in the wrong direction. Javona felt like throwing up. She dug inside her purse and touched the mirror the DEA agents had given her. Watching Blade through the mirror, Javona held onto the mirror tightly. "I need to crack a window. I'm getting sick," she said to Blade. He nodded. Javona cracked the window and with the quickness of a jewel thief and while Blade was distracted she dropped the mirror down into the car's seat, just like she'd been instructed. Javona heard it fall down into the seat, she just hoped that with the wind from the open window blowing, Blade hadn't heard it. Javona had done her part to protect herself and Lissette, she just hoped that it was good enough.

Blade pulled up to the same Park Slope house Javona had been to before with Armon.

"The boss man is waiting for you inside," he told her as he opened the car door for her and let her out. Blade walked Javona up to the door, used a key and let her inside. "You know your way around in there right?" he asked. Javona nodded. She knew the inside of that house better than they thought. Armon was sitting on the beautiful tan leather couch in the living room.

He stood up when she came into the room. His face wasn't the same. It was tight and he looked kind of stressed.

"Hey baby girl. Sorry I had to change up the plans," Armon said, grabbing her in a tight embrace. Javona inhaled his scent and she felt so safe in his arms.

"It's ok. I understand . . . duty calls," she said returning his hug.

"Yeah but I was missing you so I had Blade come get you. I wanted to do something tonight, but niggas on the streets got me stressed. Seems like some of my spots are hot right now, he replied. "I had some things to take care of so I figured we'd just stay in tonight," Armon told her. It was the first time he had ever even slightly mentioned his business around her. Javona was happy that he wanted to stay inside for the night, which meant no DEA agents trailing them. Unfortunately, they also wanted her to place a small bug inside of his cell phone. That one was going to be too hard to avoid. Now she had to figure out how she could get a hold of Armon's phone when he wasn't looking.

Chapter 7

"Damn Why They Wanna Stick Me For My Paper . . ."

"In breaking news today, the Drug Enforcement Agency reported one of its biggest raids netting almost two million dollars in drug proceeds and cocaine with an estimated street value of four million dollars. A DEA spokesperson said, there were at least twenty people arrested in conjunction with the raids, but they still haven't gotten to the top of the organization and the investigation is ongoing,"

Armon clicked off his television and looked around his basement sitting area at all of his closest crew members. "There is no fuckin' way the feds would've known where to find that stash house. It was a fuckin' old lady's

house! Y'all really fuckin' think those bastards
figured it out on their own? Nah . . . some fuckin'
body in here talkin'," Armon gritted. All of the
men in the room was struck silent. They were
afraid to breathe much less say anything to him.
"Everybody knows since back in the day when
my father ran shit, that our shit is airtight! So
this fuckin' raid could only mean one fuckin'
thing . . . like I said, one of y'all niggas is singin'
like a bird . . . somebody in this circle is snitchin',"
he said, standing up and walking amongst his
crew. He was glaring them in their eyes one by
one. All of the men looked petrified. They knew
who Armon was. The son of Tito Munoz was
not to be fucked with. All of the workers had
heard stories about Tito's reign of terror in the
New York drug game back in the days. Tito had
killed entire families behind small shit. Armon
came from a legacy of violence so nobody in
the room dared to speak. "What the fuck could
they possibly offer you for snitchin'? I take care
of all y'all niggas. I provide well . . . look out for
y'all families. What could these feds really give
you in return for being a fuckin' low life snitch?
Huh? Less jail time? Well that's a fuckin' death
sentence. My family got all the jails and prisons
from here to Texas on lock with our people! Ain't

no reason to snitch even if those muthafuckas grabbed you up on some ol' you caught shit. Y'all already know if you get knocked, I'ma get you the best lawyer and if you gotta do a bid for the family, a nigga like me gon' take care of you and yours . . . so I'm not understanding why niggas would wanna snitch . . . that would be like stickin' me for my paper! The day I can't trust my own fuckin' peoples is the day niggas gon' have to get made examples out of," Armon pontificated. Everybody in the room was shook. They all gave each other suspicious side glances trying to figure out who the snitch was amongst them. Nobody wanted to be the person accused of snitching. Armon made one more round through the men; watching them closely to see how they reacted to being near him. Armon was trying to see if he could find any signs of deception on any of their faces. When he was done walking through them, he turned his back to them. He stood for a few minutes facing the movie size projection screen that adorned one entire wall of his basement. The room was pin drop quiet. Armon's crew was scared to even breathe, much less move or try to talk. The time seemed to be ticking by almost at a standstill. No one there knew what to expect from Armon.

He didn't really ever get angry, but when he did it was off the chain. Armon turned around suddenly and swiftly with his arm extended and a .45 caliber Heckler and Koch clutched in his hand. Before anyone could react, bang! A shot reverberated off the walls. One man's body dropped and slumped to the floor, blood pouring out of a hole in the center of his forehead. Most of the dudes in the room had their eyes stretched to the limit. Some covered their ringing ears and other's covered their eyes. One of Armon's crew members even bent over and threw up, his nerves had gotten the best of him. The dead man had been standing right next to him. The fear and tension in the room was palpable.

"Now . . . that's just a sample of what niggas that snitch get. I don't know if that nigga was the snitch or not, but I guess he ain't live to tell the story. So if I got the wrong nigga, I suggest the snitch nigga go home and kill himself tonight before I do. I think I made my fuckin' point now everybody get the fuck out!!" Armon barked, flopping down on his couch as all of his crew started scrambling to get the dead body up and out of the house.

***

Javona's bladder and sphincter muscle almost released when she heard the gunshot. She had been at the top of the basement stairs listening to Armon go off on his workers. She raced back up to the third floor of Armon's brownstone where she was supposed to have been all along. With her nerves rattled to no end, Javona jumped back into the bed and covered herself up. She started to cry. If he would do that to one of his boys that he'd known for a long time for snitching, she could only imagine what he would do to her if he ever found out it was her that had led the feds right to his doorstep. Javona told herself she was going to have to find a way to get away from the situation with the feds. Maybe Lissette was right, one big lick on Armon and leave town. That plan was starting to sound more like music to Javona's ears. Whether she loved Armon or not, Javona decided she was going to call Lissette and put their plan into motion.

Dressed in all black, Lissette prepared to leave her apartment her insides rolling with excitement, fear, and thoughts of revenge. She was supposed to meet up with Bam after she had called him and told him the information Javona had gotten, together they had mapped out their entire plan. Lissette grabbed her keys off of her kitchen table and headed toward her door. Too excited to get out on the streets, Lissette didn't bother to take a peek out of her apartment window to see who was outside like she usually did. She just figured that at the corner store it would be the same ol' usual suspects out there. Lissette had too much shit on her mind right now and somewhere in the back of it was a nagging feeling of guilt for what she was about to do to Javona. Lissette figured if they murdered Armon, she would spare Javona's life if Javona agreed to keep her mouth shut. Lissette didn't know how well that would go over with Bam though, so she started mentally preparing herself for the death of her best friend.

Lissette took a deep breath and made the sign of the cross on her chest before she opened her apartment door. *God forgive me for my sins.*

With her car keys in hand, Lissette pulled back her door and stepped into her hallway. Lissette turned around to lock her apartment door when suddenly she heard rapid footsteps coming toward her. With furrowed eyebrows she turned toward the sounds. Her heartbeat sped up and she fumbled with the keys. She was going to try to get back into her apartment. The keys dropped as she looked down the hallway in horror. Three dudes were heading straight for her. Lissette scrambled for the keys but she was too nervous . . . she wasn't fast enough. Before she could retrieve her keys off the floor and get it back into the lock, wham! They were up on her.

"Aghhh," she screamed as metal slammed into her head. A sharp pain made Lissette feel like pieces of her skull had gone flying into her brain. wham! She suffered another crushing blow to the head. The sound of bone cracking echoed through the hallway. Lissette saw a bolt of light flash behind her eye sockets like someone had just taken a picture of her. Her eyes immediately began to burn as blood from her head dripped into them. "Get this bitch inside," a man growled as his accomplices assisted him with the assault. Lissette got her bearings a little bit and got ready to fight, but they were too fast. She was flattened out from another crushing blow to her head. She couldn't see, but she could tell there was more than one person surrounding her. She tried to hold on to keep them from dragging her inside, but the pain pulsing in her head rendered her too weak. "You like to rob niggas huh?" a male voice growled. Lissette tried to open her eyes to see her attackers, but tears and blood blurred her vision. "Where's my fuckin' money?" the same voice boomed. "Huh bitch! Where's my fuckin' ten Gs," he barked. Then Lissette felt a sharp pain pervade her head again. She had been either hit or stomped on, she couldn't tell which. She was seeing little squirms of light now behind her eyelids. Her ears were ringing and she could feel blood trickling out of one of her ears too. "You thought if you left the East I wasn't gon' find ya bitch ass!" her attacker barked now. Then he kicked her in the chin. The force of the kick caused Lissette's teeth to slice into her own tongue from the hit. Blood instantly filled up in her mouth. She opened her mouth to scream but the sound was stuck some place deep inside of her. Another kick, then a punch, another blow from the gun—all landed on Lissette's body at will. She could feel herself slipping toward unconsciousness. She was gurgling for air as the blood that dripped down the back of her throat threatened to drown her. "Mirk this bitch!" the man said. Bang! A loud shot rang out. Lissette's head lolled to the side and she was still. "Let's go!" he huffed. Lissette's apartment door slammed, but it wasn't locked

***

"Police! Don't fucking move! Get the fuck down now! Javona put her hands up as she had a gun shoved in her face. "Get him!! Get him now!" they screamed. Javona was on her knees now. Tears immediately started coming down her face as she looked on at the surreal scene.

"Armon! I'm sorry!" she hollered. Javona watched in horror as the DEA agents in black raid jackets with their guns drawn pulled Armon out of the bed. They threw him to the floor on his stomach roughly. Now he was next to her screaming.

"What the fuck!" Armon shouted. "What do you mean you're sorry!" Armon asked her. Javona couldn't answer him. How could she tell him this was all her fault.

"I haven't done shit! Get the fuck off me!" Armon struggled as knees were dropped into his back.

"We have a search warrant and enough evidence to put you behind bars for life!" Agent Mason said, then he let out a loud cacophonous laugh.

"Y'all ain't got shit on me!" Armon barked as his arms were forcefully yanked behind his back and handcuffs were put on him so tight he could *feel his own blood coursing through his veins under the metal.*

"Oh yeah, thanks to your little girlfriend we have plenty on you . . . right, informant Javona Blakely?" Agent Giovani said to Javona. Armon looked at Javona with hurt and disappointment but more anger in his eyes.

"You fuckin' bitch! I should've never loved you! I should've never trusted your ass! You're a dead bitch!" Armon barked as the agents roughly hoisted him up off the floor and carted him away.

"Armon!! I'm sorry!! I'm so sorry!" Javona screamed as an uncontrollable wash of tears flooded her face.

Javona jumped out of her sleep and bolted upright in the bed. Her entire body was soaked with sweat. She whirled her head around wildly touching her face. She felt that her cheeks were wet, she had really been crying in her sleep. The dream was so real that it took her a few minutes to get it together. Her sudden movement in the bed startled Armon awake. "What's up?" he said groggily, lifting his head and looking over at her strangely. Javona's heart was racing wildly, she had had that same nightmare that the feds had run up in the house two nights in a row. Javona swallowed hard as she looked over at Armon. She still couldn't speak. "You a'ight baby girl?" he asked leaning up on one elbow. Javona jumped out of the bed with her hand over her mouth and rushed to the bathroom. Once inside, she bent over the toilet and threw up the contents of her stomach. She held onto the walls for support as her head spun. Javona wanted to leave. She was so overcome by guilt that she couldn't even face Armon anymore. She struggled her way over to the sink and splashed water on her face. Looking up in the mirror, she didn't even recognize herself.

Armon came into the bathroom. "Yo . . . what's goin' on with you?" he asked seriously, touching her on the shoulder. His touch made her uncomfortable all of a sudden.

"I just need to go home . . . I will take a cab. Please don't argue with me about this," Javona said forcefully. Armon was taken aback and he lifted his hands in front of him in surrender. "A'ight whatever you want baby girl," he honored her wishes and called a car service for her. Javona treated Armon like shit right before the cab came. It was easier to put him off than have him keep treating her nicely.

***

When Javona got into the cab, she picked up her phone to dial Lissette's number. She had decided she wanted to come clean with Lissette about the feds and what she had done to some of Armon's spots. Javona wanted to make a plan to get out of town, away from the feds, away from Bam and away from Armon. Before Javona could punch in a number her phone rang. It was an unknown number.

"Hello," she breathed into the phone.

"You didn't follow our instructions. Where are you going? You're not supposed to leave Mr. Munoz's side. We want more. We want you to get us more information right away," Agent Mason said into the phone.

"I did what you asked. What more do you want? I don't know anything else. I can't stay with somebody that doesn't want me to be with him!" Javona said exasperated.

"We want you to follow instructions. You need to spend more time with him. Force your way in. We don't care how much dick you have to suck or pussy you have to give up!" Mason barked. That had struck Javona silent for a minute. *The fuckin' nerve of this bastard,* she screamed in her head. "We need to know who his supplier is, we need to know his every move. You did so well with the GPS that led us to that stash houses . . . we need more, we need some direct evidence against him," Agent Mason instructed. It was like he was possessed. He was more gun-ho than Lissette. Javona closed her eyes; she could not believe how bad everybody wanted a piece of Armon, when all she wanted was to continue being loved by him.

"That is impossible. He doesn't take me around his business stuff. I am just someone he is seeing why don't you get that through your fucking head," Javona growled into the phone.

"Well change that . . . you need to do as we say or else you go to jail and I don't know what might happen to your little friend . . . what's her name? Lissette Cruz?" Mason threatened. A cold chill shot down Javona's spine.

"You better . . ."Javona started but the line went dead.

Her cell phone immediately began ringing again. "Hello!" she barked into the receiver.

"What? Bam? I can't understand you . . . what? Lissette? No!!!" Javona screamed so loud she caused the cab driver to swerve.

"Turn around! I need to go to Kings County Hospital!" Javona screamed, her heart felt like it would explode.

When the cab pulled up on Clarkson Avenue, Javona tossed forty dollars into the front seat and scrambled out of the car doors. As she ran toward the emergency room entrance she noticed Bam walking straight toward her.

"They got her in surgery for the second time since yesterday," Bam told Javona.

"Yesterday! What the fuck happened to her?" Javona started crying now.

"Somebody shot her . . . but I was on my way to her crib and I found her just in time," Bam said. "I tried to call you but your cell went straight to voice mail," Bam continued.

Javona felt terrible, but she had to turn her phone off for fear that Mason or Giovani would call her while she was with Armon.

"I need to see her!" Javona yelled through her tears. She tried to push past Bam.

"Nah . . . they ain't lettin' nobody up there right now. They said its gonna be another two hours," Bam told her, grabbing her arm gently.

"This is all my fault," Javona cried. "I did all of this!"

Bam looked at Javona strangely when she said that. "She was at my house in East New York looking for me because I hadn't called her back and that dude Rori was looking for her . . . he must've seen her at my crib and followed her," Javona explained. But in the back of her mind she didn't know if that was what happened or if the feds were trying to send her a message. A sense of relief washed over Bam. He was glad that Javona didn't suspect him in any way. He had already fucked up the plan enough already.

"Yo . . . the lick is called off. We ain't doin' the shit no more," Javona told Bam. He nodded at her with a real grimy look on his face. She was oblivious to the deception in his eyes. She was too preoccupied with getting into the hospital to find out about Lissette's condition.

There was more than one set of eyes on Armon as he and two of his boys walked into Kings County Hospital. He went up to the sixth floor trauma unit and when he stepped off the elevators Javona jumped into his arms. "Shhh, it's gon' be a'ight," he comforted her. His boys stood off to the side to give them time together. Javona didn't know what had prompted her to call him, but he was the only other person she felt close to. She realized that calling him there might put the feds back on his tail, but Javona needed to have Armon there. He held her so tight and allowed her to melt into his embrace. It felt so good to have someone to hold her. "Do y'all know what happened to her?" Armon asked. "No . . ." Javona rasped out through sobs. It took her a while, but Javona finally told him that she didn't know who had shot Lissette but that the bullet had just barely missed her brain. She told him that the doctors were able to get the bullet out without any real brain damage. Javona and Armon walked together to Lissette's room. Javona grabbed onto Armon's arm tightly as she looked down at her best friend filled with tubes and monitors. "This is all my fault," Javona cried. Lissette's eyes fluttered like she could hear Javona's voice, but she still didn't wake up.

"Nah, its not your fault . . . niggas is just ruthless out here," Armon comforted. He didn't know the half of it. Javona looked up at him, she wanted to confess to him so badly what she had done, but the words just wouldn't come.

Chapter 8

"There's Gonna Be A lot of Slow Singin' and Flower Bringin' If My Burglar Alarm Starts Ringin' . . ."

That night Javona and Armon stayed at the hospital as late as they were allowed to stay. Lissette's eyes would flutter and Javona would get excited, but Lissette wouldn't wake up. Finally visiting hours were up. When the nurses put them out, Armon had convinced Javona to come back to his house so he could watch over her. In her vulnerable state Javona didn't protest. But in the back of her mind there was a nagging thought of the feds that were on her tail.

When Armon got her home, he poured her some wine and held her close. Javona had turned her phone off; for fear that Agent Mason and Giovani would be calling her making threats. At this point, her best friend was laying up half dead so she didn't give two flying fucks what the feds were talking about. Right now Armon was the only person she had and she still had to find a way to tell him what her real intentions were when they first started going out on dates. There was silence in the house while Armon stroked her head. She had her eyes closed . . . contemplating. Armon finally broke up the monotony. "What you think happened to your friend?" Armon asked. Javona opened her eyes and thought long and hard about his question. She inhaled deeply and exhaled. It was time for her to be honest. Fuck it, if he didn't want to be with her anymore that's what it was going to be. Javona leaned up and broke their embrace. She looked into his eyes and she started to cry. "Armon there is something I need to tell you about me," Javona said. Armon looked at her seriously. "What is it baby girl?"

"I make my living scamming, robbing, and setting niggas up . . . that's how me and Lissette been getting down since high school," Javona partly confessed. Armon touched her face. "Oh . . . that's all," he said, unfazed. Javona looked at him like he had two heads. She was shocked by his nonchalant reaction to what she'd just told him.

"Look baby girl . . . I am not just in the streets, I am of the streets. I am the streets. I knew who y'all was the day I laid eyes on y'all in Dallas. A nigga does his homework. You think I was keeping company with you that close and I didn't know who you were. I know your friend too . . . me and her got history. I bet you didn't know that," Armon said. Javona's heart started racing real fast. She was wondering now if Armon knew that she was trying to set him up or that she had been working with the feds to build a case against him. Things were spinning off axis for her right now.

"So why didn't you say anything? How did you . . . what?" Javona asked, her words were stuck.

"Because I knew at heart you were different. I knew you wasn't gonna do anything once I showed you that you could be loved. No other man has ever shown you love . . . I can tell. C'mon baby girl, if you were going to set a nigga up it woulda been done a long time ago. You ain't cut from that cloth, especially after I told you that I love you," Armon told her. Javona broke down crying even harder. He was so on point with everything he was saying. She wasn't going to go through with any of it, but there was still more he didn't know and that was about the feds. She laid her head on his shoulders. There was no place else she would rather be. She thought about the position she was in and decided it was time for a full confession. Fuck it!

"Armon . . . there are more things I need to tell you. I want you to know everything. I have to tell you everything," Javona said, her voice shaky and cracking with sobs.

"I'm listening baby girl," Armon said as he stroked her beautiful long hair. Javona opened her mouth and began to confess all of her sins. Armon listened intently.

"This is how the inside of the house looks," Bam told his little soldiers unfurling the paper he'd stolen from Lissette's battered and beaten body.

"What happens if that bitch lives and tells that it was us that missed the mark on mirkin' her ass?" one of them asked.

"Don't ask no fuckin' questions about that bitch! I'ma take care of her dumb ass once and for all when this goes down, but for now, shut the fuck up and just follow my instructions! We need to be in and out," Bam barked. Lissette's assault and missed murder was a sore spot with Bam. Bam had kicked himself over and over for fucking everything up. He thought he'd shot Lissette in the head and killed her. But apparently, he had been an awful shot and he had just delivered a flesh wound that had sent a few fragments into her face. Bam had missed a close up shot and he was the laughing stock amongst his crew. When he had heard on the streets that she had lived, he had raced up to the hospital so he could front for Javona and the police like he had no clue what had happened to her. Bam had even been the one to call Javona to tell her what had happened to Lissette. But now he had to hurry up and get the fuck out of dodge, because if Lissette came into consciousness she would be able to identify him. The police were waiting for that moment too.

Bam pulled his black hood over his head and his little cronies followed suit. His young crew consisted of boys all under the age of eighteen. Those were the only people that gave Bam the ego boost he needed. Bam was really a nobody in the streets, but the kids he ran with thought he was the man. Especially now that they were going to help him take out the most powerful dude in Brooklyn.

"We goin' in through that ground floor window right there. That's the nice thing about these fuckin' brownstones . . . windows are floor to ceiling," Bam said smiling as he looked over at the house from under his hoodie. They all watched the darkened house.

"Yo Bam you said it's a safe filled with money up in there right?" one of the boys asked excitedly. He couldn't be older than fifteen years old. Bam had them all hyped up over the possibility of how much money they were going to make.

"Damn . . . I shoulda did this shit with the two bitches. Y'all li'l niggas ask too many questions and y'all way too hype! That's how niggas get caught . . . being too hyped they start making dumb ass moves. Calm the fuck down and shut the fuck up!" Bam replied, speaking to the boys like he was their father. Just then something caught Bam's attention. He ducked down in the car seat and shushed his little crew. Bam eyed the front of the house and watched as one of Armon's crew members came out of the house, got into his ride, and rode off. "Show fuckin' time," Bam whispered. It was just like Javona had told Lissette and Lissette had told Bam; when Armon was in the house with a bitch, his boys kind of fell back so he could have some privacy. That was the perfect opportunity in Bam's eyes. His heart started hammering with excitement.

"A'ight li'l niggas . . . that was our signal. This bitch ass nigga is alone now. He running up in some pussy and we about to run up on that ass. Let's get it in," Bam announced. His little crew got amped. They all filed out of the car dressed in their black hoodies. Bam rushed across the quiet street, looking left then right to scan for possible witnesses and police. Once he made it to the house, he bent down and tugged on the first window and it easily went up.

Bam was amazed. *That was mad easy. This nigga ain't no real gangsta—leavin' windows open and shit. Lucky me.* Bam thought to himself. He had to chuckle at how stupid and lax Armon's security was. Bam pulled out his gun and climbed into the window first. There wasn't even anything obstructing his entrance; another easy feat. When Bam got inside he heard soft R&B music coming from upstairs.

Everything was working out perfectly in his assessment. Bam helped his little crew members inside the house and made sure they had the knapsack with the rope and duct tape in it. Bam was so excited now he could swear that his dick was growing hard. He silently motioned toward the ceiling, signaling his little cronies that Armon was upstairs. They all nodded their understanding. It was just like Bam had told them. They would get Armon while he was butt ass naked fucking his bitch. There was no better way to catch a nigga slippin' than with no clothes on, no access to a gun and with his defenses down from being in a pussy haze. Bam silently crept up the steps first. When he got to the top of the landing, he peeked around making sure the coast was clear. He waited for the rest of the dudes he was with as each one snuck up the stairs.

From where he stood, Bam could hear the sounds of what he believed was Armon and Javona fucking coming from the cracked door of the bedroom. His dick instantly got hard. He moved a little closer to the door and squinted his eyes, he had always wanted to see Javona's pretty ass naked. Bam smiled to himself as he watched for a few minutes. He could see Javona's bare back and ass moving up and down. Bam squeezed his dick through his pants trying to keep his hormones in check. From where he stood, Bam could see that she was riding Armon's dick. Bam started fantasizing about how

much sheer pleasure he was going to get out of
grabbing Javona's naked ass off of Armon, tying
them both up, and maybe he would fuck Javona
before he killed both of them. *That's what this
bitch gets for telling me the lick was off. Who the
fuck did she think she was! I ain't like that bitch
from day fuckin' one.* Bam thought.

"Ohhh fuck me daddy! Fuck me good! Bam
listened some more. He was growing more and
more jealous by the minute. He had had enough.
Armon's safe full of money flashed through
Bam's mind and he quickly remembered the task
at hand. He planned on getting all of that stash
money, and maybe some of those watches he
had seen Armon rocking around town too. Bam
moved his hand signaling his crew to move in.
Bam clutched his gun tight and barged full speed
ahead into the room.

"It's a stick up muthafucka!" Bam barked,
waving his gun in front of him.

"Ahhh," the female screamed. She jumped up
and turned around to face Bam and his crew.
Bock! Bock! Bock! She started letting off shots.
The real set up was going down now.

"Aghhh!" Bam screeched, dropping his
weapon and holding onto his chest. "I'm hit!"
he screamed like a girl "Oh shit! They shootin' at

us!" one of Bam's little crew members screamed as he started running for the door. Suddenly the walk-in closet in the house flew open and shots started flying from the closet. The same for the master bathroom, more shots came from there. Two of Bam's little soldiers folded to the floor like deflated balloons, one was hit in the head and one directly in the heart. The other two tried to get away. They did get as far as the hallway, but they were trapped. There was nowhere to run because they had been locked inside of the house. "Please!" one little boy begged. Nothing could save them. They were caught as some more of Armon's army came out of the back bedrooms. More shots were fired and more bodies dropped.

"This is what the fuck happens when monkeys handle guns," Blade said as he looked down at the dead bodies of Bam and all of the little teenagers that had been killed as a result of Bam's dumb ass plan. "How the fuck they gonna come to fight an army of men with little babies? Did these niggas really think Armon lived here? Don't they know this nigga would never bring people where he really rest at until they had passed all of the tests . . . I gotta laugh," Blade commented, shaking his head at tragedy. "Let's go," he called out, leading the rest of Armon's crew out of the back of the house.

***

"Bang! Bang! Bang! Police! Warrant! Open the door!" Agent Mason yelled just before he gave the signal for the agent holding the battering ram to send it slamming into the door. The front door of what they believed to be Armon's brownstone splintered open. "Police!" the DEA agents screamed as they all stomped into the house like an invading army. The agents scattered into different directions so that they could clear the house. According to the information they had received from their informant, they would find Armon in the house, along with drugs, cash, and guns. The agents converged on the house and they could be heard slamming doors and yelling out the clear signal as they found room after room downstairs empty.

"Clear down here," one of the agents yelled from the basement.

Agent Mason had his gun in hand, while he and two other agents carefully began climbing the stairs. "Police! Let me see your hands!" he called out when he noticed someone at the top of the steps on the floor. "Let me see your fuckin' hands!" He screamed again when the person didn't move. As Mason got closer, he immediately recognized the strong, pungent scent of rotting, coagulated blood. It was an unmistakable odor, like raw meat gone bad. Mason placed the sleeve of his jacket over his nose. So did the other agents. He knew right away what they were dealing with.

"Bodies! We got bodies up here!" Agent Mason screamed out. All of the agents began flooding to his location. They all did the same thing he did, cover their noses and mouths. That smell was overwhelming. They didn't know how they had missed it when they first ran up in the house.

"Call the fuckin' coroner and tell 'em we got at least five black male DOAs," Agent Mason barked.

"Don't just fuckin' stand around staring at these fuckin' bodies!! Find the fuckin' evidence that the informant said was here!" he barked at some of the other agents. He was steaming mad. He had been duped by a Munoz . . . again!

"This is a crime scene. We can't go searching and tearing up shit at a crime scene. Get a grip," Agent Giovani said, rolling her eyes at him.

"That's easy for you to say . . . your ass is not on the line," Mason retorted. It was his case not hers. He had told his superiors that he would be able to bring Armon Munoz in with enough evidence to put him away for life.

"I'm sorry you couldn't get Tito Munoz back then and now you can't get his son . . . but we're not going to do something that would compromise this fuckin' murder scene. Maybe not all drug dealers are the ghetto trash buffoons you make them out to be Mason," Agent Giovani said rubbing it in. Agent Mason bit down into his lip. He knew she was right. When Agent Mason was a newly appointed DEA agent, he was assigned to take down Tito Munoz, the most powerful drug kingpin in Spanish Harlem. Mason had failed. Munoz reigned over Harlem and the DEA could never catch him with any dirt on him. They tried planting informants, evidence, but nothing ever stuck on Munoz, he was untouchable. He remained that way until he died of throat cancer. When his son Armon Munoz took over, Mason would stop at nothing to bring him down. Once again, he had failed. Agent Mason thought for sure using Javona was going to do the trick for the takedown, but his plan had backfired. He was left holding more than the bag this time. "This shit will hit the media for sure. You better get ready to be reduced to a fuckin' academy training instructor. You'll never hit the streets again after you're humiliated over this." Agent Giovani said, chuckling at her co-worker's misfortune.

Chapter 9

"It Didn't Take Long Before I Made You My Wife . . ."

Summer 2010

Javona stared anxiously at the little white plastic device in anticipation of the answer she was looking for. She was sitting on the toilet seat inside of the new home she now shared with Armon. Her legs swung in and out as she waited with bated breath for the results of the pregnancy test. Armon wasn't home yet and she wanted to know before he got in. Her stomach churned with nerves. She had not been feeling well for about a month and decided she would get a test. At first she thought her constant nausea and restlessness was because of everything that had happened over the past few months; especially the fiasco with Lissette.

After a few minutes of waiting, Javona finally started to see something moving across the little square window. The first pink line appeared and her heart started thumping hard, but when the second line appeared Javona almost fell off the toilet. She cupped her hands over her mouth in order to contain the scream welling up inside of her. The test was positive! Javona was going to be a mother and she couldn't wait to share the news with Armon, who like her, didn't have any children.

Javona was happy but at the same time a sudden sadness came over her. This was one of those moments where she would've called Lissette to share her big news. Javona put her head in her hands while she experienced the whirl of mixed emotions. "I wish you were here with me. All of these lies and betrayal wasn't supposed to happen to us . . ."

Javona whispered out loud as if her words could somehow telepathically reach Lissette. Javona still hadn't gotten over what happened with Lissette. Then to make matters worse, when Armon's workers said they had found the layout drawing of the Park Slope brownstone that Lissette and Bam thought was Armon's house in Bam's pocket after he was dead, Javona knew there was only one place he could have gotten it and that was from Lissette. At first Javona thought maybe Bam had beaten Lissette up and taken the drawing, but when she found out that he also had the fake safe combinations Javona had given Lissette; Javona started to figure out what the real deal was. Javona was really devastated when she put two and two together and learned that her best friend in the world had planned on snaking her.

Lissette had actually planned to go through with the lick on Armon without Javona. Lissette was going to take the money, split the shit with Bam and bounce, leaving Javona for dead. That shit had incensed Javona when she found out. She didn't care that Lissette was sick and trying to recover from her injuries, Javona had gone off on her. Things were never the same after that. Gone was the seemingly unbreakable bond between the girls. Javona had confessed all of this to Armon. Luckily, he hadn't held it against her. Armon had even tried to convince her to forgive Lissette, but Javona wouldn't hear of it. It would take some time and more convincing is what she had told him.

***

It seemed to take forever for Armon to get home. Javona was more than restless now. She figured she'd probably already suffered at least ten small anxiety attacks while she waited. She had gone from one room to the next and back again in the huge house. She finally flopped down on the couch again wishing she had Lissette to talk to. Javona had to keep reminding herself of Lissette's betrayal to keep herself grounded.

Javona had fallen asleep on the couch waiting for Armon to come home. Finally she felt his soft, full lips against her cheek. She opened her eyes and moaned. She smiled when she saw his face. "I'm sorry I was late. I had some business to take care of," he said, grabbing her to help her up off the couch and to their bed.

"I have to tell you something," Javona rasped, her voice still groggy with sleep.

"Ut oh . . . last time you had to tell me something niggas was tryin'a set me up and the feds was after me . . . whatchu do now?" Armon said jokingly. Javona stopped and folded her arms across her chest. She hated when Armon brought up her past indiscretions. Those were things she wanted to put way behind her.

"Why you keep bringing that up," she pouted.

"I'm just joking baby. I know you ain't never going down that road again," he comforted. She smiled.

"This is good news this time," she said.

"What? You got a job at Saks and Neiman the places you like to shop so now you'll get a discount," Armon joked again. Javona stomped her feet like a spoiled child, but she couldn't front, his joke was not only funny it was on point. She had a love for shopping.

"A'ight . . . for real. Tell me your news," he said seriously. Javona smiled and grabbed his hand. She stood up and pulled him toward the winding staircase that sat at the center of their home. "Aww shit, this must be real good news!" Armon said excitedly thinking he was about to be seduced or something good like that. Javona smiled at him wickedly. She wanted him to think whatever he wanted. The further he was off the mark the more of a surprise her news would be.

"Oh you gon' show me better than you can tell me?" Armon asked her squeezing a handful of her ass cheeks as they came to the last few of the twenty five steps.

"You are such a freak," she joked. "Cover your eyes," she said when they got close to their master bedroom.

"Nah . . . I'ma hustla baby . . . we never close our eyes, we even sleep with all eyes open," Armon said, still joking. Javona sucked her teeth, reaching up to place one of her hands over his eyes while she led him into the master bathroom with her free hand. Once inside, she uncovered his eyes. At first, Armon looked around confused. He looked at her like she was crazy. She put her hands on her hips waiting for him to see what she wanted him to see.

"I don't get it. You want me to see you take a piss? I hope not a shit . . . let me find out you on that freak girl shit," he said laughing. "Nah for real baby girl . . . I don't get it . . . wassup?" Armon continued, crinkling his eyebrows.

"Look around . . . look around carefully," Javona instructed as she stood back. Armon whirled around twice. There was nothing on his personal sink but his straight razor and some mouthwash. All that was apparent to him on Javona's personal sink was a bunch of hair products and other female toiletries that he had no use for. There was nothing on the side of their Jacuzzi bathtub but some scented candles and decorative jars filled with bath beads and other girly shit.

"I'm sayin', I'ount see nothing. C'mon with the Merlin the Magic show and just tell me wassup," he said, growing a little impatient with the game. Javona crossed her arms and tapped her foot. She wasn't giving up her position. Armon looked carefully again. There was no way he was going to let her accuse him of not being thorough enough to find whatever she was hiding. Finally, his eyes landed on something that seemed out of place on her sink. "Ok . . . maybe I see what you selling," he whispered. He walked over closer to the sink. He squinted his eyes to make sure they weren't deceiving him. Then he turned around to face Javona. He looked back at the little test with the pink cross sign in the little window. He looked back at Javona again. His face was like stone, no reaction, no smile.

Javona didn't know what to think. Suddenly she was afraid. She looked like a deer caught in headlights. She thought that he wasn't happy. Javona became weak in the knees, she thought Armon was about to scream on her. Holding the little white test, he flexed his jaw, then he rushed over to her with a serious look on his face and grabbed her. "You trying to tell me . . . that . . . that I'm going to be a father!" he screamed, still no apparent joy behind his words. Javona was about to cry. This was not the reaction she was expecting. She couldn't even open her mouth to answer his question, her words were caught at the lump that had formed in her throat.

"Gotdamn! I'm gonna be a father!" Armon yelled excitedly. He was finally able to get his feelings out. Armon had never been so happy about anything in his entire life. A huge wave of relief washed over Javona when Armon smiled and got excited. Her tears finally began to fall. The tears of joy came down in buckets. Armon picked her up and whirled her around. She held onto his neck tightly. Javona wanted to remain in that moment forever. Armon placed her back on the floor. He told her she needed to sit down and not be stressed. Javona laughed at him. "You acting just like those white people do on those shows when they find out they're having babies. It don't usually happen like that in the hood," she told him.

"That's cuz niggas in the hood don't usually have my kind of paper and babies are usually burdens to them . . . not us!" Armon said still exhibiting his excitement. Armon walked around for a minute, then he thought about things. Suddenly his mood shifted a little bit.

"Yo, whatchu gon' do about that situation you gotta take care of? I mean . . . I don't even want you walking up in no courtroom to testify now that you pregnant with my seed. I'm sayin' that shit is gonna be mad stressful and I ain't with it," he said. Javona lowered her eyes. She knew the discussion was going to eventually shift to her impending courtroom testimony.

"I can't back out of it now. I made a deal and it cleared up everything. It's the only way to make the rest of this go away. I will be alright . . . I promise nothing will happen to the baby," Javona said sincerely. She was secretly praying that she was right. Going into a packed courtroom to testify during the highly publicized trial was the something she was dreading.

Chapter 10

"Never Trust Nobody . . .
Your Moms'll Set That Ass Up"

Fall 2010

Lissette stared up at the ceiling of the small jail cell that she had called home for the past couple of months. Some days in jail were better than others, but on the whole, the entire situation was fucked up. How she'd ended up in jail was the most fucked up part of the entire situation. Lissette had gotten over her up and down bouts of emotions regarding her best friend's apparent betrayal. Lissette figured it was karma for the grimy way she had planned to leave Javona behind on the lick against Armon.

"Cruz! Get dressed for court," the CO yelled into Lissette's cell. She rolled her eyes. It was probably being told when to eat, sleep, shit, piss and get dressed that got on her nerves the most about being in jail. Lissette got up and changed into the court clothes she had been sent. She swept her hair back into the best ponytail she could get from the soft brush they provided in jail. When she was ready Lissette was led out of her cell, down the tier. "Yo! Good luck chica! I know how it feels to have your own friends take you down," one of Lissette's tier mates screamed out. A couple of others that knew the story also put their two cents in it. Lissette left the jail and got ready to face the music for her crime.

When she arrived at the courthouse a cold sweat broke out on her body. There were throngs of people outside of the courthouse, news cameras were everywhere. Lissette knew that if any of those people in the crowd could get to her they'd probably rip her to shreds. There were fans of the NBA star camped out to show their support as well as family members and members of the general public that wanted to be nosey. Lissette's attorney had asked for a closed courtroom but his request had been denied. There would be as many people that could fit in the courtroom. More importantly, Javona would be in the courtroom, a fact that gave Lissette mixed emotions. Lissette had not seen Javona since all of the drama had gone down. Lissette had been told through a jail house kite that Javona and Armon had gotten married. That was a crazy turn of events. Lissette didn't know how she was going to feel or react when she saw her best friend.

The jail transportation van stopped at the back of the courthouse, which made Lissette glad she wouldn't have to face the crowds out front. But she couldn't be that lucky. Someone had spotted it. "Murderer!" a man's voice boomed. His outburst turned the entire angry mob toward where Lissette was going into the building.

"Move . . . move," the COs that were transporting her started to yell. They didn't want to take a chance. But they were too late. Wham! "Aggh!" Lissette screeched holding her head. The COs drew out their weapons. "Back up! Back up!" they screamed waving their weapons toward the angry crowd. When Lissette was lifted up off the ground her head was bleeding. She felt woozy. Her legs were weak. Someone had hit her in the head with a brick or a rock, she couldn't be sure which object it was since both had been tossed in her direction. Lissette was crying now. The situation was worse than she thought. She was beginning to regret everything, especially agreeing to go to trial on the case.

Lissette was seen by the courthouse medical unit. She had to get two butterfly stitches in her forehead. When she was all bandaged up, it was time for her to enter the courtroom. Lissette was not feeling well at all. Her head hurt, her stomach churned and she was not ready to face the crowd. As she was being led into the courtroom she could feel all eyes on her. The low buzzing sounds of the television cameras were very apparent to her as well. Lissette glanced over at the prosecutor's table and that is when she noticed Javona sitting behind the prosecutor. A quick pang of anger and hurt flitted through Lissette's chest. She flexed her jaw and tried to catch eye contact with Javona. Javona would not look up. "Fuckin' coward," Lissette grumbled, breaking her neck to stare at Javona, waiting for even a half a second of eye contact. Nothing. Javona stared down the entire time.

"All rise," the court officer called out announcing the judge into the courtroom. The shuffle of clothes and feet gave Lissette a chill. She kept staring at Javona. Lissette raised her eyebrows slightly when she noticed the small bulge in Javona's clothes. As angry as she was, Lissette felt a fleeting moment of happiness for Javona. They had always talked about who would have kids first. Both girls had promised each other that they'd be the godmother for each other's children. Lissette wondered for a minute it Javona would ever make her the godmother now.

The judge banged her gavel to signal the beginning of the proceedings in the State of Texas vs. Lissette Cruz for the manslaughter of Garrison O'Neil.

Javona had purposely avoided eye contact with Lissette. It would have just made things harder and Javona didn't want to complicate things now. She had been going over things over and over in her mind, preparing for this day. But as soon as she had stepped into the courtroom everything she had rehearsed had gone out of her mind. Javona turned around slightly and looked at all of Armon's people that were there in support of her. Armon had chosen not to come to the court proceedings. He didn't want to associate with anything that had to do with court, cops, or anything of the like. He had made sure she was escorted under very tight security though. She looked down at her cell phone screen and noticed a text message from Armon, "It's all going to go down just like its supposed to. I love you and be strong." Javona smiled slightly. He was so damn sweet. The judge was talking, then the prosecutor and then the defense attorney. They were talking about exhibits, witnesses, and yada, yada, yada. Javona wasn't listening, but she did hear it crystal clear when they called her name out.

"We call state's witness Javona Blakely to the stand," the prosecutor announced loudly. His words garnered hushed murmurs and deep grumbles from some of the people that were squeezed tightly into the jam-packed courtroom. A cold chill shot down Javona's spine as she heard herself referred to as the states witness, which in the hood, equaled snitch. Javona would have rather be known as a terrorist than a snitch. Javona's legs felt like lead pipes and her feet like cinder blocks as she walked slowly toward the boxed in wooden sitting area to the left of the judge's bench. She could feel the heat from all of the eyes on her, burning holes into her. She wouldn't dare look out into the crowd. Where she came from, snitching of any kind, especially testifying in court was like a cardinal sin. Javona looked down at her hands as she finally took her seat.

"Ms. Blakely, please raise your right hand," a tall, slender court officer told her. Javona raised her right hand and answered yes when he asked her if she swore to tell the truth. "Would you state your entire name for the record," the prosecutor said. Javona mumbled her name, barely wanting to speak out loud. She felt like she had eaten an entire jar of paste, her tongue was heaving and stuck to the roof of her mouth. Her throat also felt dry as the desert. "Ms. Blakely you will have to speak up," the judge announced.

"Snitch bitch!"

Before Javona could say her name for the record a loud scream erupted from some place in the back of the courtroom. Javona jumped, her heart thundering fiercely. She looked out in to the crowd for the first time. Damn! There was more than one scowling face staring back at her. She recognized the faces of a few dudes; one put two fingers up to his head mimicking a gun and acted like he was pulling the trigger.

"Order!" the judge screamed as the court officer's raced to the back of the room to find the troublemaker. A few guys and girls were shuffled out of the courtroom doors.

Javona finally sat down in the snitch box as it was referred to in the hood. She had to place her hands under her thighs in order to keep her nerves at bay. The prosecutor asked her a few questions about things she knew first hand.

"Ms. Blakely is the person responsible for the murder in this courtroom today?" the prosecutor asked her. Javona shook her head in the affirmative. "Can you point to that person for the court? He followed up. Javona's eyes grew wide. This wasn't what she had rehearsed with the prosecutor. He had promised her that she would be able to focus her attention on him and she wouldn't have to look into the familiar face of the person she was ultimately betraying. Javona froze. She couldn't move. Her instincts were telling her to bolt out of the chair and run far away, but she was actually frozen, catatonic.

"Ms. Blakely you need to follow the instructions," the judge said jolting Javona into action.

Javona lifted her arm slowly and extended her pointer finger toward the defense table.

"There," she whispered. "That's the person who did it. Lissette Cruz was responsible for the death of Garrison O'Neil."

"You fuckin' snitch bitch! You fuckin' traitor ass bitch! After all I did for you! I fuckin' made you! I saved you! You ain't hear about what they did to Sammy the Bull . . . ain't no such thing as witness protection! The fuckin' feds can't protect you!" Lissette jumped up and screamed. Javona was finally forced to look into the familiar eyes of her best friend. They were cold and unforgiving, a far cry from the way they used to greet her.

"Order! Order!" the judge screamed. "Counselor you will control your client or I will impose a contempt of court sanction that will send both of you to jail even if you get an acquittal!" the judge yelled out.

Javona was shaking all over as the pandemonium that had erupted in the courtroom started to die down. She thought the judge would ask for a recess, but no such luck. The prosecutor just kept right at it. Making her look more and more like the biggest turncoat in the world. He was throwing questions at her like hard, fast balls. None of this shit was her fault. Lissette had forced her into this shit. Javona was pissed. According to what everybody in the streets believed, she would be living the rest of her life in witness protection.

"Ms. Blakely. Why don't you recount for the court what you remember about how this all came about," the prosecutor said.

Javona opened her mouth to speak as a flood of memories came rushing back into her mind.

Chapter 11

"Your Nobody
'Til Somebody Kills You"

Spring 2011

"Cruz! Let's go. They turning your ass loose today," the CO yelled out. He didn't have to tell Lissette that it was her day to leave that hell hole, she already knew. Lissette had her shit all ready to go. She walked out of her cell and told all of her prison friends good-bye. She signed off on her release paperwork with a big smile on her face. She was finally free.

Lissette walked out of the prison doors and inhaled deeply. "Ahh, fresh air!" she exclaimed stretching her arms upwards. Lissette didn't have a pot to piss in or a window to throw it out of but she was happy to be free.

"Bitch if you don't c'mon I'ma curse your ass out," a voice screamed out from a black BMW X6. Lissette started laughing and rushed toward the vehicle. She jumped into the passenger seat with a huge smile on her face.

"I ain't gon' be too many bitches! Not after I just did a bid to keep ya man from suffering the takedown!" Lissette said. Then she reached over and hugged Javona tightly.

"Yeah, you right. It was a pretty good deal in the end though. The feds were pissed because I wouldn't help them so they pinned that murder on us . . . but you was real stand up when you took the fall for the shit so they couldn't muscle me. But, you can't front . . . it was the least you could do after you tried to snake me out of the lick," Javona recounted.

"Well you still ain't have to fuckin' live with dirty-ass hoes for a year . . . its all good though. Armon paid for the best attorney around . . . so its all gravy," Lissette said as they pulled out.

"Not only that . . . this nigga is about to take care of you. He got you a crib, some loot, you good. I'm sure you won't need to do anymore illegal licks," Javona said.

"Let me see that damn pretty ass baby," Lissette said turning toward the backseat. "Damn she looks just like your model ass," Lissette sang, admiring Javona and Armon's beautiful daughter. Lissette turned back around and looked at her friend.

"For real, I'm real happy for you Javona. You always deserved this type of life. Good man . . . living large. It was always in the cards for you," Lissette said somberly.

"C'mon don't start all of that sad talk shit. Whatever I deserve you deserve too. I'm gonna make it happen for you too. We gon' fly back to Brooklyn tomorrow and life will begin," Javona told Lissette.

They spent two days in Dallas and then they boarded a flight back to New York. It was like old times for Javona and Lissette. Both girls had seemed to bury the hatchet and there seemed to be no hard feelings. When they landed at JFK, Blade and Armon picked them up. The mood was light and even happy. They pulled up to a beautiful new condo building downtown near Atlantic center where Jay-Z was planning on putting a new basketball stadium when the Nets changed from the New Jersey Nets to the Brooklyn Nets.

"Yo' I could never repay y'all for this shit right here," Lissette said as she looked around at the beautiful fully furnished pad. She walked through it and admired the hardwood floors, large airy windows and all of the ultra modern furniture.

"You don't have to repay us, but you do have to come and party with the Munoz family tonight . . . in your honor," Armon said smiling. Lissette's face got serious for a minute.

"You ok?" Javona asked when she noticed Lissette's facial expression. Lissette seemed to snap out of whatever it was that caused her reaction. She shook her head from left to right real quick.

"Shit . . . girl I'm more than alright. I'm fuckin' overjoyed!" Lissette exclaimed. Something about her words seemed phony to Javona. She knew Lissette very well. But, Javona wasn't going to argue or press the issue right now.

"We'll be here to pick you up at eight p.m. for your party. Be ready," Armon told Lissette.

"A'ight. I'll be ready," Lissette said as she watched the Munoz family leave.

Blade picked Lissette up as planned. When they pulled up to the club in the city, Lissette's heart fluttered. She hadn't partied in so long. She went inside and noticed how beautifully the place was decorated. There was a huge neon sign that said "Welcome Home." Lissette smiled when she saw Javona. "That outfit turned out to be perfect for you . . . you look hot," Javona complimented Lissette on the beautiful Diane Von Furstenberg shirt and jeans she had left for Lissette to wear.

"Yeah but these shoes right here are hard as hell," Lissette complained jokingly.

"Bitch those are Christian Louboutins you better not complain about them shits . . . they cost a grip," Javona laughed. They went to the VIP section and let the party begin. There were plenty of drinks passing amongst them. There was a beautiful cake too.

"Let me say a toast," Javona stood up. It was midway through the night and her words were slurring already. "To my girl Lissette who is a real rider. She rode for our family and that is why we are all able to be here today," Javona slurred some more. "Bitch you a real friend," Javona said, knocking her glass against Lissette's. Armon was laughing at his drunken wife.

Just then Lissette stood up. She was rocking on her feet too. She had one hand up holding her glass and one hand behind her back. Everybody looked on with lazy grins on their faces. They were all bent.

"I just want to thank y'all for keeping my commissary piling while I did that bid. I also want to say that sometimes revenge takes longer than we think," Lissette said. She pulled her hand from behind her back.

"Oh shit!" somebody screamed but it was too late. Bam! Bam! Two shots rang out. "That's for the sins of your father. He killed my family," Lissette belted out after she let the shots off. Screams erupted everywhere and people started scattering in every direction.

"Get that bitch!" Blade screamed. More than fifty shots rang out after that. Lissette's body crumpled to the floor.

"Help! Help!" Javona exploded. She was holding Armon's limp body in her arms rocking. His chest was completely wet with blood. "No! Armon you can't die!" she hollered. All she could do now was hope that he would live.

Beauty and The Streets

by

JaQuavis Coleman

Prologue

Madison lay naked on the king size hotel bed while counting stacks of hundred dollar bills. While lying on her stomach, she glanced back at Jah who was running the cash through the money machine. Jah passed a stack of bills to Madison so that she could recount it and put it in rubber bands. A tightly rolled blunt hung from his lip as he stood shirtless with a pair of baggy denims on. The butt of Jah's chrome .45 pistol stuck out of his waistline as he took a long drag of his blunt and blew smoke circles. Madison smiled and admired her man who was a natural born hustler. He was just over 300 pounds and six-foot-three, most people would call him a "big boy", but his swagger and charisma made him the most sought after hustler in Detroit. Jah's baldhead and neat full-beard turned Madison on every time she looked at him.

"I love you Jah." Madison said sexily as she wrapped a G-stack in a rubber band and tossed it in the duffel bag at the foot of the bed.

"I love you too," Jah said in his deep raspy voice. Jah always took his time when he talked and his words come out slow and slurred. Jah ran the last stack through the machine and then took a deep pull of the spliff. He passed the last stack to Madison and then blew out the smoke. "We did it baby. That should be a million even, right there." Jah said as he sat next to his woman while she flipped through the bills.

"We did it baby!" she repeated as she banded the last G-stack and wrapped her arms around Jah's neck. They passionately kissed and Jah sat the blunt in the ashtray and grabbed the bottle of Moët Chandon from the ice bucket on the dresser. He popped the cork and took a swig of the champagne. That night was to be a night of celebration, because it was the night that Jah would officially retire from the streets and start his new life with Madison.

"I can't believe we are finally about to leave Flint for good. I wonder what Los Angeles is going to be like." Madison thought out loud as she continued to rub Jah.

"It's going to be beautiful." Jah said as he stood up and turned around so that he could face Madison. He pulled off the gun on his waist and sat the bottle on the dresser. He grabbed both of Madison's hands and took a deep breath. "Baby, you been down with me for so long and you are the only person that I ever loved or trusted. You ain't built like these other females and I admire that. What I'm trying to say is . . . I want to be with you forever." Jah said as he reached into his pocket and pulled out a small box.

Madison couldn't believe what she was seeing. He's about to ask me to marry him, she thought as she put both of her hands over her mouth and tears formed in her eyes. The only man she ever loved was about to make her the happiest woman in the world. Her hands began to shake as she watched Jah get on one knee and hold up the box in front of him.

"Oh my God, Jah." She said in a shaky voice as she looked into Jah's dark brown eyes. He displayed his perfect smile as he popped the box open, showing Madison the blinging four-carat diamond ring.

"Madison, will you be my wife?"

"Yes! Yes, I will!" Madison screamed as she threw her arms around her man and hugged him with all her might. Tears of joy flowed freely down her cheek as she hugged him and rocked back and forth. Just as she released him so that she could try on the ring, a loud shotgun blast ripped through the hotel's aluminum door. Two masked men entered immediately after; and before Jah could even reach for his pistol, the gunmen filled his body with slugs from the shotgun. One shot to the chest. Madison screamed at the top of her lungs as she saw the love of her life getting blown back from the blast.

"Noooo!" Madison screamed at the top of her lungs as she lunged for Jah. She immediately jumped on Jah's twitching body and watched helplessly as his eyes began to roll in the back of his head. "Jah!" she yelled—disregarding the masked men's orders for her to get up. She watched as Jah's life slowly left his body. His eyes stopped rolling and the twitching ended. His big brown eyes stared into space as he took his last breath. Madison cried and screamed as she gripped his corpse. She couldn't even hear what the men were instructing her to do; her only concern was her man.

A single shot rang out. A bullet went through Madison's back and she laid face to face with her love. In death, they eloped.

Chapter One

The Beginning

1994

"Jaheem, come help momma," Fallon said as she tied the belt around her arm and frantically searched for a vein. Jah sat in front of the TV. with tears in his eyes, knowing that it was time to help her mother take her "medicine". Fallon's fragile 105 pound body barely sat up straight in the wooden chair. "Come on, now." She added.

"Momma, I don't wanna do that anymore." He pleaded as he held his head down, trying not to witness what his mother was doing.

"Please baby. Help momma take her stuff so she won't get sick." She said in her kindest voice. Jah was only ten, but he knew that his mother was a heroin addict.

"Momma, please don't make do it. I hate do-ing that. It always makes you act weird." He said as he twiddled his fingers and let his tears fall freely. Fallon, tired of pleading with her young son, became angry. She snapped her head back and gave him a look that displayed hatred.

"Get yo' fat ass over here and help me!" she yelled degrading him as she frequently did.

Jah slowly and reluctantly walked over to his mother with his head buried in his chest.

"There you go baby. Be a good boy for momma." Fallon said as she tightened the belt around her arm and smiled. "Now, you know how momma likes it. Hold it nice and tight so I can find a vein for my medicine," she ordered. Jah had been helping his mother hold the belt for years and it hurt him more and more every time. The young Jah cried as he watched his mother poison herself with the dope.

Gino sat in front of the TV with a fifth of Jack Daniels in his hands. He had been drinking for hours and was waiting for his daughter to return home from school. He had been building up animosity most of the afternoon and he was anxiously waiting for Madison's return. The sound of the blasting television traveled through the small apartment

Madison walked through the door and she immediately recognized the strange look in her father's eyes. She then looked down on the floor and saw the bottle of liquor next to her father. She instantly tried to rush to her room to avoid the inevitable, but he stopped her.

"Madison!" he yelled in a drunken slur. "Come sit on Daddy's lap and tell me about school today. To avoid getting a beating, she didn't protest. She dropped her book bag on the floor and slowly walked over to her father. The closer she got, the stronger the scent of liquor invaded her nose. She reluctantly climbed his lap as he requested. Gino ran his hand through Madison's long thick hair.

Gino looked at his beautiful daughter and flashes of her mother popped in his head. He couldn't believe how much she resembled her mother. Her mahogany brown skin tone and jet black hair was exactly like her deceased mother. He smiled, remembering how much he was in love with Madison's mother when she was alive. She had been his wife of fifteen years before she passed. His smile quickly turned into a frown when he remembered how much he now hated her mother. It was her fault that he was infected with HIV. Her promiscuous ways caught up with her and she brought home the monster. He picked up his bottle and took a gigantic gulp of liquor before focusing on Madison's slightly developed breast. He slipped his hand under her shirt and she cringed at his touch.

"What's wrong? You know you like how that feels." He said as he began to fondle her.

"Daddy, I have homework to do," she said trying to elude what was about to happen.

Gino forcefully grabbed Madison's face and harshly squeezed her cheeks together.

"You know you like the way that feels. You're a whore! Just like your fuckin' mother!" He said just before backhanding her, causing her to fall off his lap and onto the floor. Gino stood over her and slid off his belt.

"No Daddy! Please don't! Please don't hit me." Madison pleaded as she balled up and held her hands up in attempt to shield herself. Gino paid no attention to her cries and struck her across the back twice, releasing his rage at her expense. She was about to feel the pain and agony that her mother had brought him. It was a twisted-type therapy for Gino to see Madison suffer. In his mind, he was hitting her mother and not her.

After minutes of beating her he pulled down his pants and pulled out his manhood. Madison was crying, but not because of the pain in her belly, but because of what she knew she had to do next. She rose to her knees and prepared to give her sick father oral sex. At the age of ten she was forced to please her father, completely stripping her of her innocence. He had never penetrated her, but if someone didn't stop the abuse soon—it was sure to come.

Chapter Two

Jah stood at the top of his apartment building and looked down at the rundown projects. His eyes watered as he thought about his mother's habit. He went to the rooftop every night, usually after his mother caught her "dope-fiend lean" and nodded off. The sound of the big metal rooftop door opening echoed and Jah didn't even look back, because he already knew who it was. He quickly tried to wipe his tears away so Madison wouldn't think he was a punk. She walked up behind him with tears also in her eyes and didn't say a word. She just stood next to him and looked below at the housing projects that they called home. Gino had finally passed out, allowing Madison to sneak out and meet Jah on the rooftop. After two minutes of silence, Jah finally looked over at Madison and noticed that her eyes were red from crying. At that point he already knew what had happened. Rage

overcame him and he balled up his small fist and
spoke.

"When I get bigger, I won't let 'em touch
you anymore. Just watch!" he said through his
clenched teeth. Jah and Madison had been best
friends since they were both seven and they
naturally clicked. They both lived in the same
building and were their parent's only child.
They both knew each other's dark secrets and
although they were both only ten years of age,
they both were forced to grow up much quicker
than the average adolescent.

Madison looked into Jah's eyes and understood that they shared the same pain. Just as
Madison was about to say something, the sound
of a man screaming stopped her. Both of their
eyes shot to the door that led to the rooftop.
Someone was coming up. Jah quickly grabbed
Madison's hand and pulled her behind one of the
chimneys to hide. The way the man was screaming, he knew something bad was happening.

The doors flew open and they saw two men
come up, one grabbing a bloody man by the
collar and practically dragging him to the roof.
A few seconds later another man followed close
behind. Jah immediately noticed the man's face.
It was Jah's idol, Brock Hartman. Brock ran the

whole city of Detroit and was a well known dope man in their community. Jah looked like he had seen a ghost, because it was rare that people had a chance to see Brock. Brock had on a dress shirt with his tie unloosened and his sleeves were rolled up. His worker dragged the yelling man over to the edge and held him by his collar, hanging the upper-half of his body over the ledge. They were inches away from Jah and Madison, but they didn't notice them. Madison was shaking and she gasped in fear as she thought about the possibility of a man dying right before her eyes. Jah put his hand over Madison's mouth and whispered, "Shhh be quiet. I got you."

The sounds of Brock's gators clicked the cement as he slowly walked over to the two men. Brock took a deep breath and looked at the projects that lay before him. A slight smile formed on his face as he looked at the man who begged for his life.

"Brock, please! Man, don't kill me man. I—" The man said just before Brock stopped him by waving his hand.

"Don't beg. At least have some mu'fuckin pride, nigga. Stop crying and man up. Let me ask you a question. Who gave you a job when you first got out of the joint, huh? When nobody would hire you!" Brock asked calmly. The man doubletalked trying to explain why he had been skimming off of the top and profiting off of Brock's heroin operation. Brock cut the man's begging off and repeated his question. "Who gave you a job and looked out for you?" Brock yelled as he reached in for his gun that was in the small of his back.

The man looked at Brock and hesitantly admitted, "You did Brock . . . you did."

Before the man could say anything else Brock sent a single shot through his forehead. Brock's henchman, Charlie B, pushed the man off the roof, launching him fifteen stories to the cement portion of the playground. Madison cringed at the sound of the gun blast and Jah held her tight trying to comfort her. He knew if Brock noticed them, they would be next.

"Shhh," Jah whispered again, when Madison began to breathe heavily. They watched as Brock wiped off the gun and tossed it behind the chimney right beside them. Brock and his worker exited the roof talking to each other, as if nothing happened.

"Oh my God, oh my God." Madison whispered as she rushed over to the edge and looked down at the man. Her young eyes glued to the man as he lay awkwardly on the ground stories below her. Blood surrounded his body and it was, by far, the most gruesome thing she had ever witnessed. Jah picked up the gun and stared at it. He didn't even pay attention to what Madison was saying, he just gripped the gun. A feeling of power overcame him as he clenched the iron in his palm. It was his first time ever feeling the cold steel of a gun in his hand. He pointed it and clenched one eye as if he was aiming at a target.

"Jah! Are you crazy? Put that thing down and let's get out of here." Madison yelled, snapping Jah out of his brief daydream. Jah looked at Madison who was staring down at the dead body and slyly slid the gun into his waistline.

"Madison, let's get out of here." He said as he felt the hot tip of the gun burning his inner thigh. The gun was still hot from the shooting. Jah was young, but he wasn't naïve to what would happen to them if they had told anyone about what they saw. He knew how powerful Brock was. He grabbed Madison by the hand and noticed that she was shaking uncontrollably and tears were in her young eyes.

Jah walked Madison to her door in silence. They both wanted to talk about what they just witnessed, but neither of them had the courage to say anything to each other. When they reached Madison's apartment door, she slowly turned the knob trying to not wake her father. Jah gently grabbed Madison's arm and whispered, "Don't tell anyone about what you saw tonight. Brock would kill us if we snitch, so keep your mouth shut—okay Madison?" Madison nodded her head in agreement right before she kissed him on his cheek. Jah watched as Madison slipped in trying to make the least noise possible. Jah blushed as he watched her close the door. He had a crush on Madison and he had been waiting for a long time to get the kiss that he had just received.

"That's going to by my girl, watch" he said to himself as he stared at the apartment's door.

"Yo' li'l ass think you slick, huh?" Gino said as he sat at the kitchen table, watching Madison attempt to sneak back into the apartment." Where the fuck have you been?" he asked sternly.

Madison's heart began to beat rapidly as she tried to think of a quick lie, but nothing came to mind.

"Me and Jah were—" She tried to say before he cut her off.

"Yo' li'l fast ass was with that boy from down the hall, huh!" he asked as he stood up and walked toward her. Madison instantly dropped her head and avoided eye contact with the monster she called her father. She didn't want to make him angry and feared that he wanted an encore from earlier that day.

"Answer me!" he yelled as he forcefully yanked her arm.

"Daddy, we were just on the roof." She said as she cringed from the tight grasp he had on her.

"Yo' li'l fast ass opening yo' legs huh? You think you grown? Well I'ma show you how to be grown." Gino suddenly pictured his wife and thought about Madison following in her infamous footsteps. So he backhanded her, making her fall onto the hard floor. He scolded her at the top of his lungs and began to unbuckle his pants. He was about to make Madison a grown woman in his mind. *She wants to be grown. . . . I'ma show her what grown women do*, he thought as he dropped his pants. Madison's cries for help fell on deaf ears as he climbed on top of her, violently ripping off her clothes.

"Daddy no!" she yelled as she tried to keep him off of her, but he was much too powerful for her young muscles. Gino placed his sweaty hands over Madison's mouth, while using his free hand to release himself from his boxers, and prepared to take over his own flesh and blood's virginity. One last muffled cry for help escaped Madison's mouth before Gino got the chance to cover it up completely. Just before Gino got a chance to penetrate, a loud thud startled him and the image of a young man pointing a gun at him appeared. It was Jah. Madison had forgotten to lock the door when she entered.

"Get the fuck off of her," Jah said as he stood there without a drop of fear in his heart. He held the gun steady, pointed directly at Gino's head.

"What the fuck you think you going to do with that li'l nigga? Huh? You going to shoot me? Boy, you better take yo' ass back down the hall to Fallon, before I tell her you've been a bad boy," Gino said as he stood up and inched toward the young boy. "Now, give me the gun."

"I ain't giving you nothing, homeboy. You okay, Madison?" he asked as he glanced down at Madison who remained on the ground weeping. Gino took advantage of the opportunity and lunged for Jah during the brief moment he took his eyes off of him. The loud boom from the .45 caliber pistol echoed throughout the small apartment. Jah dropped the smoking gun out of fear and watched as Gino flew back from a gun blast to the mid-section.

An uncomfortable silence arose as Madison and Jah watched as Gino struggled for air and blood leaked from his mouth. Jah's adrenaline began to pump and his legs trembled as he realized what he had just done. His chest felt like it had a baboon inside of it, trying to pound itself out. Madison stared at her father with a blank expression on her face, not knowing how to feel or react. She wanted to feel terrified, but her true emotions took control, and a sense of relief overcame her. While fighting for his life, Gino stared into the eyes of his only daughter—the one that he continually abused and molested for years. The gaze in Madison's eyes was that of hate and at that moment it was the first time he had felt guilt for what he had done. At that instant, Gino stop fighting and faced the inevitable. His body stopped moving and he reunited with his wife.

Madison sat on the stoop as flashing red, white, and blue lights gleamed everywhere around her. Yellow tape circled the front of the building and bystanders gathered around gossiping. Madison could overhear some of the older women giving their account on what happened.

"Yeah, that's Fallon's boy that their arresting. He just snapped and killed two niggas. Shit, he threw one off the rooftop! I knew that boy wasn't right in the head. With a momma like Fallon, you can't blame him."

Madison watched as the police restrained a yelling, kicking, and screaming Fallon so that they could cart Jah away. A female social worker was sitting next to Madison asking her questions, but she couldn't hear anything she was saying because her focus was on her best friend leaving her. She watched the police car pull-off and Jah glanced at her. They locked eyes and Madison watched until he was out of sight. She then she glanced over at the bloodstained, white sheet that covered the dead man from the rooftop. She quickly turned her head trying not to see the gruesome sight. Her mind instantly went on Jah and how he had slayed the monster that she called her father. Jah was her savior and she would always remember that.

A week later, Jah was sitting in front of a juvenile judge waiting to hear his sentence for murder. His young mind couldn't grasp the magnitude of what he had done a week earlier.

It was all like a daze to him—getting put in a cell, talking to a court appointed lawyer, and going through the motions. He kept hoping that his mother would come and save him but she never did. Actually she was in an alley getting high at the same exact time that he was standing in front of the judge.

"Do you have anything to say before the court sentences you?" the female judge asked as she looked down at the young Jaheem. Jaheem looked back at the courtroom—just to check and see if his mother was there, but of course she wasn't. However, he did see Brock and one of his right hand men, Charlie B, in the audience. Jaheem's eyes locked on Brock's and it seemed as if he was stuck. They locked stares and Brock released a small grin followed by a gesture. Brock put his index finger over his lip and then winked at Jaheem. For some reason, Jah felt safe. The look that Brock gave him said more than any words could. It was as if Brock was saying, "Keep your mouth closed and I will take care of everything else." Jah smiled back at Brock and then looked at the judge.

"No ma'am, I have nothing to say." He said in his low tone.

"I sentence you to incarceration at the Detroit Boysville Center until eighteen years of age." She said just before dropping her hammer on the gavel. The two guards took Jah by the arm and escorted him out. Just before they reached the door, Brock stepped in the path of them.

He grabbed Jaheem by the cheeks as if he was a concerned parent and bent down as if he was about to kiss him on the cheek. However, he whispered in Jaheem's ear. "You did good, son. You stood up like a man and didn't rat. I'ma take care of everything, trust me. I will see you soon." Brock said just before rising up and stepping to the side. Jaheem couldn't describe the feeling in his chest; he was unfamiliar with that feeling. He just got complimented by the man he idolized and wanted to be like. Although he was about to go into lockup, he felt on top of the world. He was now connected.

Immediately after checking into the detention center Jaheem could tell that he wasn't treated equally as the other juveniles. Upon entering, he got approached by a male guard letting him know that anything he needed would be provided for him and he didn't have to worry about anything. Brock had already made inside connections to ensure that Jaheem would have a smooth sentence. The other guards even began calling him "Brock's boy" and he received special treatment by all—even the warden.

The first time Brock came to visit Jaheem was about two weeks into his sentence. Brock came walking in and all eyes were on him. It was mid-winter, so Brock sported a long peacoat with the finest thread underneath. Brock resembled a lawyer more than a gangster, but somehow no one ever got it confused. His hood swagger reeked from out of his pours and his walk screamed "boss". He had a strong presence that was felt by everyone he came into contact with. The scent of Brock's cologne filled the room and the clean fresh scent made the males envy and the ladies lust. Jaheem sat at the visitor's table with butterflies in the pit of his gut, not knowing what to expect.

Brock sat across from Jaheem and smiled, gazing at the young boy trying to feel him out. Jaheem's chubby cheeks still showed his strong jaw line as he clenched his teeth trying to look as tough as he could.

"Do you know who I am?" Brock asked before he sat down.

"Yeah, everybody in the city knows who you are," Jah replied.

"How you doing li'l man?" Brock asked as he slid off his leather gloves. He chuckled at Jah as he tried his best to give him a tough-guy look.

"I'm good," Jah replied as he stuck his chin up and poked out his chest. Brock couldn't help himself. He released a chuckle and shook his head from side to side. Jaheem couldn't understand what was so funny, so he became agitated.

"What's so damn funny?" Jaheem said without fear, feeling slightly embarrassed.

Brock began to wave his hand in the air while lightly chuckling.

"Naw fam, I'm not laughing at you. You just remind me of myself so much. You are not scared of anything . . . you're fearless." Brock said. "I appreciate what you did for me and I will never forget that. You realer than a lot of so called gangsters and you are going to be a boss one day. Did you get those Jordans I sent you?" Brock asked.

"Yeah, thanks."

"And the money?" Brock asked referring to the thousand dollars he put in Jaheem's commissary. Jaheem nodded his head and lightened up a bit. "You don't have to worry about anything while you're in here. I got you. If you do this little stretch for me and keep your mouth closed, when you get out I will make it worth your while. If you need anything, let Lester know and I will make it happen for you." Brock said, referring to the guard that he had on payroll.

Jah had so many questions for Brock, but only one came to mind. "Can I ask you something?"

"Sure, anything."

Jaheem leaned in close to ensure no one else could hear what he was about to ask Brock. "Why did you shoot that man on the roof? What did he do that was so bad?"

Brock took his time before speaking and then took a deep breath.

"Sometimes you have to do things that you don't want to do. But as a man, you have to do it. It's rules to the game and if someone breaks them—" Brock stopped mid-sentence and knew that Jaheem's juvenile mind couldn't comprehend what he was trying to convey. He continued, "You will understand when you get a little bit older." Brock said, answering it the best way he knew how. Brock quickly changed the subject and began to explain to Jah that he was a made guy now. Brock promised Jah eternal loyalty and from that day forward Jah and Brock were family.

As for Fallon, six months after Jah was locked up she was found dead in her apartment from a drug overdose. This didn't come as a big surprise to anyone that knew her. With her heavy drug habit, it was inevitable. The facility released Jah for a day so that he could attend his mother's funeral and Brock was right there with his li'l man showing support. Shortly after, Brock became Jah's only family and he visited him everyday and made sure he was okay. Brock was only grooming him for the boss he would be when he was older.

Chapter Three

Madison's situation didn't turn out so nice either. After her father's death she ended up living with her grandmother who stayed in the same neighborhood. She thought about Jah everyday and always wondered about how he was and how he was doing. When Jah first went in, she would write him weekly but life eventually got in the way. Every week turned into once a month and once a month turned into once a year. Their bond slowly parted and the two best friends were strangers. Nonetheless, the old saying is: out of sight out of mind, and while Jah was away, Madison grew up.

Eight years later

Madison lay sprawled out on the king-sized bed completely naked. She stared at the ceiling fan spinning slowly and it sort of put her in a trance as she breathed heavily trying to catch her breath. She had just received the greatest oral sex from her man and he gave her a quick passionate workout. She watched as Brock, completely naked, walked over to his cherry oak desk that sat in the corner of his spacious bedroom. He opened up his candy jar and dumped a small pile of pure coke onto the table. Madison's eyes instantly grew as she became overly interested.

"Daddy, I want some," she said as she sat up and stared at the coke that sat before Brock.

"Oh you do huh," Brock asked sarcastically as he leaned over the table and used his nose as a vacuum for the blow. He quickly rose up and tilted his head back to prevent his nose from running.

"Come on. Make me a line, Daddy," Madison said in almost a whining voice as she stepped off the bed and displayed her curvaceous figure. Her small B-cups were perky and just a handful. But what she lacked in the chest, she surely made up for it in her ass. Brock stared at Madison's physique and the two plump melons that sat on her backside. Brock licked his lips and fantasized about being inside Madison once again. He had watched her grow from a little girl into a gorgeous woman and Brock had been enjoying Madison since her eighteenth birthday.

"You want another line baby? Come get it," he said as he dumped another pile on the table for her. Just as Madison was motioning toward him, Brock stopped her by holding up his hand. "Uh-uh. Crawl to me," he demanded as his eyes were glued to her neatly shaved lovebox. Without hesitation, Madison dropped to her knees and began to seductively crawl toward Brock. It was as if she was a lion seeking her prey. But in this case, the prey was the white content that waited for her on that desk. Madison reached Brock's feet and slowly began to run her tongue up his leg and onto his crotch. She took him into her mouth, making sure it was as wet as can be. Brock's toes curled as he looked down at Madison making his manhood disappear and re-appear while slurping him skillfully. Madison suddenly stopped and slowly rose to her feet. She used his pinkie to make a straight line with the blow and ran her nose down the line, getting every bit of the drug as her nose swept by it. Madison quickly threw her head back and smiled as the drug's magic instantly ran its course. She slowly began to walk over to the bed, switching hard, and making her assets jiggle with each step.

She knew that Brock's eyes were glued on her as she put on the visual show for him. She crawled onto the bed on all fours, showing her pinkness to him, knowing just what he liked. The blow had Madison on fire as her love button throbbed and her anticipation for intercourse began to build. Brock smiled as he held his rock hard tool in his hands and walked over to Madison. He was ready to put in work.

He quickly dropped his Armani slacks and then his silk boxers hit the floor. He made his way over to Madison, who was still on all fours and entered her from the rear. Madison threw her head back in pleasure as a small grunt escaped her lips. The sounds of her wet box echoed throughout the spacious master bedroom, only turning Brock on even more. Brock's pole was hard and thick; his veins showing through his tool as he went in and out of his younger lover. He thrust harder and his balls swung and smacked Madison's clitoris with each stroke. Madison was so horny and the drugs had her in a dream-like state. Brock's pace began to speed up and Madison's grunts turned into loud moans. Just as Madison began to feel an orgasmic sensation, Brock grunted loudly and fell on top of her.

"No, no, no," Madison whined and she pounded on the bed with one fist as if she was a kid. *Not again, this nigga only gives me two minutes . . . every time! Fuck!* She thought as she watched as he rolled over on his back breathing heavily.

"Come on daddy, let me get my nut." Madison pleaded, but it was to no avail because Brock was chasing sleep. Madison jumped up in anger and stormed to the shower. The lack of performance blew her high and she hadn't had a penis induced orgasm since she had been with Brock. I'm tired of this shit! *The nigga cannot hang,* she thought as she turned on the shower and stood under the hot water.

Her thoughts began to drift and the image of her father Gino trying to rape her emerged. She began to scrub her body, trying to scrub the smell of sex off of her which always reminded her of the gruesome experience Gino cursed her with. The thought of Jah shooting her father entered her mind and a small smile formed on her face. "Thank you Jah," she whispered as she did every night just before she said her prayers. In her mind, Jah saved her life and she would be forever thankful to him. The thought of him made her realize that he would be getting out soon. She couldn't wait to see her old friend.

***

Jah walked out of the facility with a plastic bag containing his walking papers and the clothes on his back. As the gates of the prison closed behind him he smiled as he experienced being free for the first time since he was twelve-years-old. He had stayed in juvenile until he was eighteen and then was shipped to Jackson Penitentiary on his eighteenth birthday. Jah smiled when he saw Charlie B leaning against a cocaine-white luxury Maybach with his arms crossed, smiling. Charlie B was Brock's right hand man and throughout the frequent visits, Jah had grown to love Charlie as well as Brock. They were the only people that came to see him and Brock had always promised Jaheem that once he was released he would take care of him for not snitching.

"What's good family?" Charlie said as he threw both of his arms up greeting Jah.

"What up nigga," Jah said as he approached Charlie, smacked hands, and embraced him.

"Welcome home," Charlie B said as he playfully punched Jah in the chest.

"Thanks, thanks," Jah said. "Where's the boss," Jah asked as he glanced into the back seat of the car, only seeing the black limo tint and his reflection.

"Oh yeah, he had to handle some shit back home. But he's waiting for you. He's going to be happy to see you, fam. Let's roll," Charlie B said as he walked over to the driver's side of the car.

"Cool," Jah said as he was just about to get in the passenger side.

"Jah! Yo, hop in the back." Charlie B said as he smiled and got into the car.

"For what? Jah thought as he shook his head and got into the back. As soon as Jah opened the back door he saw a pair of caramel legs with red pumps. He smiled as he got into the car finding three caramel colored women in the back with nothing but G-strings on. Jah already knew what was about to go down compliments of his man Brock.

Jah didn't get a chance to say two words before the trio of beautiful women pounced on him, licking him anywhere they could get their tongues on. Jaheem had been in lockup for most of his teen years, so sex didn't come often. He did have an experience with a girl a couple summers back when the female juveniles visited their camp for an annual baseball game, but other than that; he was inexperienced. One girl began to unbuckle his pants while the other one sucked on his neck, ripping off his button-up shirt. Jah squirmed as he was overwhelmed by the groping hands and tongues on different parts of his body. Before he knew it, his pants were pulled down, exposing his soft rod. One girl took Jah into her mouth, making his back arch in pleasure while another girl kissed him passionately. It wasn't long before Jah was erect displaying his curved pipe. Before the driver could even get off the block, Jah was involved in an all-out orgy. As one girl rode Jaheem's face, the other one sucked his balls—giving him an out-of-body experience. The third woman sat next to Jaheem and masturbated while softly moaning Jaheem's name. The sounds of her wet box drowned out the soft sound of Usher that played through the speakers. Her legs were spread as far as they could possibly go and her fat, bald lovebox was totally exposed.

Jah had physical and visual stimulation simultaneously and he was harder than he had ever been. His eyes went back and forth from the woman bouncing on his lap to the woman playing with herself. He reached over to help the third girl masturbate and seconds later she yelled out in pleasure as a small squirt launched into the air and her body began to quiver feverishly. The three girls alternated positions and not one second went by that Jah was not getting stimulated in some form. Brock really laid out the red carpet for Jah, showing his gratitude.

"Thanks Brock," Jah whispered as he lay sprawled out in the backseat catching his breath.

Madison walked around the house to make sure everything was perfect for Jah's homecoming. Balloons, champagne, and banners decorated Brock's luxurious home all in anticipation of Jah's return. Brock had invited his whole entourage to help him welcome the newest member of the crew, Jaheem. Although none of the goons knew Jah, Brock had talked about him for years and always called him the "king in the making" and Jah had respect because of that.

As Madison was putting the finishing touches on the decorations, Brock walked in the door.

"Hey baby," Madison said as she looked over her shoulder while she was taping a balloon to the wall.

"Hello beautiful," Brock said as he walked in.

"Hey Brock! He's not here yet, right?" Madison asked as she walked over to Brock and jumped into his arms, landing a big wet kiss on him. Madison was eighteen years old and her body had developed voluptuously. Her smooth ebony complexion and big brown eyes were any man's weakness. Her cinnamon highlights complemented her skin perfectly and to say the least—she was beautiful. She was heavy in all the right places and was the street's most wanted. That was the reason Brock had taken her under his wing and made her his woman. She was the hottest thing in the streets of Flint and Brock claimed her before she was even legal.

"What time is Jah coming?" Madison asked as she had excitement in her eyes and voice.

"Charlie B and the boys are picking him up now," Brock said. He looked down at his Movado watch and then at Madison's thick curves in the tight jeans she was wearing. His manhood began to rise as he thought about having her legs in the air while he gave her a tongue lashing. He loved the way her butt cheeks hung low and the sight alone was enough to make him orgasm. He grabbed her butt and pulled her close to him. "We still have time to get it in before they get here." Brock suggested as he looked down at her.

Madison looked up at the handsome man that stood before her and smiled. She loved his salt and pepper beard, displaying his maturity. His Gucci cologne reeked off of his neck and instantly turned Madison on. She grew up hearing gangster stories and myths about Brock and he was in front of her, in the flesh. He was the man of life and contained so much power; it was mesmerizing. She saw him for the second time when she was sixteen while on the block. He pulled up in a luxury blue Maybach, all-black tint. When the car pulled on the block, everyone knew who it was. You could feel the power coming from the car. When Brock rolled down the back window and called for Madison to come—it was a wrap. Madison had been with him ever since. Brock was a gentleman and never made love to her until she was eighteen, but by then he had already had her mind, body, and soul.

"Anything for you, Brock," Madison whispered as she dropped to her knees and began to unzip Brock's designer slacks. She pulled down his pants and just as usual Brock had brief drawers. Madison pulled out his slightly erect penis and took him into her warm mouth. Brock gently placed his hand on the back of her head and threw his head back in pleasure as he let her go to work. Madison gently rubbed Brock's balls as he slowly went up and down his shaft. She hummed while in action so he could feel the vibrations.

"Damn girl," Brock whispered as he began to stroke her mouth as if it was a vagina. He reached down and lifted up her blouse and bra so that her long erect nipples could show. He began to rub her nipples and palm her B-cups. "Let me taste that pussy," Brock said under his breath as he slid his dick out of Madison's mouth. Madison lay on the wooden floor, quickly unzipped her pants, and slid off her jeans. She wore no panties, so Brock didn't have to waste any time to get on his mission. Madison stuck her legs straight in the air just like Brock liked it. Her chubby lovebox sat up and her slightly pink clitoris peeked out of her lips, making Brock only hornier as he dropped to his knees and went to work.

Brock began to work his tongue, swiftly swiping it back and forth over her button as her juices began to trickle down to her other hole. Madison began moving her mid-section in circles as she gripped the back of Brock's neatly waved hair. "Ooh," she crooned as he stuck his two middle fingers inside of her and gently massaged her inside while searching for her G-spot.

"Brock you the best," she said as she felt a small orgasm approaching. Brock stopped in the middle of it all, and rose up. He was ready to penetrate her. Madison quickly rolled her eyes . She knew that the only way she would nut was if she did it by herself. Brock had a premature ejaculation problem and it never failed. Damn, why this nigga stop eating my pussy, she thought to herself as she put on a fake smile trying to stroke his ego. Brock was a master oral pleaser but his dick game was horrible. Madison knew that this ride would be short lived. Brock entered her and began to stroke her slowly. Madison moaned loudly as she spread her legs as wide as they could go. She grabbed his butt cheeks making him go deeper into her. Just like a charm, after the seventh or eighth stroke Brock was quivering and ready to explode. He pulled out and shot his creamy load on her stomach. He let out a loud grunt and he rolled over while sweating profusely. Madison screamed, faking an orgasm as she did every time they had sex. She quickly jumped up so that she could finish the job on her own in the bathroom.

"I'm about to go jump in the shower before everyone gets here," Brock nodded his head and watched as her plump backside disappeared into the hallway.

"Whoa, that girl goin' be the death of me," he said and he smiled and shook his head.

Chapter Four

Jah looked out the limo's window as they pulled into a gated community. It was a beautiful property in the suburbs of Grand Blanc, only a few miles outside the ghettos of Flint. Jah was feeling relaxed and slightly tired after his phenomenal sexual encounter. Their vehicle pulled inside the gate and parked outside a lovely string of condos. The driver got out to open the door for Jah while the girls continued to get dressed. Jah jumped out, leaving the girls in the car. Just as he stepped out, Charlie B pulled up behind him. Charlie jumped out smiling with a set of keys in his hands.

"Y'all doing it big. This is where Brock lives?" Jah asked as he got out and stretched while looking at the immaculate building.

"Naw, young blood. This is where you live. You already set-up in 40-A." Charlie said as he tossed the keys to Brock. Jah caught the keys and released a small grin. He nodded his head in approval and looked at Charlie in disbelief.

"Straight up?" Jah asked as he stared at the keys as if they were gold.

"Oh yeah. That's your Benz parked over there too. Compliments of Brock. Go up and get fresh. The limo will be waiting for you to take you to see Brock. We got something put together for you," Charlie said as he heading back to the car. Charlie signaled for the girls to jump in the car with him and just like that—they were gone. Jah stood there in awe as he smiled and looked at the brand new raven-black Benz that sat on chrome twenty-two-inch rims. "My nigga," he whispered as he made his way into the building.

Jah walked into the building and took the elevator to the fourth floor. The hallway was made of all marble floors and walls. The condos were soundproof, so silence filled the air as he strolled the halls. Jah had never seen anything like it. He felt like a million dollars as he approached 40-A. He entered the key in the keyhole and as soon as he walked in he was amazed. The spacious layout was fully furnished and the front glass window over looked the man-made lake that sat in the middle of the district. Jah smiled as he closed the door and began to observe his new place. He walked into the kitchen which was also open styled and ran his hands over the marble countertop.

"This is what I'm talking about," he said as he made his way into the living room where a leather sectional and circular glass end tables were. A fifty-inch flat screen was perfectly centered on the wall. He sat down and took a deep breath as he enjoyed his first day of freedom in a very long time. Flashbacks of the night he took Gino's life resurfaced in his mind. The main thing he remembered was the look of relief on Madison's face when Gino was on the ground breathless. Then he remembered the look in her eyes when the police officer drove away with him in the backseat. She looked heartbroken and there wasn't one night that passed that he didn't think of that beautiful face. He took a deep breath and promised himself he would find Madison once he got himself together.

He stood up and decided to take a look in the back to check out the rest of the condo. He peeked in the bathroom and it looked like a million bucks with porcelain everything. He thought to himself, *Brock overdid it with this one.* He went to the back bedroom and peeked into it and it was also fully furnace and draped in all beige and creme with a queen-sized bed. He was definitely amazed when he walked in. He plopped on the bed and felt the padded mattress against his back. He hadn't felt a bed so soft his entire life. "This shit feels great," he said as he closed his eyes and enjoyed the moment. However, it was short lived because he heard a noise coming from the other room. He quickly jumped up and looked around suspiciously. He listened closer and once again he heard movement in the next room. Jah slowly stood up and his mind began to churn. He didn't know who the fuck was in the condo with him. *Is Brock trying to kill me,* he thought to himself as he tried to figure out what was going on. He grabbed the steel candle holder off of the dresser and approached the door cautiously. He quickly opened the door and scanned the long hallway. He saw that it was another bedroom with the door closed. He slowly crept to the door and placed his ear on the door. He heard a cell phone buzz and he instantly knew indeed that someone was in there. He took a deep breath and bust into the door. What he saw, he couldn't believe—

"Ooh Jaheem. What took you so long?" the mystery lady asked. A thick Spanish girl with silky hair was naked with the exception of her red stilettos. Her legs were spread wide and her bald plump lovebox sat up and was smiling at Jah. She held a vibrator to her clitoris as it buzzed against her lovebox. She had been patiently waiting for Jah to enter so that she could please him. Brock had instructed her to give Jah any and everything he wanted; she planned on doing just that. Jah had barely recouped from the foursome he had just had in the limo. Brock was really laying out the red carpet for Jaheem and Jah wasn't mad at it.

"That wasn't a cell phone I heard," Jah said to himself as he licked his lips and stared at her thick body.

"What?' she asked in between moans.

"Nothing ma, nothing." He said as he dropped his pants and approached her. She took him on a wild ride and Jah was living heaven on earth.

Hours later, Jah had just stepped out of the shower and noticed that the girl was gone. He walked over to the bed and saw that she had left him a note. Don't worry, I let myself out. Had a wonderful time, the note red with a kiss print at the bottom for a signature. Jah was more than fine with that. He didn't have to have an awkward moment with the girl by asking her to leave, so he was content. He walked over to the closet and noticed that it was full of designer clothes, all his size. He had suits, street gear, and jogging suits to choose from. Jah was in awe at the magnitude of generosity Brock displayed. Jah slipped on designer jeans and a black hoodie, and at the bottom of the closet was his choice of everything from Timberlands to Gucci slippers. Of course, he opted for the Timbs and made his way down to the curb. Just as Charlie B promised, the limo was waiting to escort him to Brock's palace.

Brock, Madison, Charlie B, and various members of Brock's crew were in attendance as they awaited for their newest member to walk through the door. Brock had been waiting on this day for years and he wanted to show his gratitude to Jah for not snitching.

Madison was in her own thoughts as she contemplated about Jah. She never told Brock that she frequently thought of Jah, in fear that he would get jealous. *I wonder how he looks now. That boy saved my life,* Madison thought as she sipped on the glass flute that contained champagne. She often wondered how life would have been if Jah never came to her rescue and her father continued to raise her. For that reason alone, she would always have a place in her heart for Jah. She also knew that Jah was unaware that she was now Brock's woman. She didn't know how he would take it.

Anxiety overcame her and her heart began to pound quickly. She swiftly dipped into the bathroom to try to calm herself. She turned on the faucet, dipped her head over the sink, and splashed water in her face. She held up her head and looked into the mirror and into her own eyes. She saw the traces of red in her eyes and quickly looked away not wanting to look at herself. She knew that the long night of doing blow and drinking had given her a worn-out appearance. "Jah doesn't want you. You're a fuckin coke head," she admitted as she reached into her blouse and pulled out a small vial of powder. She quickly emptied the contents in between her thumb and pointer finger and used her nose as a vacuum. She knew that the drug would ease her up and make her more like herself. And just like a charm, she felt good. She made sure her hair was on point, put on lip gloss, and headed out to the party. Brock grabbed her by the waist and leaned into her ear.

"Slow down on that shit today. You've been sniffing that shit all day." Brock said, knowing why she had taken a little bathroom break. Madison sucked her teeth and rolled her eyes at Brock's remark and was about to say something back but Charlie B interrupted.

"He's pulling up!" he yelled as he peeked out of the window. Everyone got quiet and waited for the man of the hour to walk through the door. A few moments later the driver opened the door and in walked Jah.

"There's my boy!" Brock yelled as a cigar rested in between his teeth. He popped a bottle of champagne and the suds spilled onto the floor and eventually into a glass for Jah. Everyone clapped and welcomed him with open arms. Jah didn't smile, just nodded in approval as he made his way over to Brock's arms. Brock hugged him tightly and kissed him on the forehead. "Welcome home," Brock said with a gigantic smile on his face.

"Thanks," Jah said as he finally unleashed a small grin and took the glass of bubbly from his hero.

"Come on. Let me introduce you to the crew," Brock said as he threw his arm around Jah and only introduced him to his head street workers. "You know my man Charlie B already. This is Lola, she runs the fifth ward. This is my man Fat

Rat, he holds down the Southside. This is Black from Merrill Hood and this is—" Brock said as he paused and turned around so that they could face Madison.

"Madison," Jah said finishing Brock's sentence.

"Jah!" Madison screamed as she hugged him tightly. Jah wrapped his arms around her and closed his eyes enjoying the moment. They unleashed their embrace and Madison stepped next to Brock and he threw his arm around her waist.

"Oh yeah. Madison did mention that you guys were friends when you were kids," Brock said, blowing off their once close bond. Brock leaned down and kissed Madison as she rested her hand on his chest and giggled. That sight sent daggers through Jah's heart. However, he did his best not to display his broken heart and smiled to mask the pain.

"Yeah, something like that," Jah said as he looked into Madison's eyes and noticed that she avoided eye contact with him. On the inside he was bothered but he downed the champagne and didn't show his cards.

"Yo, listen up! I want to make a toast!" Brock announced as he held the bottle up. Everyone followed suit and did the same as all eyes were on Brock.

"This is to my man Jah. One of the realest niggas I know. He is cut from the same cloth as the old school gangsters and the true hustlers that wrote the rules to the game that these young cats live by today. He stood up and didn't fold like most cats would. For that . . . I am forever grateful. Jah will be the man one day soon. He is the future! To Jah!"

"To Jah!" everyone yelled in unison as they all lifted up their glasses and then downed their drink in honor of Jah. Jah also downed another glass of champagne and glanced over at Madison who snuck a sniff of blow while everyone toasted. His heart dropped as he saw her in that way. He knew at that point that she was off limits and too far gone. All he could do at that point is sit and watch her self-destruct.

The next couple of days was like a fog to Jah. The only thing he could think about was seeing Madison dip her head and sniff the cocaine. Nevertheless, he was out of lockup and it was time to make his own way. Brock had instructed him to meet on the North side of Flint so that he could put him down with the family business. Jah, no license and all, pushed the black Mercedes Benz down North Saginaw Street. The Dramatics lightly pumped through the subwoofers serenading Jah. Although a young man, he had an old soul. Brock understood that, so he left his favorite CD in there for Jah to bump. He slowly nodded his head to the beat, leaned back in the seat, while resting his right hand on the wood-grained steering wheel. In his eyes, the world was already his—he just had to go take it. He pulled up on Twelfth Street and just as promised, Brock was there waiting for him, leaning on his pearly white Cadillac truck.

Brock looked down at his Movado watch and smiled. "Right on time," he mumbled as Jah met him there at 12:00 P.M. on the dot. Jah pulled to the curb and hopped out.

"Good afternoon," Brock said smoothly as he rubbed his salt and pepper beard.

"Sup, big homie," Jah responded as he briefly locked hands with Brock.

"You ready?" Brock asked.

Jah just nodded his head in approval and they proceeded to go into the brick two-story house. As they walked into the house, the stench of cooked cocaine entered their nostrils and the sounds of water boiling perked their ears.

"This is your new spot. This is a twenty-dollar house, nothing more, nothing less. We keep it moving over here. We don't take no shorts," Brock said as he gave Jah a tour of the house. As they entered the kitchen they saw a skinny woman that looked to be in her early sixties with a robe on, house shoes, and a Newport cigarette sticking out of the left side of her mouth.

"Hey Brockie," she said as she rested her right hand on her hip and the other one stirred the cocaine that was in the Pyrex jar.

"Hey Lu Lu, I want you to meet Jah." Brock turned to Jah and continued. "Jah, this is Lu Lu. She got the best wrist game in the city. She does all the cooking and owns the house."

Jah nodded his head and stepped to her with his hand out. Lu Lu chuckled and slapped his hand away. "Boy come over here and give me a hug. I've been hearing about you for ten years. It feels like I already know you. Come give me some sugar," she said as she gently tapped her cheek. Jah smiled and stepped to her, giving her a peck on the cheek and a hug.

"Brockie I got it from here. You can gone and have a seat."

Brock threw up his hand and conceded. "I'm not gonna argue with you. Do your thing."

Although Lu Lu was an older woman and skinny, she still had her hips. Gucci house shoes were on her feet and she wore big hoop earrings accented with flawless diamonds. Her ear holes slightly sagged because of years of wearing big earrings but she wore them well. She dumped the crack cocaine onto the napkin so that they could dry and proceeded to go into the living room. "Follow me."

Jah did as he was told and within two hours he was up on game. She introduced him to all his workers and the procedures of the crack house. Jah's job was to make sure that everything ran smoothly and collect the money, never letting the stash get over $10,000. Once the money got to that point he would take it to Brock's stash spot so that it could eventually be put into Brock's safe.

Within a month's time, Jah had the house booming. He changed up the rules and let the fiends smoke inside the house so that it could be a one-stop shop; cop the crack, smoke the crack, and buy again. This was something that Brock never thought of, but Jah saw the potential and put the new policy in motion.

***

Madison noticed how Jah didn't show any interest in her and the lust that she had for him slowly drifted away as she focused on her drugs and shopping. Little did she know, Jah only ignored her out of respect for Brock and didn't want to catch feelings for her. With the new-found rejection she went harder on the drugs; which in turn dampened her soul. With her increased blow use, her sex drive went sky high and Brock was not the answer. Although they sexed nearly every day, she hadn't orgasmed on a dick in months. Her orgasms were always self-inflicted and it was building up a fire that she was going to eventually have to put out.

Chapter Five

Madison was sprawled out on the bed, moaning in pleasure, as she slowly moved her fingers in swift circular motion over her clitoris. The insatiable urge to orgasm overcame her when she woke up alone in Brock's bed. Brock fled earlier that morning for a business meeting with the construction company and left Madison unfulfilled. The lack-luster performance he put on last night wasn't merely enough for Madison, so she woke up ready to explode. Madison often had to go behind Brock and please herself just to get off and it frustrated her to the core. As she continued to play with herself her climax began to near, then—the doorbell sounded.

"Fuck!" Madison spat as the doorbell threw her off and interrupted her much needed sexual release. Madison, completely naked and frustrated, hopped out of the bed. She grabbed her silk robe off the vanity and quickly covered herself. As she stomped down the porcelain stairs, she cursed out whoever stood on the opposite side of the door for interrupting her session. As she made her way to the door, she tied her robe tightly making sure that she wasn't exposed. Madison opened the door and a familiar face was on the opposite side of the door.

"Oh, it's just you," Madison said without enthusiasm as she looked at Charlie B.

"Yeah, whatever," Charlie said as he slightly smiled. "Yo, where Brock at? His phone going straight to voice mail."

"He went to a meeting earlier. He said he would be back later this evening," Madison responded as she gripped her robe, covering herself up. Charlie B's eyes wandered down to Madison nipples which were slightly erect and showing through the robe. Involuntarily, he licked his lips and Madison watched as he did his best LL impersonation. Madison curled her toes as the sight alone turned her on. Her lovebox was already soaking wet, but now it began to pulsate. She never looked at Charlie B in a sexual nature, but her clitoris was rock hard and the slightest gesture made her pulsate. Charlie B noticed her sudden discomfort and he looked down at her toes and saw that she had curled them. He was an OG and he knew what that meant o' too well. He then looked at the silhouette of her figure through the robe and he too got aroused. His rod's prints began to show through his Armani slacks and Madison couldn't help but to look. Her eyes got big as she saw how well endowed he was. She cleared her throat and tried to not seem so obvious.

"Well, I will tell him you came by." Madison said wanting to end the inappropriate encounter.

"Yeah, you do that." Charlie B said slyly with a smile. Madison returned the grin and slowly began to close the door. Madison was horny as ever and was ready to go upstairs and masturbate to the thought of what she had seen in Charlie B's pants. Just before she closed the door, she saw Charlie's foot stick in. She quickly opened the door back.

"May, I help you?" she asked as she looked at Charlie B who was once again licking his lips.

"I really have to piss. Can I use the bathroom?" he asked.

"Yeah, but hurry up. You know Brock doesn't like anyone here if he's not home." She added.

"I'll make it quick." Charlie B said as he stepped in and made his way into the house. Charlie took another glance at Madison's hard nipples and brushed passed her making sure his elbow rubbed across them. Madison closed her eyes as the tingly sensation shot down her back and went down to her clitoris.

"Ooh," she whispered, not being able to contain herself. It was as if the words slip out of her mouth. Charlie continued to the bathroom and began unzipping his pants while walking to the half bathroom just off to the left of the kitchen. At that point, Madison was drenched wet. Her inner thighs were soaked and couldn't wait until Charlie left so she could get herself off properly. Charlie B disappeared into the bathroom and Madison couldn't stop her hands from making their way down to her lovebox. Just the slightest touch would make her explode and she couldn't wait. She quickly snatched her hand back up and decided to go get some water out of the kitchen. As she walked past the bathroom door, she took a glance and what she saw made her stop dead in her tracks. Charlie B's meaty rod was in his hand as he stood in front of the toilet. He purposely left the bathroom door open, hoping she would walk by—and she did. Charlie turned so that he would be facing Madison and slowly stroked his rod which was growing by the second. Veins began to show throughout his manhood and he stood firm.

"I won't tell if you won't," Charlie B whispered, knowing he had Madison in the palm of his hands. Nine times out of ten, Madison would have dismissed the advance, but she was so horny and in need of a hard dick she could not resist. Madison dropped her robe, exposing her thick naked body, and began to slowly rub her clit while exposing her pinkness. She looked down at Charlie's rod and noticed how thick and juicy he was. He had Brock beat and she wanted to get some good dick for a change. She slowly walked to the kitchen counter, switching hard, making her thick butt cheeks shift weight from side to side for Charlie B to watch. Charlie B followed while letting his pants hit the floor. Madison jumped bent over the counter and spread her legs widely.

"We have to hurry up. Come on daddy," she said as she began to play with herself, rubbing herself furiously, striking her love button with every motion. Wet slurping noises echoed throughout the kitchen and small moans escaped Madison's lips in pleasure. Charlie had always wanted to sex Madison but never attempted because of his strong bond with Brock. But he wasn't about to let this opportunity pass to sex a beautiful woman half his age. He saw her chubby, neatly shaved lovebox hanging from the back and made his way over. He slid into her from the rear as the loud slurping noise filled the air.

"Oh my God!" Madison screamed as she felt his thickness enter her. She parted her legs wider for easier access. She began to move her hips as if she was dancing and she smacked her butt against Charlie's pelvis making loud clapping noises. Charlie B looked down at the young woman working him and the rippling effects going through her ass seemed like ocean waves.

"Just like that, baby," he coached as he began to pump. His balls swung back and forth with each stroke, each time hitting his love button. Madison began to moan louder and Charlie B couldn't control himself. He quickly pulled out and ejaculated on the floor as his legs began to wobble. "Oh shit," he said as he stroked himself and jerked violently as he released himself.

"No in the fuck you didn't," Madison said as she turned around with a major attitude. Can't fucking believe this shit," she said as she—once again—was deprived of an orgasm. "I can't believe y'all niggas!" Madison said as she stormed over to her robe and covered herself back up. Charlie B was looking confused not knowing what she meant about "Y'all" and he couldn't find the words to defend himself.

"You can show yourself out!" Madison said as she stormed out of the room and up the stairs mumbling under her breath. *That wasn't even worth cheating,* she thought as she made her way to the bedroom and to the candy jar. Maybe a line of coke would make her feel better—since Charlie B could not.

"Great! Thank you, Mr. Williams," the burly white man said as he shook Brock's hand. They stood on a construction site sealing the deal, all of them wearing hardhats. Jah was also in company. Brock wanted to expose Jah to the business-side of the game as well as the drug distribution portion.

"No problem, Dan. Nice doing business with you," Brock answered just before he walked away with Jah.

"This new sports bar is going to be what I need to retire from the game," Brock said as he put his hand on Jah's shoulders. Jah remained quiet but nodded in approval. "The dope game is a young man's game," Brock added, as he stopped just as they were out of earshot of Dan. "Once this bar gets built—I'm done with the game.

"You are going to really let your empire go?" Jah asked not understanding how Brock could let his whole operation go so easily.

"No, I'm not going to let it go exactly . . . I'ma pass it down to you." Brock answered.

"What?" Jah asked not believing what he was hearing.

"Yeah, it's time for you to come into your own. You were built for this. Niggas like you are cut from a different cloth. You are young, but you move like a wise man and live by principles. I knew you since you were a little boy and I know that you are one hundred percent. You didn't fold, you didn't rat. I am forever indebted to you. If this is the life you want to lead, I'ma set you up right. It's your time to be the boss. I knew you were going to be a boss since you were a youngin." Brock said, meaning every single word he said. "So, you ready?" Brock asked.

"I'm ready," Jah confirmed as a slight grin formed on his face. Brock was ready to give it all to Jah. Only time could tell if he could handle it or not.

On the ride home Jah rode shotgun as old school Marvin Gaye bumped through Brock's speakers. They both remained silent and bobbed their head in unison to the smooth music that the legend created. Jah loved Brock's smooth style and knew that one day he would sit behind the wheel of a luxury car just as Brock did, wearing the finest threads and with the world in his palms. Power was alluring and it was what Brock had. Jah was turned-out already. As they were riding, Brock's phone rang. He slightly turned down the volume to the system and answered.

"Hello," Brock said in a low even tone. Brock paused and listened to the person on the other end of the phone. He smiled and thought about what he was going to do when he got home. It was one of his many women on the other end telling him how horny she was and wanted him to come and lay it down. "I can take care of that," he said just before he told her bye and hung up the phone. The thought of sexing a woman made him think of Madison who was at home.

"You and Madison used to be real tight back in the day, right?" Brock said remembering that Madison had mentioned how close they were. Brock also knew that Jah had killed her father on her behalf.

"Yeah, something like that. That was a long-time ago though," Jah said brushing off his true feelings. Jah always thought about how he would find and wife Madison when he was released, but never in his wildest dream would he have thought that she would end up with Brock. But that's how life was sometimes—the unexpected had become a reality. The one girl that Jah had always loved was now the lover of Brock. Brock was the only person that held Jah down while he was locked up and Jah would always remember that. He was loyal to Brock and vice versa.

"That li'l bitch is wild, you hear me?"Brock said as he shook his head from side to side and smirked. Jah gritted his teeth at the sound of Brock calling Madison a bitch but he quickly relaxed not wanting to show that he cared.

"Oh yeah, why you say that? Ain't that your girl?" Jah asked trying to find out the real.

"Hell no, that's not my girl. I'm a rolling stone, young blood." Brock said as he slowly bent the corner. "I just keep the bitch around because she got a good shot of pussy. I keep her ass high and she keeps me fucked good. We have a good arrangement," Brock said proudly. Jah sat back and listened and realized that Brock didn't give a damn about Madison and she was just his sex toy. He knew that Brock was taking advantage of Madison—just keeping her around to sex her and it bothered him. Madison thought that Brock was her man, but Brock couldn't care less about her.

"So, she's just your—" Jah started but was cut off by Brock.

"My li'l bitch. I just keep her around because I can. She's a fuckin coke head and wild as ever. She crashed three of my cars this year. Driving fucked up and high—not giving a fuck. At least once a week I have to send one of my goons to a club to pick her up because she's passed out at the bar. Tell the truth, I'm getting tired of her ass," Brock admitted.

"Well, cancel that bitch," Jah said trying to cover up his true feelings for Madison. Jah knew how bad Madison had it as a kid and felt as if he was her protector. He wanted Madison to get away from Brock because he was helping her spiral downward by feeding her the drugs.

Just like Brock felt indebted to Jah—Jah felt the same way toward Madison. He was supposed to be her protector and the guilt of being absent burdened Jah. He had to figure a way to save Madison from herself. He just had to figure out how he was going to accomplish that.

"How is that spot I set up for you?" Brock asked referring to the dope house on the eastside of Flint that Brock had given him.

"We are doing numbers. I can't complain." Jah said modestly. Brock smiled and knew that

Jah was made for the streets. Jah was copping twice as much dope weekly than Brock's other lieutenants and was moving up in the ranks fast. Jah had only been out for three months and he was already copping half bricks. Not a bad quality for an eighteen year old.

"What are your plans for tonight?" Brock asked as he briefly looked over at Jah.

"Nothing too important." Jah answered.

"I need you to make a run with me." Brock said as he reached into his ashtray and pulled out a perfectly rolled joint.

"Enough said."

Chapter Six

It was just before midnight and Brock and Jah were strolling down the sidewalk along the Flint River near downtown. The sound of the water was the only noise that could be heard and the moon's blue light illuminated the area. Brock had asked Jah to join him on that night and Jah didn't know why, but he would soon find out. Brock had been less talkative than usual and it seemed as if something was on his mind and bothering him. Jah tried his best to read Brock and find out what was the issue with him.

"It's a beautiful night," Brock said as he strolled carefree while having his hands stuffed into his Armani slacks. Jah remained silent as his hands were stuffed into his hoodie, right hand on the chrome .45 Brock had given him.

"I know you didn't call me out here to talk about the weather. What's up?" Jah asked modestly but getting straight to the point. Brock chuckled.

"That's what I like about you. You don't fuck around," Brock said smiling. "I wanted to talk about the future. I am getting too old for this game and I see the end. Everybody thinks Charlie is the next in line to takeover—I think otherwise."

"What are you saying?" Jah asked. Brock stopped walking and turned toward Jah.

"I want to introduce you to someone," Brock said as he looked over the river's dock. It was a man on the boardwalk with a fishing pole. Jah didn't understand, but he soon would learn that Brock was plugging him with his out-of-town heroin connect. Jah was about to step into a world that all dope boys dreamed about.

Madison pushed Brock's drop-top Porsche down I-75 doing just over one hundred miles per hour. She dipped her head down to take a line of coke that sat on the dollar bill in her lap. "Whew!" she screamed as she jerked her head up and sniffed. It was Saturday night and she was ready to party like a rock star as she did almost every night on Brock's dime. The perk to being Brock's woman was the luxury cars, money to blow, and grade-A cocaine to sniff at her leisure.

Madison was living the life. Madison had only seen Brock briefly that day and he was in and out, so that was good for her. The guilt of sexing Charlie overwhelmed her and she decided to go out and try to forget the deception.

She looked over at her passenger who was a female she had just met earlier that day. Madison didn't even know her name but she didn't care because she just needed someone to party with. Her only true friend was the blow that she rammed into her nose daily.

"What's your name again?" she asked.

"Tawana, for the millionth time," she said with a smile as she sniffed coke off of the nook between her thumb and pointer finger.

"Oh yeah . . . Tawana. Let's hit the Purple Moon next," Madison said referring to the second club they would have visited that night. Madison sped down the highway and got off on the exit of the club. As usual, it was packed and the line was around the building.

Madison pulled up to the front where the valets flocked to her car, noticing the luxury vehicle and Madison's familiar face. Madison always tipped well and the valets were all battling for the chance to get the tip. Tires screeched and all eyes were on Madison as she hopped out of the car and tossed her keys in the crowd of valet boys. They all lunged for the keys similar to desperate women at a bouquet toss. Madison smiled as she bypassed the long line and headed to the front. She approached the doorman and smiled.

"Hey Bernie," she said as she stuffed a hundred dollar bill into his top pocket making him smile. He immediately opened up the velvet rope for Madison and her friend to enter the packed club.

"Good evening, Miss Madison." Bernie yelled as he caught a glimpse of her body in the black tube dress that she wore. It hugged her hips so tightly; it left nothing for the imagination. Her black stilettos only enhanced the look of her fat rear end which made every man lust and every female envy her. She headed into the club and the bass of the DJ's subwoofers made the floor tremble. Madison headed straight for the bar and had a seat. She left the girl she entered the club with, not caring where she went.

"Give me a double shot of Patron, Darese," she said to the bartender. Darese rolled his eyes knowing that that was the beginning of many shots and he would have to pick her up off the floor after she got hammered as he usually did every weekend. The end result would be him having to tell the owner, who was friends with Brock, to call him to have someone pick Madison up. Darese rolled his eyes and hesitantly poured her the shots and would have denied her but he didn't want her to go and tell Brock and have his life in danger. Brock ran the city—and theoretically, so did Madison.

Madison slammed the shots and asked for a couple more. Before long she was tipsy and feeling good. She danced in her chair as she put both hands in the air feeling the sounds of Rihanna's newest single. She swayed her hips back and forth while sitting down, gaining the attention of a young hustler by the name of Harry-O. The dark skinned, slim built man approached Madison after watching her all night. He loved her curves and wanted to see what she was about.

"How you doing, ma?" he asked as he leaned into her ear while having a bottle of Moët in his hand.

"What? Boy, you betta gone," Madison spat back while waving her hand in dismissal. She knew that every little thing she did got back to Brock in some way or fashion. She was shocked that a nigga even approached her. Everyone in the city knew she was Brock's girl so she didn't get approached often, especially in the club Purple Moon—an establishment Brock co-owned.

"It's like that?" the hustler asked as he stepped even closer to her, letting her smell his Creed cologne.

"Do you know who I am?" Madison asked conceitedly as she took a sip of her Long Island Iced Tea.

"No, I don't. If I did—I wouldn't have asked for your name." he said as he moved the toothpick that was hanging from the corner of his mouth. He extended his hand and continued. "Anyway, I'm Harry-O. I'm kind of a big deal." He said only half jokingly.

Madison couldn't help but to laugh and she shook her head at his arrogance. "If you knew what was good for you, you would keep it moving. I belong to Brock. You know him, right? Madison asked, already knowing the answer.

· "Yeah, I know who he is." Harry-O said just before he took a swallow of his champagne. "But I don't give a fuck about that nigga. I got money too." He said as he smiled.

"You crazy, you know that?" Madison asked as she looked around to see if anyone was watching.

"Yeah, I know. But listen, I see you not interested now, but if you ever do get interested—here is my number." He said before he reached into his pocket and pulled out a napkin. He put it on the bar and Madison just looked at the napkin while sipping her drink. "Look under that napkin," Harry-O suggested.

Madison was curious and did as she was told. She peeked and saw a small baggy full of blow. Harry-O had watched Madison sniff blow all night and saw it was an opportunity to get in good with her. He would love to have the bragging rights to bagging Brock's girl and he knew that the door of opportunity opened that night—so he stepped straight through it. Madison saw the fish scale look in the coke and quickly slid the napkin and blow into her purse. She smiled and winked at Harry-O just before spinning toward the bar and finishing her drink. Harry-O smiled back and walked away, hoping to hear from her again.

Brock and Jah were approaching Brock's car, each with two duffel bags in their hands. Brock had just introduced Jah to the Dominican connect and was setting him up for the future. In twenty years, Brock had never introduced anyone to his plug, but he knew that Jah was the exception. He was now grooming Jah to be the next big thing. Just as they loaded up the car and put the duffel bags in the trunk, a car slowly pulled down the street. Jah quickly closed the trunk and put his hand on his banger that was concealed in the front pocket of his hoodie. As the car got closer Jah saw that it was a police car. His heart began to beat rapidly and the only thing he could think about was how much prison time that the dope could get them if caught.

"Heads-up," Jah whispered as he threw his head in the direction of the approaching cruiser. Brock slowly stepped to the curb of the street as the cop approached.

"You got my li'l man over here nervous," Brock said to the black cop who rested in the driver's side of the cruiser. They enjoyed a chuckle, just before Brock reached to the back door of his car and opened the door. Brock reached in, retrieving the bulky brown paper bag. He then tossed it in the car quickly and just as quick as the police officer pulled up—he was gone.

"Let's get out of here," Brock said as he just showed Jah how to cover his ass from all angles. "One hand washes the other. You have to make sure everybody eat in this business if you want to be successful." Brock said as he started his car and smoothly pulled off.

Brock's phone began to buzz on his hip and he quickly retrieved it. He sat and listened to the person who talked on the other end and began to shake his head in disgust. He quickly pushed the end button on his iPhone and continued to shake his head.

"Yo, I need a favor." Brock said as he looked over at his protégé.

"What up," Jah asked.

"Go get that dumb bitch. She un' passed out at the bar again," Brock said as he picked up his phone to dial up another one of his mistresses for entertainment that night. He didn't feel like dealing with Madison that night anyway, he had a surprise for her that he was planning the next day. He didn't want to see her until then.

"I got you," Jah said.

"Let's drop these off at the spot first," Brock said right before he pulled off.

The club was mostly empty and the lights were on as Madison rested her head on the bar. Darese was cleaning the bar top, getting ready to finish his shift. Jah walked in and a guard was at the door. He attempted to search Jah, but he wasn't having it. He shot the guard a cold stare and let the butt of his gun be noticed as he slightly pulled it out of his front hoodie. The security guard stepped to the side, not wanting any part of Jah. Jah looked over to the bar and Darese immediately knew who he was looking for. Darese waved him over and Jah preceded to the bar. Jah approached Madison and shook his head from side to side as he looked at her drool on the bar while having her hair all over her head.

"She's been out for almost an hour," Darese said as he stopped wiping the bar and rested both of his hands on the countertop. Jah reached into his pocket and pulled out a hundred dollar bill and laid it on the bar top for Darese. He began to lightly smack Madison on the face trying to wake her up from her drunken slumber.

"Come on ma. Let's get you home," Jah whispered in Madison's eyes, making her slightly raise her head. He threw her arm around his shoulder and scooped her up. He held her close and although Madison was belligerent—it felt good to hold her. He grabbed her tightly and carried her across the floor as he made his exit.

Madison clung to him tightly and drunkenly whispered, "Thank you Jah," her gratitude sent chills up his back. Although Madison was wild, spoiled, and turned out; Jah still had a deep love for her. She was the only woman that he had ever loved in his whole entire life and it seemed like all of her flaws made her more alluring. Jah took her to the car and sat her in the passenger's seat. He gently closed the door and made his way to the driver's side. Before he reached the other side, Madison had opened the door and threw up all of her drinks.

"Oh God," Madison yelled as she sweat and breathed heavily. She began gagging and heaving and the second round shot out of her mouth like a faucet. Jah rushed over and pulled her hair back. "Don't get it on my car," Jah said as he slightly laughed at her heaving.

"Shut up Jaheem," Madison said as she smiled and looked up at him. "I'm not going to mess up your car." Madison felt a tad better after she released. She was more embarrassed than anything. She spit and then sat back in the car. Jaheem closed the door for her and then returned to the driver's side and got in. She ran her fingers through her hair trying to fix herself up. "I know I look a mess." She said.

"Yeah, you fucked up," Jah said as he pulled out of the parking lot.

"Whatever." Madison said.

"You good now?" Jah asked in concern.

"Yeah, I'm okay. Why you act like you care anyway?" Madison asked in a slurred voice as she continued to run her fingers through her hair.

"What are you talking about? You're drunk Madison," Jah said.

"So! You don't care! If you did . . . you wouldn't have left me." Madison screamed belligerently.

"What . . ." Jah asked as her words served as daggers straight to his heart.

"I needed you. You were my protector. You were all I had," Madison said. Although she was drunk, Jah knew that the words were coming from her heart. Jah was her only protector and when he got locked up he involuntarily sent her to the wolves. Madison leaned her head against the passenger's glass window and stared outside. Her big brown eyes were like kryptonite to Jah. He glanced over and for a slight second, he envisioned her as a little girl—The same girl that he fell in love with, the same girl that he rescued from her perverted father. Jah focused back on the road and he felt his heartache because he knew that he was right.

"Madison . . . I didn't mean to leave you. Honestly, if I had to do it over, I wouldn't change a thing. Those years I spent locked up were well worth it. What that man did to you, he deserved to die. I know that you have had a rough life but you don't have to let your past dictate your future. I see the path you going on and it doesn't look good. When I look at you I still see that beautiful little girl that . . ." he paused and looked over at Madison and saw that she had fallen asleep. He smiled at how quickly she had nodded and finished his sentence.

"That I loved." He took her home and put her in the bed just as Brock had asked. Just before he left, he kissed her forehead and whispered in her ear.

"I still love you."

Chapter Seven

Madison woke up to a banging headache as the morning sunrays crept through the window blinds. She sat up and rubbed her temples as her head pounded heavily.

"I feel like shit," she said as she tried to block the sunlight from her sensitive eyes. She looked to the left to check for the time and noticed it was just a few ticks before noon. She honestly couldn't remember how she had gotten home. The last thing she remembered was taking patron shots at the bar with some girl. She saw a glass of water and two aspirins on the night stand.

"Thanks Brock," she whispered as she knew that he had left them for her. She quickly took the medicine and grimaced as the throbbing of her head continued.

The smell of bacon and eggs invaded her nose and sounds of food sizzling in the pan filled the air. Madison grabbed her robe and slowly made her way down the stairs. To her surprise, Brock was cooking. She smiled as she watched him maneuver his way through the kitchen like a veteran chef. Madison stopped halfway down the stairs and just smiled at Brock while he prepared the first meal of the day. His designer dress shirt was in tack while his sleeves were rolled up displaying his chiseled forearms. The apron on Brock fit well and he looked like the man of Madison's dreams.

Just as he poured the eggs onto two separate plates, he caught a glimpse of Madison staring at him from the stairwell.

"Good morning beautiful," Brock said as he released his nearly perfect smile. He quickly snatched off the apron and grabbed both plates off the counter. "Sit and have breakfast with me," Brock suggested.

"Aw, this is so sweet," Madison said as she made her way down the stairs. This was out of Brock's character and it really gave Madison butterflies. Her headache seemed to slowly drift away as she approached him. Brock, still having both plates in his hands, gave her a kiss on the forehead.

"Have a seat. Let's eat," he said as he made his way over to the glass kitchen table. As they sat down, Brock looked into Madison's eyes, without blinking once. Madison sat down, grabbed a fork, and began to eat her eggs.

"How did you sleep?" Brock asked.

"As you can see . . . I had a rough night." Madison said as she smiled and shook her head from side to side. Brock smirked and began to eat.

"Yeah, I know. You need to slow down baby." Brock said as he stuffed bacon into his mouth.

"Yeah I know," Madison admitted.

"I wanted to have a talk with you this morning." Brock said as he grabbed a napkin and wiped his hands and mouth.

"What's up," Madison answered.

"I have known you since you were a young girl. I remember the first day I seen you. You were only a baby. I knew that once you got older that you would be mine." Brock said as he gently brushed his hand over her forehead, removing the hair from her face. He continued, "Since you were eighteen years old, I have taken you under my wing and treated you like a first lady . . . first lady of the streets. You drive and crash the best cars, wear the finest clothes, and sniff the purest cocaine."

"I appreciate all of that Brock. What exactly are you getting at?" Madison asked not really understanding Brock's angle.

He continued as if he didn't even hear Madison. "All I ever asked of you is to never give my pussy away." Brock said as his slight grin turned into a scowl. Madison's heart began to pound rapidly as the words slid off his tongue.

"I wouldn't dare do that, Brock," Madison said as she thought about the small encounter she had with Charlie B.

"You promise?" Brock asked.

"I promise," she lied through her teeth.

"Madison baby," he said as he rubbed her and smiled at her. "I love you, Madison." He said.

"Love you too daddy."

"Let me show you something," Brock said as he smiled and reached out his hand for Madison. She grabbed willingly and followed him as he led her to the basement door. Madison was surprised because Brock never let her go into the basement where he claimed he handled business.

"Oh my God. You're letting me into your man cave," Madison asked as she felt anxious like an excited young girl who was getting a gift.

"Yes, baby girl. Today is a special day. I have a big surprise for you." Brock said as he opened the door and stepped to the side so Madison could go first. "Ah ah . . . don't peek," Brock said playfully as he gently placed his hands over her eyes and walked behind her.

"This is so nice daddy. What is it?" Madison asked as she smiled from ear to ear.

"You'll see in a second. Did it just for you, baby girl." Brock said as he guided her down the stairs. They finally reached the bottom of the stairs and Madison couldn't wait to see what Brock had for her.

"Are you ready?" Brock asked as he stood behind her. Madison could smell the Gucci cologne lingering off Brock and she loved every minute of it.

"Yes! Let me see," Madison said as she clapped her hands together joyfully. Brock slowly slid his hands away from Madison's face and let Madison see the big surprise he had for her. As soon as Madison opened her eyes, her knees got weak, and her mouth nearly hit the ground. What she saw was something that would be etched into her memory forever. Brock slowly walked around and stood next to the hanging body of Charlie B. His hands was shackled by chains and hanging from a steel pipe. His body was battered and bruised while completely naked. Brock had beaten him all night and morning because of his disloyalty. He was barely breathing and covered in his own blood. A socked was jammed so deep in Charlie's mouth that only a small portion of it stuck out from his lips. Two of Brock's goons came from the back with bats in their hands. Madison dropped to her knees in shock and looked at Brock. Brock's small grin had transformed into a menacing stare as he took off his shirt so he wouldn't get blood on it.

"Hand me that," he ordered one of the goons. The goon handed Brock the steel baseball bat and Brock began to circle Charlie.

"I only wanted loyalty from you Charlie. You have been my right hand man for twenty years and this is how you repay me. I gave you love and you gave me your ass to kiss. You couldn't keep your nasty little hands off of my bitch huh?" Brock said as he continued to circle him while shaking his head from side to side. Charlie B mumbled something but he was incoherent and muffled. At that point, there was nothing that Charlie could say to Brock to alter his own destiny on that day.

"And you . . ." Brock continued as he turned his attention to Madison who was on her knees with tears in her eyes. "You ungrateful hood rat ass bitch. You think I didn't have cameras all around this palace? I'm the king of this town. Don't nothing move or happen in this city and I don't know about it. And for you to think I wouldn't find out something that happened in my house? You thought I wouldn't find out?"

"Brock, it didn't mean . . ." Madison tried to explain.

"Shut up bitch!" Brock said as he pointed the bat at Madison. "I just want you to sit and watch!" Brock barked just before he signaled for one of his goons to grab Madison and make her watch what he was about to do to his former best friend. The goon grabbed Madison and grabbed her chin so she was looking directly at Brock while he put his murder game down.

Boom! Brock hit Charlie directly in his balls with the bat. "You want to fuck my bitch, huh?" he asked as he delivered another blow to Charlie B, but this time in the torso. "I checked my damn cameras and saw you behind my woman. . . . I can not believe you!" Brock screamed and he swung again connecting with Charlie's mouth, busting out his whole front row of teeth and making blood squirt everywhere. When Madison heard the part about the hidden camera she knew that she couldn't lie out of the current situation and fear overcame her. She lost control of herself and pissed on herself as pure fear set in and overtook her body. The more Brock thought about his former friend sexing his woman, the more he became enraged and began to beat him brutally. At first Charlie B squirmed and cried in agonizing pain, but after a couple of head shots the movement ceased and his eyes began to roll in the back of his head. Shortly after, Charlie lost his life at the hands of Brock and his crazed rampage. Madison cried and witnessed her second murder as she watched a man get beat to death.

Brock was sweating profusely and breathing heavily by the time he was done. "Get this mu'fucka done and out of my house," Brock said before he stood in front of Charlie's lifeless body and spit in his face. He then focused his attention on Madison. "Drop her," he ordered. The goons let Madison fall to her knees and he walked over to her, hovering over her.

"Please, don't kill me Brock—please," Madison said as she scurried to the corner of the room.

"I'm not going to kill you . . ." Brock said as he slid off his belt and looked at Madison with a sinister stare. "But when I'm done, you are going to wish you were dead."

Chapter Eight

Jah jumped up out of his sleep and grabbed the gun that sat on his nightstand. The banging on his door startled him as he got out of the bed and crept to the door. Jah approached his front door, gun in hand. "Who is it?" he yelled.

"It's me, open up," a female voice said on the opposite side of the door. Jah looked through the peep hole and saw that it was Madison. He quickly lowered his gun and opened the door. Immediately he saw her battered face and swollen lip.

"What happened?" he asked in concern as he pulled her in the door.

She fell into his arms and cried like a little girl as she began to hyperventilate, not getting her words out clearly.

"Calm down, calm down," Jah said softly as he closed the door and began to stroke her hair. He held her closely and rubbed her back until she calmed down. "Now, tell me what happened."

They walked over to his couch and had a seat. Jah gave her a box of tissues to wipe her tears and waited for her to explain what was going on.

"It was Brock!" she screamed. "He beat me like I was a nigga on the street. He was trying to kill me! He threw me out and told me to never come back."

"What?" Jah asked, not understanding what had gone wrong.

"He saw the tape and he went crazy. He killed Charlie B. He beat him to death with a baseball bat . . . blood was everywhere."

"What? Charlie B? The tape? What the fuck are you talking about?" he asked.

Madison took her time so that she could calm down and she told him the truth. Jah sat, listening closely, and got the full details of what had gone on.

So that's what was wrong with Brock. That's why he introduced me to the connect and not Charlie B, he thought as he sat in deep contemplation while rubbing his chin. Jah placed his hand on Madison's shoulder. "Do you want me to keep it real with you? I would have beat your ass too. What you did was foul. Let's keep it real."

"It was just an accident Jah! If he was laying the pipe right I wouldn't have fucked with

Charlie B. He just caught me at the right time. I was lonely and I needed somebody," she replied.

"It's just certain things you don't do. Charlie B was foul and he deserved what he got," Jah said.

"You just don't understand Jah," she said as she buried her face in her hands. "I need to calm my nerves." She sat up and reached into her bra and pulled out a small vial of blow. "I need to get my mind right and figure out what I'm going to do next." Madison said as she scrambled to get her purse so she could retrieve her nose candy. Jah watched in disbelief as she emptied the contents on his coffee table and pulled out a dollar bill so that she could use her nose as a vacuum. Madison quickly dipped her head and did a line. Jah was speechless as he just shook his head and watched as she destroyed herself.

Madison jerked her head back to prevent her nose from running as she sniffed the snot that was attempting to drip. Her eyes got big as if a light bulb had gone off in her head. "I have an idea!" she said as she stood up and began to pace the room like a mad scientist at work. Jah remained quiet and just watched Madison go into her own little frenzy.

"That nigga put his hands on the wrong bitch! I got something for his ass." Madison said as she stopped in her tracks and looked at Jah. Madison then looked at the table and saw the other line. She quickly bent down and sniffed it up like a pro. She grew a smile on her face as she thought about the possibilities. "I know the combination to his safe. The safe where he keeps his stars. I know it's over a million dollars in there," Madison suggested. She hurried over to Jah and sat next to him. "We always wanted to be together right? This is our chance," she said as her nose ran and white residue was on the tip of her nose. She smiled and tried to kiss Jah, but he quickly turned his head and stood up.

"You got me fucked up! Why would you try to rob Brock? He's the only one who looked out for you," Jah asked not understanding Madison's disloyalty.

"I knew you would be scared," Madison said as she walked to her purse and grabbed another vial full of blow. Jah stormed over to her and slapped it out of her hands making the small tube slid across the floor, spilling its contents.

"You need to leave that shit alone. That's your damn problem right there Madison," Jah screamed as he began to form veins in his forehead. He had heard enough and was tired of keeping his cool. In his eyes, Madison was going insane.

"What the fuck are you doing? Why did you do that?" Madison said as she looked at the blow scattered all over the floor.

"Because Madison! You're getting out of control. You're talking crazy!" Jah said as he roughly grabbed Madison by her shoulders.

"Get your fucking hands off of me!" Madison yelled with bloodshot red eyes. She snatched away from him and began to breathe heavily. "You're not my damn father!" she yelled and it struck a chord with the both of them because the room got quiet and her words sunk in. They both were reminded of the night that Jah killed Gino.

"I know I'm not your father," Jah said lowering his voice. Madison's eyes began to water and she grabbed hes purse.

"I'm out of here! You're scared of Brock! I knew it!" she said as she headed for the door.

"Madison!" Jah yelled. "Madison!" However, she did not turn around. The loud sound of the door being slammed echoed throughout the condo and she left Jah standing in the middle of the room, wondering what she was going to do.

"Damn," he whispered as he saw the woman he secretly loved leave him.

Chapter Nine

The ringing of Jah's cell phone woke him from his light slumber. Jah looked over at his nightstand and Brock's name popped up on the caller ID. Jah sat up, cleared his voice, and picked up the phone.

"Yo," Jah said in a groggy voice. "Wake up! That bitch robbed me!" Brock said on the other end.

"What?" Jah asked as he wiped the cold out of his eye. He could not believe what he was hearing. *She actually did it,* he thought as he stood up.

"Madison! The bitch robbed me! I went for a jog this morning and when I came back, my stash was gone. The bitch had the nerve to leave her lip prints on my bathroom mirror. The bitch dirty! She's dead! That's my word," Brock said with rage in his voice.

"Hold on. She did what?" Jah said trying to decide whether or not he was going to tell Brock that she had visited him a couple of nights before. Brock retold him what he already knew. Brock explained to him everything from him catching her and Charlie B on camera, to the way he beat her ass, and then he told him about the robbery. He left out the part about Charlie B because he didn't want to talk about murder over the phone.

"Put this out in the streets: anybody who brings me that bitch . . . I got one hundred grand for them! I run this mu'fuckin city, so she can't hide for long. I need to catch that bitch before she tries to skip town with my money." Brock demanded as he fumed over the betrayal.

"I got you. That shit is foul," said Jah.

"Just meet me at my house in thirty minutes," Brock said just before leaving him with a dial tone. Jah knew at that point that Madison's life was on a countdown.

Madison dipped her head in the powder that pulled up on the desk. She was completely naked and high out of her mind. She looked over at Harry-O who was on the bed counting the money that they had stolen from Brock. He was also naked and had just given her two hours of good hard pipe. After seeing that Jah wasn't down for robbing Brock, she gave Harry-O a call. Once Harry-O heard the plan, he jumped at the opportunity. He also supplied Madison with good coke which kept her happy.

They were in a small hotel on the Southside of Flint hiding out. They both knew that Brock would be looking for Madison all over the city, so they stayed there until they figured out the next move.

"I thought you said he had a million stashed. This is more like $200,000," he said as he flicked through the bills and rubber banded them.'

"I guess he took some out and moved it last night," Madison said as she held her head back to stop her nose from running.

"I have to admit . . . I didn't think you were serious when you called me." Harry-O said as he stood up and slid off his boxers. He stroked his dick as he looked at Madison's body. He couldn't believe that he was sexing Brock's woman and stealing Brock's money at the same time.

"Let me get some more of that good pussy," he said blatantly as he began to walk toward her. Madison was already high out of her mind and was willing to do whatever. She turned toward Harry-O and took him into her mouth. She began masturbating while in the chair. Her oral sex made slurping noises as well as her wet lovebox. Harry-O forcefully jammed his rod into her mouth and grabbed the back of her head. He began to pump harder and faster being overly aggressive with her as he treated her mouth as if it was a vagina. She moaned in pleasure as she continued to please him. He was rough but she enjoyed it thoroughly. Madison closed her eyes and sped up her hand that she used to please herself.

"Oooh," she crooned as she felt an orgasm approaching. But just before she could release herself she felt a glob of semen shoot into the back of her throat. Harry-O grunted as he shoved his whole shaft into her mouth and began to quiver. He slid out of her mouth and Madison continued without him. She leaned back in the chair and spread her legs wider as she tried to chase the nut that she wanted so badly. Harry-O walked away and let her do her thing.

Madison was so into her session, she didn't have a clue what was in store for her. Harry-O grabbed his gun that was on the dresser and violently struck her over the head, sending her crashing into the floor.

"Aghhh!" she screamed as blood leaked from the right side of her mouth. Another hit struck her, this time catching her in the back of the head. Her vision became blurred and only a silhouette of Harry-O's body was visible. "What are you doing?" Madison mumbled as she tried to regain her vision.

"Bitch, you thought you were all that," Harry-O said, remembering the night she played him at the club. He took it personally and it bruised his ego. He was surprised when he got the call from her and he was about to make her pay. He powerfully kicked her in her mid-section with all his might. Madison balled-up into a fetal position in pure agony. She began to cry and it was music to Harry-O's ears. "You're not so tough now—are you, bitch?" he said before he let out a sinister laugh. He began to put on his clothes and put the money it the duffel bag it came out of. Within a minute, he was dressed and ready to walk out of the door while Madison was still on the floor dazed and in pain.

"Thanks for the head. It was great!" he said sarcastically just before he punched her again, landing a good shot to her temples. With that, he walked out $200,000 richer. That last shot knocked her out cold; leaving her naked, limp body in the middle of the hotel's floor. Now Madison was left with no money, no friends, and no soul. Karma had come back full circle and bit her instantly. Life's a bitch.

Chapter Ten

Jah sat on Brock's couch and watched as Brock paced the floor with his hands behind his back. You could literally see the veins forming in his forehead. "I can't believe this bitch had the audacity to take from me," Brock said. His goons were scattered throughout the room, waiting for a command from Brock. "This is what I want to happen. I'm putting a price on her head," Brock said through his clenched teeth. He began barking orders. "You, put the word out to the streets that I got a hundred stacks for whoever brings her to me." He said just before he turned to another goon. "You, go to the clubs and let the owners know to keep an eye out for her." Brock turned to Jah. "Jah, come with me."

They headed to the basement where Brock's office was and Jah took a seat. Brock was beside himself and all he could see was red. The phone on his desk began to ring. Brock sat down in his chair and picked up the phone.

"Hello," he said into the phone. "This is he." He listened carefully to the valuable information that was given to him on the other end and a slow smile began to grow on his face. "I got her!" Brock said as he hung up the phone and began to rub his hands together.

"What up?" Jah asked trying to figure out what he meant by saying that.

"I know where the bitch at. She used my credit card to book a room at the Holiday Inn on the Southside. I put an alert on my card; once she robbed me I knew the dumb bitch would use the card I gave her. Let's go!" Brock said as he reached into his drawer, pulling out a snub nose .45 pistol. Jah's mind began to spin. He knew that he had to get to Madison before Brock did. Jah didn't want to show his true colors, so he had to think of something quick to save Madison.

"Yo, let me go!" Jah said as he stood up and patted his gun on his hip. "You don't want to show your face like that. You the boss," Jah said as he tried his best to persuade Brock.

"Yeah, you right. You right. Smart thinking kid. Bring that bitch to me and I'ma show her something." Brock said as he sat down and smiled.

"I can't want till you dead that foul bitch," Jah said lying through his teeth. It hurt him inside to even call Madison a bitch. Although Madison did deserve to get punished, Jah couldn't see himself letting any harm happen to her.

"Yo, take one of my goons with you." Brock ordered as he sat back in his chair waiting to see Madison. He was already planning what he would do to her.

Jah hurried up the stairs and out of the door, purposely leaving the goon behind. He had to go save Madison before one of them got a hold of her. He pushed his Benz down I-75 going nearly 100 miles per hour, hoping that he would catch her before she had left. *What was this girl thinking? It's my fault. I should have never left her. It's my fault,* he thought as he maneuvered through the thick traffic trying to get to his love.

Madison crawled to the sink breathing heavily and was disoriented. Her lip leaked blood and it left a trail across the floor. She couldn't believe that Harry-O had beaten her the way he did. She immediately began to regret calling him, but she didn't have anyone else and just like every abused girl, she wanted a man to provide comfort and a sense of security. Dealing with a scorned Brock, she knew that she was going to need someone to protect her. Unfortunately for her, Harry-O had a hidden agenda. She struggled to pull herself onto the sink and she looked into the mirror, seeing her swollen face. The sight alone made her bust into tears. "Why me? Why me God?" she cried as she broke down. Just as she began to cry, a knock at the door startled her and her heart began to beat rapidly. *Is that Brock? Is that Harry-O coming to finish what he started?* She thought as she dropped to her knees and covered her mouth as she cried in sheer fear. She was so scared that she urinated on herself. She was having a panic attack as her chest felt tight and her breaths were shallow. She sat on the floor and rocked back and forth, hoping that the knocking would eventually stop. Knock, knock, knock . . . the thuds got louder and her fear grew. Madison tried her best not to move so the person on the other side of the door would leave. After a minute of complete silence, Madison stood up. I think they're gone, she thought as she looked at the door and wondered if someone was there or not. All of a sudden a loud gun blast sounded blowing the lock clean off. Jah walked in with his gun drawn. He stepped in cautiously and looked over at Madison.

"Where's the money, Madison!" Jah asked as he looked over the room searching for the cash.

"It's gone! He took it all," she said as she covered herself.

"Who took it? What the fuck are you talking about?" Jah asked as he frowned up. He looked closer at Madison and saw that she was high as a kite. He grabbed her arm and pulled her close. "This stops today!" he said as he grabbed her clothes. "Let's get the fuck out of here before Brock's goons come." He said as he flipped over the table, spilling the coke pile on the floor.

"Okay, Jah," she said in a conceding tone. She knew that she had nobody else. He was her only hope. She quickly got dressed while Jah kept peeking out of the blinds. Madison finally was ready and began to wipe the blood from her mouth with a wet cloth.

"Listen to me," Jah said as he hugged her close and looked into her eyes. The sight of her battered face almost brought tears to his eyes. "I won't let anything happen to you. You have to just promise me that you will follow me. Let me lead you." He said with the most sincerity.

"I will, Jah. I will," Madison said as a tear slid down her face. Jah gently kissed her forehead and closed his eyes, embracing the moment. They fled out and hit the highway—Jah had a plan.

Chapter Eleven

Jah looked over at Madison who rested her head against the window asleep and looking comfortable. She looked so peaceful, so serene. Jah couldn't believe what Madison had just told him hours before. She explained to him how Harry-O had robbed her and took all of Brock's money. Originally, Jah was going to find Madison, get the money, and return it to Brock; in hopes that he could smooth things over and ask Brock to give Madison a pass. Jah understood that Madison was at a point of no return with Brock. He had to make a big decision but when he looked at Madison, he knew that it was worth it. He owed this much to her.

He looked in the backseat and saw the three duffel bags that sat in the seats. Two of them were filled with his and Madison's clothes and the last one had ten bricks of raw cocaine that he had taken from Brock's crack house that he ran for him. Jah had crossed his former mentor so that he could save the love of his life. Many people would call it grimy, but in Jah's heart he was doing the right thing. They were on their way to a new city, with a new view on life. Jah honestly believed that he could bring Madison back to the innocent girl that he fell in love with and if he couldn't he vowed to die trying. As for Harry-O, he would see him once again to settle the score but he let that pass to focus on the future.

With the bricks in the backseat, Jah decided to start over in another state in a new town, and build something special with Madison. Jah looked at the sign that said, "Welcome to the Beautiful State of Ohio" and he smiled. He had a good feeling and although he knew it would be a hard journey with Madison, he looked forward to taking it with her. She pledged to him that she would stop using coke and turn over a new leaf.

"This is how it was supposed to be," he whispered as he continued to drive into the sunset.

Epilogue

Madison lay naked on the king-sized hotel bed while counting stacks of hundred dollar bills. While lying on her stomach, she glanced back at Jah who was running the cash through the money machine. Jah passed a stack of bills to Madison so that she could recount it and put it in rubber bands. A tightly rolled blunt hung from his lip as he stood shirtless with a pair of baggy denims on. The butt of Jah's chrome .45 pistol stuck out of his waistline as he took a long drag of his blunt and blew smoke circles. Madison smiled and admired her man, who was a natural born hustler.

"I love you Jah." Madison said sexily as she wrapped a G-stack in a rubber band and tossed it in the duffel bag at the foot of the bed.

"I love you too" Jah said in his deep raspy voice. Jah always took his time when he talked and his words come out slow and slurred. Jah ran the last stack through the machine and then took a deep pull of the spliff. He passed the last stack to Madison and then blew out the smoke. "We did it baby. That should be a million even, right there." Jah said as he sat next to his woman while she flipped through the bills.

"We did it baby!" she repeated as she banded the last G-stack and wrapped her arms around Jah's neck. They passionately kissed and Jah sat the blunt in the ashtray and grabbed the bottle of Moët Chandon from the ice bucket on the dresser. He popped the cork and took a swig of the champagne. That night was to be a night of celebration, because it was the night that Jah would officially retire from the streets and start his new life with Madison. They could leave the past behind them and move forward with no worries and no regrets.

"I can't believe we are finally about to leave Ohio for good. I wonder what Los Angeles is going to be like." Madison thought out loud as she continued to rub Jah.

"It's going to be beautiful." Jah said as he stood up and turned around so that he could face

Madison. He pulled off the gun on his waist and sat the bottle on the dresser. He grabbed both of Madison's hands and took a deep breath. "Baby, you been down with me for so long and you are the only person that I ever loved or trusted. You ain't built like these other females and I admire that. What I'm trying to say is . . . I want to be with you forever." Jah said as he reached into his pocket and pulled out a small box.

Madison couldn't believe what she was seeing. He's about to ask me to marry him, she thought as she put both of her hands over her mouth and tears formed in her eyes. The only man she ever loved was about to make her the happiest woman in the world. Her hands began to shake as she watched Jah get on one knee and hold up the box up in front of him.

"Oh my God, Jah." She said in a shaky voice as she looked into Jah's dark brown eyes. He displayed his perfect smile as he popped the box open, showing Madison the blinging four-carat diamond ring.

"Madison, will you be my wife?"

"Yes! Yes, I will!" Madison screamed as she threw her arms around her man and hugged him with all her might. Tears of joy flowed freely down her cheeks as she hugged him and rocked back and forth. Just as she released him so that she could try on the ring, a loud shotgun blast ripped through the hotel's aluminum door. Two masked men entered immediately after; and before Jah could even reach for his pistol, the gunmen filled his body with slugs from the shotgun. One shot to the chest. Madison screamed at the top of her lungs as she saw the love of her life getting blown back from the blast.

"Noooo!" Madison screamed at the top of her lungs as she lunged for Jah. She immediately jumped on Jah's twitching body and watched helplessly as his eyes began to roll in the back of his head. "Jah!" she yelled—disregarding the masked men's orders for her to get up. She watched as Jah's life slowly left his body. His eyes stopped rolling and the twitching ended. His big brown eyes stared into space as he took his last breath. Madison cried and screamed as she gripped his corpse. She couldn't even hear what the men were instructing her to do; her only concern was her man.

A single shot rang out. A bullet went through Madison's back and she laid face to face with her love. In death, they eloped. They laid in their own blood breathless and staring into space. It was their end . . . it was their fate.

***

Brock sat patiently with two of his goons with him. His tinted van parked only a couple spots down from the hotel's door. He smiled as the sounds of guns being cocked and loaded serenaded his ears. After a year of searching, he had finally caught up with his two old friends Jah and Madison and he wanted to repay them for everything they had done for him. He was going to make it special for them, just as he did for his former best friend Charlie B. Like the old proverb says: what goes around eventually comes around. He couldn't wait to see his former protégé and the beauty that once was his woman to teach them a lesson they would never forget.

www.ashleyjaquavis.com

Notes

Notes

Notes

Notes